BRIAN WELLS

REPUBLICINK

CINCINNATI, OHIO

First Edition

Printed in the United States of America

Library of Congress Control Number: 2016930993

ISBN 978-0-9972270-0-0 (hardback)

Visit LeagueAndLantern.com

For Nancy.

You are beautiful and amazing.
More than a feeling, it's the power of love.

THE BIG DO-OVER

"IS HE DEAD?"

The voice was muffled and fuzzy. It sounded like a girl to Jake, but he wasn't quite sure. Everything was black and spinning.

"No way. Not dead."

Definitely a guy's voice this time, and much closer. Everything was still muffled though, as if Jake were hearing it through a pile of pillows. If he could just get his eyes open, maybe he—

"How would you know?" It was the girl's voice again.

"No crazy stare," said the guy. "Dead guys always have this crazy stare."

"I said *dead*, not zombie. You watch too much TV."

The voices were getting clearer. And there was gurgling, maybe water. Voices, murmuring, and gurgling . . . and blackness, everything still black.

"How old is he, like eleven or twelve?"

"I don't know, but he's a scrawny one. And what's with the hair? He looks like a wet poodle. Wait, is that drool? Yep. We have a drooler."

The fog in Jake's head was beginning to lift. Things were getting brighter. What was he lying on? He felt a tug at his side.

"There's something smashed all over the kid's shirt. It looks like, I don't know, maybe dead squirrel."

"Ewwwwww! Don't touch him! Dead things have diseases and stuff."

"You mean the kid or the squirrel?"

"Both!"

"Nope, never mind. Not squirrel. I think . . . I think it's corn dog. Yep, dead corn dog."

The voice was closer now, almost in his ear. A bell chimed somewhere above him. Chimes and murmuring and gurgling. Definitely gurgling.

"We should do the Heimlich or a tourniquet or something," the guy said.

"Right, Einstein. The Heimlich is for choking and tourniquets for bloody stumps. Just call 911."

"Nah, I got this."

Jake felt arms wrap around his waist.

"What are you doing? Put him down!"

As Jake was hauled to his feet, he felt a fist thrust into his gut.

"*Aakkkkkkkhh!*" Jake yelped as he coughed forcefully. His eyes popped open and he launched a spray of saliva, corn dog, and mustard into the air.

"Yessss, I knew it! *Not* dead." The boy dropped him back into the shallow fountain pool. "No crazy stare."

Jake sprawled on his backpack, flailing like a flipped turtle in the water. He scrambled to his side and lurched to his feet. "Aahh-aahh-*choooooo!*" He launched a sneeze, and his soaked hair sent a mist across the assembled crowd.

"OK, OK, OK," he sputtered. "I'm OK. I'm OK." He regained his footing and stumbled out of the stone fountain, tumbling into the boy who had lifted him up.

"Watch it, Corn Dog!" The boy shoved him back toward the fountain where Jake collapsed on the stone lip.

Jake squinted, trying to get his bearings. The late summer sun was beginning to set behind the imposing limestone towers anchoring the university courtyard. A small crowd of college students encircled him, though the blond kid staring down at Jake barely even looked like a high schooler. He wore the name "Greg" on his bright orange shirt and was standing next to a blond girl with a matching shirt that read "Amy." They both had disgusted looks on their faces.

"What's going on here?" A police officer on a Segway broke through the crowd. He stopped in front of Jake and eyed him suspiciously before turning to the boy and girl. "What's with your friend?"

"Whoa," Greg said. "Not my friend. Never seen the kid before. I think he was messing around in the fountain."

"What? No! No." Jake stood up. "That's not what—*Ahh-choo!*" He sneezed violently, stumbling back into the fountain.

"OK," the officer said, turning to the crowd. "I've got this. Everyone move along."

The boy and girl stepped back before drifting away with the crowd. Jake heard somebody whisper something about drugs as they passed by.

"Do you have some kind of ID, son?"

"Definitely, yes sir," Jake said, climbing out of the fountain. He pried a school ID out of his soaked pocket and handed it to the officer. "Not the greatest picture. Need to work on my smile. Looks more like a mug shot. Um, not that I would *know*, I mean, I *would* know, just not *personally*, you know."

The officer scanned the ID and then glanced up at Jake, pausing as he noticed Jake's mismatched eyes.

"Heterochromia iridum," Jake explained.

"Excuse me?"

"One blue eye and one gray eye. My Uncle Gabe says it's a gift. Makes me see things differently."

The officer looked back down at Jake's ID. "So, Jake Herndon, what's the sign say?"

"Presented by University of Chicago Class of 1922."

"The other sign."

"Keep Out of Fountain. This Means You."

"And that means?"

"It means you. I mean, sorry, sir, it means me. But it's not like that. You see—"

"Son, I'm going to need you to step over here." The officer pointed to the edge of the walkway. "Walk this line for me."

"Officer, I can assure you I'm not under the influence of—"

"Son, the line."

"Yes, sir. Standard protocol. I can respect that. The old

walk and turn." Jake walked the line perfectly. "What's next? One-leg stand? Horizontal gaze?"

"Breathe," the officer said, leaning in close to Jake's face.

"You know, sir, I'm not sure you want that. I mean—"

"Just breathe, son."

Jake took a deep breath and exhaled.

The policeman flinched when Jake's breath hit him.

"Sorry, sir. Mad Hungarian. Corn dog with Budapest fire mustard. Kind of sticks with you. Flat-out nasty. Breath mints don't stand a chance."

"OK. You seem clean . . . so to speak." The officer pulled a notebook out of his back pocket. "So, was this some kind of prank gone wrong? Your friends ditch you?"

"No, sir. No friends. I mean I *have* friends, just none my age, not at the present moment. I guess you could say sixth grade wasn't a big win socially, if you know what I mean. Tough crowd, but I'm working on it."

Jake paused and looked down at the ground, then back up, a little defiantly. "This year's a big do-over that I'm confident will remedy the situation. In fact, curious thing, that's exactly where I was headed, my Big Do-Over, a middle school reboot of sorts where I . . ."

He looked momentarily stunned. "Wait, prank? No, sir. No prank. Not trying to create a spectacle. As I was saying, I was on my way to a school thing. University Prep Middle School. Summer's Over Sleepover. You may have heard of it. Seventh grade orientation thing. They call it a sleepover, but word is there's not a lot of sleeping. Just cheesy team-building stuff. Sorry, that sounds negative, I mean, it could be the beginning of greatness, right? An epic quest for me, you never know, right?"

The officer stared at Jake.

"So anyway, I'm late. I'm taking a shortcut and there's this, uh, there's this kid." Jake looked for a reaction, but the officer simply continued staring at him silently. "Soooo, yes sir, there's this, uh, this little kid. And, uh, he was crying. Yes, he was crying, like he's in crisis or something."

"A little kid? In crisis?"

"Yes, sir, a crisis of some sort, a traumatic situation. At this point we don't really know. So I said, 'Hey kid, what's wrong?' but he wasn't speaking English, maybe Chinese. Yeah, I think it was probably Chinese."

"A Chinese kid in crisis?"

"Yes, sir, I believe so. Maybe about five. He wasn't saying anything. He just points. And that's when I saw it."

"You saw it?" The policeman started writing in his pad.

Jake was staring at the Chicago Cubs sticker on the officer's Segway, moving his lips while thinking. "Yes, sir." He looked back up at the man. "Cubs hat, right in the fountain. Poor kid must have dropped it."

"And this little kid, where were his parents?"

"My question exactly. Great minds think alike, right sir? Who was it that said that, anyway?"

The officer didn't look up from his pad.

"So, anyway, I'm in a hurry. You know how that is I'm sure, being Chicago's finest and all."

No response.

"But then I said to myself, 'Hey wait a minute, Jake.

What's a guy if he can't help a little kid? I mean where are all the heroes?' Defining moment here. A worthy endeavor. A chance to step up and be a dude. So I went in for the hat but I must have leaned over too far and, wham! Yes, sir, head first. Which surprised me as much as anyone. I mean, I'm not the biggest guy, but my wrestling coach says I've got catlike reflexes. Which makes for mad skills, even if you're undersized. Won sixth grade regionals in my weight class last year. Had my name in the paper. Perhaps you read about it."

"So you're a hero on a mission to rescue this alleged Chinese kid's hat?"

"Well, I'll leave the hero part for others to decide. Real dudes don't brag, right? My Uncle Gabe says, 'Pride goeth before a destruction.' Not that I think that God would just jack me in the head for bragging, but hey, why risk—wait, what do you mean 'alleged'?"

"And how did you end up unconscious?"

"Hmmm. Well, see, I snagged the hat and, I, uh . . . I don't know. Maybe I leaned over too far? I started to feel a little dizzy. I stumbled. Anyway, the next thing I know, this blond kid's pulling me up and doing this violent Heimlich thing with his fist. Not that I don't appreciate the effort, but—"

"So, this little kid. Where is he? And what about the hat?"

"Again, great question. Not your first time at the rodeo, is it, sir? Wait . . . what are you writing, sir? Is that a ticket?"

No answer.

"Yes, sir. The missing kid. I have a theory. I think he . . ." Jake paused in deep thought. "I think he . . . he grabbed the hat. Yes, I think he grabbed it and then sometime during all the commotion, he found his parents and they went on their way."

"And the smashed corn dog on your shirt? How does that fit into your story?"

"Oh, that. Right. The corn dog shrapnel. So I mentioned the Mad Hungarian? Right before the little kid situation, I had a little run-in with my lunch. Accidentally smashed a bit of the corn dog goodness on my shirt. It wouldn't have been so bad but then there was the Heimlich thing. Did I mention that? Yeah, that didn't help."

"Look, son, I've heard it all. A kid losing his hat? Not even a top-ten story."

The officer tore out a ticket and handed it to Jake. "You'll need to appear at the juvenile desk with a parent. You've got thirty days."

"Wait, sir, maybe there's another theory that would—"

"It's for impeding pedestrian traffic." The officer was already stepping back onto his Segway. "I could have made it for trespassing. It's your lucky day." And with that, he sped away.

"Yeah. My lucky day," Jake muttered as he scraped bits of corn dog from his shirt. As if the ticket wasn't bad enough, he had now gone from maybe-late to flat-out late. He turned to run but smacked right into an old woman. An old Chinese woman. She was smiling, her arm draped around a small boy clutching a wet Cubs hat.

"Thank you, young man!" she said with a smile.

Jake gave them a thumbs-up and smiled weakly before breaking into a jog. Not good. So much for the Big Do-Over.

His chance to snatch middle-school victory from the jaws of last year's debacle was not starting as planned. And now he was late. Late, soaking wet, and reeking like a Mad Hungarian.

FIGHTING EINSTEINS

JAKE HUSTLED ACROSS the cobblestone courtyard, weaving in and out between streams of college students with overloaded backpacks and stuffed messenger bags. While his clothes had started to dry, he couldn't say the same for his water-logged backpack, which left a small stream behind him. He dodged a guy with dreadlocks who was juggling a soccer ball with his feet and ducked through an ancient, ivy-covered archway. He raced across the university lawn and crossed the street as a bell tower chimed in the distance.

This was most definitely not going as planned. At least it was only Level 2 humiliation—in public, but with strangers. Manageable. But now there was impending lateness.

The sidewalk was an obstacle course of bookstore crates and café tables. When he finally passed the Fifty-Ninth Street train station, he knew he'd make it. This might be his first day at Uni Prep Middle School, but he was no stranger to the neighborhood.

Jake was out of breath by the time he reached the soaring Greek columns of the museum. He scowled as he caught his reflection in the revolving door. *Who was it that said, "You never get a second chance to make a first impression?" Was it Gandhi? Or a shampoo commercial?* He tried to finger-comb his mop of curly black hair into submission but failed miserably.

The last of the sun's rays disappeared over Lake Michigan as Jake entered the Museum of Science and Industry and rushed up the escalator into the enormous lobby. Even after all the Saturday mornings here with Uncle Gabe, it never got old. The cavernous space was laid out like a huge plus sign, with four wings spreading out from the massive center rotunda. Each wing had a main floor, then a balcony with more exhibits extending up to the ceiling. Jake stood in the center and spun around, taking it all in as the last of the day's visiting families swarmed past. Straight ahead was the rickety cage elevator that ran down to the underground coal mine. To his left, a 727 airliner jutted out from the east wing's balcony high overhead, appearing to soar over the lobby. Jake's favorite was the towering man-made tornado swirling inside a glass column in the west wing. But he loved all of it. Then he saw the banner on the table: "Summer's Over Sleepover Registration"—reminding him that tonight wasn't about the usual fun.

The Summer's Over Sleepover was a simple concept: The new seventh graders meet their classmates the weekend before school starts, with the eighth graders leading them through a bunch of games. It was a simple concept that any seventh grader could tell you is absolutely ridiculous, another bad idea from an adult who had completely forgotten the brutal reality known as middle school. Put the seventh graders in their pajamas and under the thumb of eighth graders still working out their own issues from last year. It usually takes about fifteen minutes for this kind of thing to go from fun and games to *The Hunger Games*.

Nope. Jake caught himself. *Not going negative. Fresh start. Do-over. Be positive.*

The last of the families streamed out of the closing museum as Jake approached the table. A woman in a University Prep sweatshirt was finishing packing up.

"I'm sorry, sweetie," she said, glancing up at Jake and his mustard-splotched shirt. "I think the 'Fun with Food' camp was earlier today."

"What? No, ma'am. I'm here for the sleepover deal. Jake, Jake Herndon."

She looked him over once more, eyebrows raised as her eyes settled on his mustard stains.

"Oh, this." Jake pulled at his T-shirt. "There was an incident. Little kid. I tried to do the right thing. You know, rise to the occasion. But it went south. And then there was an over-aggressive Heimlich. But I—"

"Well, let me check," she said as she scanned her clipboard. "Wait. Jake Herndon. There you are! You're new. That's . . . well, that's just great!" Her voice rose two octaves and she made a mock salute. "I'm Mrs. Everjoy and I'll be your cruise director for this trip!"

Jake smiled and dropped his soaked backpack on the table

like a bag of wet noodles. "Sorry, ma'am. Collateral damage. Maybe there's a dryer in the building?"

Mrs. Everjoy slid the wet backpack behind the table and gave Jake the classic "you poor thing" smile. She grabbed a walkie-talkie. "Alby, we've got a Tardy Tony who needs a bit of a makeover. Could you bring over one of those shirts from the gift shop?" She glanced back at Jake. "Extra small if you've got it."

"Small's fine. I don't need extra—"

She waved Jake off. "And maybe a wet wipe too." She stepped out from behind the table, cleared her throat, and motioned to the banner as if it were a new car. "Welcome to the Summer's Over Sleepover!"

Jake gasped as he felt himself being squeezed and lifted off the ground from behind. When his feet returned to the floor, he spun around to find himself in the awkward embrace of a mascot with a white lab coat and an oversized head.

"That's what we call an Alby Welcome!" Mrs. Everjoy said, going in for an unsuccessful fist bump with the character who apparently couldn't see her fist from inside his giant head. The mascot had a fuzzy white mustache and crazy gray hair; it looked like he had been electrocuted. The front pocket of his lab coat was stuffed with pens, mechanical pencils, and a slide rule. He released Jake and turned to Mrs. Everjoy, handing her a plastic bag dramatically, as if it were a major award.

"Thank you, kind sir!"

Alby waved an oversized gloved hand at Jake and scurried away.

"Alby?" Jake asked. "Is your mascot dude Albert—"

"Yes, sir. We're the Fighting Einsteins." She peeked in the bag. "Well, shoot it all. I guess these are the only smalls they had left. Better than a poke in the eye with a sharp stick, though. You can change in there," she said, pointing to a bathroom. "But hurry up. When you hear the music, you'll know we're starting." She motioned to a stage in the corner of the lobby where kids were gathering. "You don't want to be the Late Great Jake!"

Jake ducked into the bathroom, passing a janitor replacing the paper towels. He stepped close to the mirror. *Whoa. What was that twisted mushroom on his head?* Oh, yeah, his hair. *Should have gone for that back-to-school haircut. A quick sink-shower should help.* The janitor gave him a strange look as Jake stripped off his matted shirt and threw it in the trash. Jake splashed his hair and chest and patted dry with a few paper towels. After a second attempt to get his hair to obey, he gave up and pulled the T-shirt out of the bag.

"*Nooooooo!*" Jake cried out as he looked at the shirt. He spun for the trash can. Empty. He swung open the bathroom door and leaned out. No janitor. In fact, there was no one at all. Then the music cranked up. Jake dropped his head. *OK. Salvageable situation. Review your options. A: Go in shirtless. Bold move, but high potential for Level 3 Humiliation—Public and In Front of People You'll See Again. B: Sneak away. Pursue homeschooling. C: Suck it up and put on the stupid shirt.*

LEVEL 3

JAKE FOLLOWED THE SOUNDS back to the stage area. Dance music bounced off the marble walls while blue spotlights circled the rotunda dome high overhead. A hundred nervous kids gathered around several folding tables stuffed with pizzas and drinks. This was it. This would be his world, his people. Pop quizzes, field trips, forced fun, the whole deal. He just wished he wasn't entering this brave new world a half hour late, wearing mustard-stained cargo shorts and a pink Hello Kitty astronaut T-shirt.

The kids swarmed the pizza like jackals descending on a fallen antelope. Jake jostled his way through the crowd and just barely managed to grab one of the last pieces. He wasn't sure how this would mix with the Mad Hungarian still rumbling in his stomach but he wasn't going to pass up free pizza. He pulled a hot sauce packet from his damp pocket and squirted it on the slice.

Now the mingling. The dreaded mingling. What was it

his teacher had said? Nimble. He needed to be more socially nimble. He rolled his shoulders and surveyed the room. Basic middle-school stuff. Everyone huddled with their friends, like pioneers circling their wagons against hostile invaders. He moved toward the closest group, hovering just outside their circle. The indirect approach. He followed the conversation. He laughed when they laughed. Then there was a pause. Perfect time to jump in. What was that opening line he'd come up with last night? Something about that song that kids liked so much this summer. But before he could step in, the group moved as a pack to the drink table.

No problem. Jake spied another cluster. He guessed that they were Level 2 social strata. Not the cool crowd, but somewhere in the middle. Definitely attainable. He inched closer. He still couldn't remember the line. He'd have to freestyle it.

"What's that smell?" one of the kids asked, sniffing the air. They made pained faces and moved away.

Awkward. Note to self: More Old Spice, less Budapest fire mustard.

He scanned the room. Maybe there was another lone wolf who hadn't found a pack. How about that tall kid in the corner? The one working the "hang by the food table" strategy. *Wait, is he wearing a Captain America T-shirt?* Yes. A good reminder. Just what Jake needed. Not the T-shirt, already had it. Wished he was wearing it right now.

No, what Jake needed was a quest. A quest would be just the thing. It's how all the greats became great in the first place. It's how scrawny Steve Rogers became Captain America. It's how Dr. Jones became Indiana Jones. Even in Gabe's favorite—*The Princess Bride*—just one worthy quest turned Westley into a hero.

Yes, that was the missing piece. He just needed a quest of his own. A moment to step up and be a dude. He knew he could do it. He just needed the chance. Rescue the princess from the tower, crush the evil empire, restore order and justice to the universe. But first he should probably lose the Hello Kitty T-shirt. Jake was halfway into a daydream where he was saving the entire girls' soccer team from Nazi robots when he glanced back toward the kid in the Captain America shirt. What was that kid doing? Jake watched the boy pull a tube of hand sanitizing gel out of his pocket and rub it all over his hands, twice, before picking up his pizza. *OK, maybe not the right sidekick.*

The music faded and Mrs. Everjoy bounded onto the stage. "What up, what up, young bucks?" She made a big game show motion with her hands. "I'm Mrs. Everjoy, your humble class advisor and new bestie!"

What up young bucks? Bestie? Classic BFF advisor proto-type. Trying too hard.

"Tonight, you join the long, prestigious line of University Preparatory Middle School students. Tonight you are arriving as one hundred individuals. But Sunday afternoon you will leave as a class, a family. And what a class you will be." She read from a list in her hand. "Seventy-five of you scored in the top 1 percent on the National Middle School Aptitude test. Three of you are world-class pianists, four are accomplished violinists, and we have more than a few ballerinas, junior champion tennis players, swimmers, and fencers. The rest of you, I guess, are straight-up slackers! JK. JK. Whewww." She wiped her head with a handkerchief and returned to her list. "Eighty of you are coming up from our prestigious University Grade School. Please stand so all our new friends this year can get a good look at you."

She led the room in applause, accompanied by a "Woo-woo" from a teacher in the back. "Another seventeen of you are part of our international exchange program. Please stand." There was more applause and light woo-wooing. "Welcome from Dubai, London, Shanghai, Paris, Mumbai, and Mexico City."

Jake looked around the room. They may have been from all over the world but everyone looked like they shopped at the same store. Everyone except a dark-haired girl sitting in front of him. Her shirt was a funky patchwork of colorful animal and flower symbols stitched together. She had an exotic-looking woven band on one wrist and a silver bracelet engraved with some kind of tribal markings on the other.

"Well, welcome all. Tonight is—" Mrs. Everjoy suddenly stopped, squinting through the spotlight toward the back of the room. "Oh yes, did I forget something?" The teacher who had been woo-wooing was saying something to her.

"My bad, my bad. Eighty of you are coming up from our grade school, seventeen are international exchanges, and there's three of you who are . . ." She looked down at her clipboard. "Well, it doesn't say, but there's three 'others.' Would you wonderful, beautiful others please stand?"

Jake didn't want to stand, but as everyone's eyes settled on him, he gave in. He slowly rose to polite applause along with the dark-haired girl in front of him and the tall kid in the Captain America T-shirt. All three quickly sat back down.

"Well, again, welcome. And oh, yes, that reminds me—this year is especially exciting because I'm proud to say that this is the first year of our Everyday Einstein Scholarship, which opens our class to one student who might not get the chance otherwise."

For some reason, Jake felt like everyone's eyes were settling on him again.

"Alrighty. Now before we break up for the Einstein Pride Scavenger Hunt, I need everyone to grab a sticker out of the bag that's passing by, slap it on your cell phones, and drop them in the bag. That's right, homies! We're kickin' it old-school tonight. Confiscating yo cellies."

A scavenger hunt, thought Jake as the bags passed through the aisles. *This might not be so bad. Maybe it won't be the usual team-building nonsense*, like those awful trust falls. Whoever came up with the idea of having strangers catch you as you fall backwards into their arms? Maybe Jake just had trust issues. Or maybe it was because Wayne Browning wasn't fully engaged at Camp Greenwood last summer, and Jake's trust fall became a lot more "fall" than "trust."

Mrs. Everjoy dropped the bag of phones into a footlocker and slapped a padlock on it.

"OK, let's get this party started! Crews, go ahead and huddle up with your eighth grade ambassadors for your first clue."

As the kids quickly gathered in groups, it became obvious that Jake and the two "others" didn't know where to go.

Mrs. Everjoy stepped back to the mike. "Oh, and if you're

one of our wonderful others, you can join the orange crew for tonight."

The next three seconds were a blur, as if Jake were in a slow-motion dream . . . a very bad dream.

What are the chances? Actually, in Jake's short twelve years, the chance of this kind of thing seemed to be pretty high. He tried to melt into the wall as Greg and Amy, in their matching orange shirts, waved him over to their crew.

CRACKING THE CODE

JAKE JOINED THE GROUP, doing his best to hide in the back of the huddle. *OK, now I'm glad I changed my shirt. Even Hello Kitty is better than them recognizing me.*

"Gather round, munchkins." Greg blew a whistle that was completely unnecessary. "You heard Mrs. Everjoy say this stuff about getting to know each other and it not being about who wins. Well, that's fine for the other teams, but not for us. For us, it's about winning. We'll get to know each other by winning. Everyone else will get to know each other by losing. Any questions? Great, let's talk tactics and strategy."

"Hey, shouldn't we do names?" one of the seventh grade girls asked.

"Sorry. When I said 'any questions,' I meant no questions."

"It's just that, I think we'll work better as a team if we, you know, know each other's names?"

Greg gave her an icy stare. "OK, we've got a few minutes

before they give us the first clue. Knock yourselves out. Why don't you start, Miss Team-Building Expert?"

"OK," she said, either missing Greg's sarcasm or choosing to ignore it. "I'm Sevita Bahkta, which is a Hindi name from my father's side. My dad teaches physics at—"

"OK, Chatty Cathy! Don't need the life story," Greg interrupted. "How about you, big guy? Why don't you go next?" He pointed to the tall African-American boy in the Captain America T-shirt who had stood as one of the "others" earlier.

"Sure. TJ McDonald," the boy responded.

"Welcome, Cap," Greg said, referring to TJ's shirt while reaching out and shaking his hand. "Looking forward to seeing what you have on the court. Our seventh and eighth grade teams are combined."

TJ looked at him, confused, while pulling a small bottle of sanitizer out of his pocket and squirting gel on the hand he had shaken with.

"Basketball," Greg said. "Basketball."

"Right. Not my game." TJ responded with a sigh. It was clear this wasn't the first time he'd been asked this.

"Sorry," said Greg. "I just thought, because you're, well . . ."

"Tall? Dark? Handsome?" said TJ. "Guilty, guilty, guilty. But no basketball. I do know my way around a saber though, second place in the under-14 category at nationals. They scored it as third, but I was robbed. It was second. So fencing, and if there's a Quidditch club, I'm all in."

"Great," Greg interrupted, rolling his eyes. "So if we run into any pirates or wizards, we're good."

While Greg cut off each seventh grader as they introduced

themselves, Jake slipped behind a support column to turn his Hello Kitty T-shirt inside out.

Greg motioned to the dark-haired girl Jake had noticed earlier.

"Lucy Garcia," she said, stepping forward. "We just moved back to the States from Nepal." She gave everyone a small smile.

"OK," Greg said. "Now that we're all feeling the love—"

"You missed someone." Lucy motioned to Jake behind the column. The kids moved aside, exposing him as he was halfway through pulling his shirt back on.

Greg broke into a huge grin, nudging Amy. "Corn Dog!"

So much for do-overs. Level 2 meet Level 3.

"OK, Corn Dog, give us your name and your favorite condiment. Well, never mind," Greg said, pointing to the mustard on Jake's shorts. "I guess we just need the name."

"Ahem, Jake Herndon. Excuse the clothing, there was a situation. An incident, really, a crisis. A corn dog, a little kid in peril, I didn't have time to—"

"OK, again, life story? Not needed. But hey, this is great. We've got Captain America *and* Captain Corn Dog. How can we lose? Avengers unite!"

"Assemble," Jake muttered under his breath.

"What was that?" Greg asked.

"Assemble," TJ jumped in. "He said *assemble*. It's 'Avengers assemble!' Not unite. Unite would be X-Men. *X-Men United*. Although that's really just from the second movie. And even then most just call it *X-2*."

Jake nodded in agreement.

"O . . . K . . ." Greg said, rolling his eyes.

Captain Corn Dog, thought Jake. *This could be a problem*. Jake had become somewhat of an expert on embarrassing nicknames. This one had potential to stick. Funny story? Check. Short and catchy? Check. Created by an overconfident loudmouth? Check. Definite stickiness. *Better just ignore it*.

Jake smiled his "I get it, I can take it" smile.

"OK, crews!" Mrs. Everjoy was back at the microphone. Your ambassadors all have their first clue. On the count of three, you can open your envelope. We'll see you at the finish line for the Epic Einstein Ice Cream Bash! One . . . two . . ."

On the count of two, Greg tore open his envelope and read the card aloud: "'Their loss is our gain. We cracked the code just the same.' OK, I have no idea what that means, but it doesn't matter." Greg tossed the clue card to the floor. "Here's the deal, newbies: I know how this works from last year. They start each team with a different clue. You get a different token at each clue station. First team to collect all the tokens wins. Instead of messing with our clue, we'll split up into three groups and follow the other teams. When they get their first token, we'll grab one too. Meet back here as soon as you have it. Then we'll start on our clue. We'll be way ahead."

"You know . . ." Jake raised his hand. "I don't think that's the spirit of—"

"That's why you're not supposed to think, Corn Dog. I'm the team leader, I'll do the thinking. You just do the doing."

Greg pulled three of the boys next to him. "We'll hit the lower level." He grabbed Sevita and two other girls and shoved them toward Amy. "Chatty Cathy, you go with Amy to the balcony floor. And you three others," he motioned to Jake, TJ, and Lucy, "cover this main floor. As soon as you have your token, meet back here."

They all raced out, leaving Jake, TJ, and Lucy standing in the middle of the room. Jake was staring at the floor, silently moving his lips and talking to himself.

TJ plopped down in one of the seats. "Look, I say we grab a few Yoo-hoos from the vending machine and chill out until it's ice cream time."

"Ahem." Jake cleared his throat, still staring at the floor. "Maybe we should try to do it—you know, solve the clues. If we flat-out crushed it, that would be gigantic, right?"

"OK. I guess that's one way to go," TJ said. "We'll call that Option B. Chilling with Yoo-hoos is Option A. Solving the clues, a solid Option B."

Jake read the clue off the floor. "'Their loss is our gain. We cracked the code just the same.' So what do they have here that was lost?"

"Probably a lot of things. But first, how about we vote on that Yoo-hoo proposal?" TJ looked around, realizing that Lucy was gone. "Hey, where's the Nicaragua girl?"

"Nepal," Jake said.

"What?"

"Nepal," Jake repeated. "She said she just moved back from Nepal." Jake turned to see Lucy on the other side of the room, jiggling the handle of the "Staff Only" footlocker.

"If I can get my mobile back, we can Google the clues," Lucy said.

Jake lost his train of thought. He wasn't sure if it was

because of the way she pronounced "mobile" (MOH-bile) or because he was just now seeing her up close. She was a little taller than Jake, though not so much as to make him feel short. But her eyes—they were the most intense green eyes he had ever seen. She twisted a paper clip and jammed it into the lock.

"Whatthewhat?" TJ stood up. "Not sure what a 'MOH-bile' is, but I'm pretty sure there's an official lockdown on those cell phones. I don't how they roll in Nigeria, but I'm not looking to add 'breaking and entering' to my college application."

"Nepal," Lucy corrected.

"Right. Well, ixnay on the breaking and entering, Miss Nepal," said TJ.

"Lucy," she said, standing up and turning back to the boys.

"Hmm?" asked TJ.

"My name is Lucy. Use my name and I'll use yours. Or would you prefer Captain What's-His-Name?"

"Uhh, uhh, uhh." TJ appeared to be losing his breath. "Captain What's-His-Name?"

"The little cartoon on your shirt."

"Really? Little cartoon?" TJ looked to Jake, who grimaced uncomfortably. "It's America. Captain AMERICA. Like the land of the free, home of the brave, the first Avenger. Need I go on?"

"So, TJ it is," said Lucy, tossing the paper clip into the trash can. "That's not going to work. It's a double-pin lock. I could open it, but I'd need to break it."

Jake was staring at the floor again, muttering to himself.

"'Their loss' and 'our gain.' I've been to every exhibit here, more than once, and I can't think of . . . Wait! The U-505 submarine downstairs. Stellar! They captured it from the Germans in World War II. It was their loss and our gain."

"Sounds like a stretch," Lucy said. "What's that have to do with a cracked code?"

Jake grinned. "Germany's secret code machine was onboard. It helped us win the war."

"I guess that's worth a shot," said Lucy as Jake picked up the clue card and pointed across the lobby to the stairwell.

Lucy headed for the stairwell with Jake close behind. TJ brought up the rear, muttering something about Yoo-hoos and Option A.

AS ABOVE, SO BELOW

WHEN THEY EXITED THE STAIRWELL, they arrived in the cavernous lower level, a sprawling cement room as big as a stadium. In the center a massive German submarine, nearly three stories tall, was bathed in floodlights and docked as if it had been captured yesterday.

"I'll bet it's somewhere over here." Jake walked to a glass display case. Inside was a strange typewriter-looking machine.

Lucy read the card next to the machine. "M4 Enigma machine taken from the U-505 German submarine. The Enigma and its codebooks were rushed to Washington, D.C., to help the Allied code-breaking effort."

"Their loss was our gain," Jake said.

"We cracked the code just the same," Lucy replied with a smile.

TJ spotted a yellow clue box under the display. "Bam! Ten points for Gryffindor!"

Before he could open the box, Lucy reached in and pulled out the bright yellow envelope. She tore it open and tossed the envelope to TJ, keeping the card. TJ flinched but managed to catch it.

"Next clue." Lucy read from the card. "'As above, so below.'"

"Great," said TJ, throwing the crumpled envelope back to Lucy. "Weirder and weirder. Next thing you know, Mr. Wonka's going to take us on a psychedelic boat ride."

Lucy gave TJ a puzzled look.

"You know," TJ said, squirting his hands with more gel. "Willy Wonka? Oompa Loompas?"

Lucy's look of confusion didn't change.

"Wow! Avengers I kind of understand, but no Willy Wonka in Namibia either?"

"Focus," Lucy said, not commenting on the fact that TJ still couldn't remember Nepal. "'As above.' I'll check out the exhibits on the balcony. Why don't you two see if there's anything on the main floor. Meet back here in ten."

"Whoa," TJ said. "I don't remember electing you Supreme Commander."

"Suit yourself," Lucy called over her shoulder as she headed toward the stairwell.

"OK. And then there were two," TJ said, turning to Jake. "Now how about those Yoo-hoos?"

Jake was staring at the floor, his lips moving silently. He looked up at TJ. "She's not right."

"Who? Funky Thai girl? I agree, on so many levels."

"No, I mean about 'so below.'" Jake headed across the

room. "Let's check out the first floor but I think we might need a different strategy."

"OK, so that's a pause on the Yoo-hoos for now." TJ followed Jake into the elevator.

When the doors opened, the two boys stepped out into the north wing of the enormous main lobby where a sea of half-opened shipping crates surrounded a towering Ferris wheel.

A huge poster reading "Chicago: Then and Now" was stretched along the massive far wall. "Temporary exhibit opening Monday," Jake said, looking for any signs of a yellow envelope. "Supposed to be flat-out classic."

He pointed to the Ferris wheel. "That's a replica from the 1893 Chicago World's Fair. They've also got choice stuff from the Civil War, the Bears' Super Bowl trophy, Michael Jordan's shoes, even props from movies made in Chicago."

Two security guards stood by a large opened crate.

"No way." TJ stepped toward a gleaming red and blue metallic robot over thirty feet tall. "Optimus Prime?"

It's from the *Transformers* movie they filmed here," Jake said.

"Really? Awesome. How do you know about all this?" TJ couldn't take his eyes off the robot.

"My Uncle Gabe works here sometimes. We're coming to the exhibit when it opens next week."

They walked to the center of the floor where a security guard with curly red hair stood next to an industrial-looking steel cabinet. The front was marked "Lincoln Library" just above a high-tech keypad.

"Whoa," TJ said. "That case looks like it could survive a nuclear explosion. What's in it? The crown jewels?"

"You could say that. I think it's why Uncle Gabe wants to come," Jake said. "He's really into the Civil War. It's President Lincoln's hat and gloves."

"Cool, although I think a life-size Optimus Prime might be the real crown jewels."

"It's the hat and gloves the president wore the night he was assassinated. Complete with blood stains."

"What? Weird. Cool, I guess. But weird. But cool, I think. But still weird."

The red-haired security guard turned to the boys. "Hey kids, you're not allowed in this area."

"I can respect that, sir," Jake said. "But we're on a bit of an official exercise here. The Uni Prep Scavenger Hunt. You may have received a memo. Anyway, we plan to be the victors and we think—"

"Not here. Not tonight. This wing is no access until it's set up."

"Sorry, sir," Jake said as he and TJ turned back. "I have another 'so below' thought I want to check out. See if Lucy found anything upstairs. Meet back here in ten?"

"I still like the Yoo-hoo plan better," TJ said, stepping into the elevator. "But if you say so." He added, as the elevator doors closed, "Captain Corn Dog."

It should just die if I ignore it, right? Jake thought as he crossed the lobby to the coal mine wing. *Just ignore it.*

So below. As Jake approached the old cage elevator, he re-membered how scary the trip down into the coal mine had

31

been when he was little. The rickety chain elevator and the dark walls seeping with water were almost too much. Now it was one of his favorite exhibits. When the elevator reached the shaft floor, he slid the cage open and stepped into the passageway as the cool, damp air enveloped him.

His eyes slowly adjusted to the dim light coming from the wall lanterns and he began edging down the stone path. He passed an open room with crusty miner equipment and headgear hanging on the walls. A small wooden table stood in the center, covered with old lamps they'd used to detect poisonous fumes. Jake remembered that this was where the guides would light a lamp as part of the demonstration. He scanned the room but there was no sign of any clues.

When the path ended at the entrance to the mine train, Jake realized he hadn't seen an employee down here, not a single one. As he turned back toward the elevator, he felt an extra chill. On his next step a thunderous explosion rocked the tunnel. The lights shattered and the cave was plunged into darkness. Broken glass and dust rained down on Jake's head as he was slammed to the floor.

CAVE DARK

THERE'S DARK AND THEN THERE'S CAVE DARK. The kind of dark you only get where there's absolutely no light. The kind of dark you can feel. Jake choked through the swirling dust and rose to his knees. He held one hand in front of his face. He couldn't even see his wiggling fingers. *Cave dark.*

He tried to stand but fell back to the floor, his ears still ringing from the explosion as he wiped dirt from his eyes and spit dust out of his mouth. Had the explosion knocked out all the power, or just down in the mine? What had caused the explosion? Would there be more?

Not wanting to wait to find out, he stumbled to his feet and fumbled his way to the wall. He could feel the cool, damp air and hear the water trickling further ahead.

This is totally manageable. Just scoot my feet slowly along the wall and I won't fall onto the tracks.

He shuffled for about ten minutes before reaching what he hoped was the way back through the tunnel. His hunch was confirmed as he felt the stone wall become damp, then slick with water. Jake moved more quickly as the narrow passage began to expand, though everything was still pitch black. Jake thought his eyes would have adjusted by now, but without even a hint of light, it didn't matter.

He finally came to an opening. He let go of the wall and took a careful step. If his memory was correct he should— *oomph.* The table's edge painfully confirmed his hunch. He was in the demonstration room and headed in the right direction. He leaned against the table. Why was he breathing so hard? *Stay calm. Be positive.* Slowly his breathing returned to normal. *What was that?* He'd thought he heard someone. No, not exactly heard, more like felt. He could feel the room's air moving slowly across his neck, as if someone else, or something else, was breathing. He stood completely still. Nothing. *Maybe cave dark makes you cave crazy?*

He eased his hands along the tabletop. He had an idea. His fingers finally landed on a small box the size of a matchbox. *Exactly* the size of a matchbox, because it was a matchbox.

Yes. Now the lamp. He swept his hands across the tabletop. He felt the cold metal of the lantern just before he knocked it off the table. The sound of the shattering glass echoed off the stone walls.

So now we have a good news/bad news situation. Good news: I found the lamp. Bad news: I smashed it into tiny pieces and I'm now going to die a slow, painful death in the dark. Jake slowly searched through the broken glass with his foot. On one swipe he managed to kick the base of the lamp. He leaned down and gingerly picked through the pieces. The glass was definitely toast and the top was dented, but the rest seemed to be intact.

Slowly, carefully, Jake pulled a match out of the box. He fumbled for the right end before striking the match against the side. There was a scraping noise followed by the match snapping in two. Not even a spark. He tried again. And again. Same result. He had one match left.

"Use the Force, Luke. Use the Force," he quietly mouthed to himself. He carefully dragged the last match along the side of the box.

First, there was the unmistakably crisp sound of a flame sparking to life as a burst of light filled the chamber. This was immediately followed by a boot flashing from the shadows and slamming into Jake's forehead, sending him crashing back to the floor. The ancient lamp clanged along the stone floor, casting a flickering shadow onto Jake as a dark figure hovered over his crumpled body.

DON'T PANIC

THIS TIME IT WAS JAKE'S EARS that came to life first . . . sort of.

"Surhwhirrrworrrrrrrr."

"Surhwhiworrrr," the muffled sound echoed somewhere in his head.

Jake opened his eyes. The glow from the lantern blinded him before he snapped his eyes shut. His sense of smell kicked in next. *Green apple?*

"Surwhirrwirreee."

He tried to open his eyes again. This time he was able to keep them open just a crack, adjusting to the lantern glare. He began to make out a blurry figure standing over him.

"Soworeeee."

The sound was growing clearer.

"I'm soreeeee."

"I'm sooo sorry!"

He blinked again, both eyes fully functioning as he squinted up into two deep green eyes.

"I'm so sorry! I'm so sorry!" Lucy hovered over him, staring down with a concerned look.

"Whaaa?" Jake was confused but he recovered quickly, sitting up, trying to sound cool. "I'm OK. I'm OK."

"I'm so sorry," Lucy repeated. "You know you have two different colored eyes?"

"What happened?" Jake realized his lip was bleeding.

"I heard someone breathing," Lucy said. "Then this crash. I thought you were one of them."

"One of who? What hit me?" Jake sat up.

"I did."

"You punched me?"

"It wasn't a punch."

"Huh?"

"Mawashi-geri."

Jake was getting more confused, not less.

"Martial arts. Basically a roundhouse kick," Lucy said, grabbing Jake's hand and pulling him to his feet. "I'm glad you're OK. No serious injuries."

"I don't know. That might be a premature conclusion," Jake said, dabbing the blood off his lip.

"But you're OK, right?"

"I guess, but—"

"We need to get out of here."

Lucy grabbed the lantern and walked into the tunnel. She paused, noticing that Jake was still dabbing his lip. "Are you going to be weird about this?"

"Weird? I don't know. I mean, I've been assaulted and—"

"You have a hard time letting go of stuff or something?"

"I don't think I would call—Wait, what did you mean by 'one of them'? The museum is closed. Just our group and the museum security."

"Don't really know," Lucy said as they reached the elevator room. "I was upstairs when something blew up. Lights went out. People were running. Someone yelled, 'Stop! Put your hands up!' Then I heard a couple of loud bursts. No more yelling."

What?" Jake couldn't believe what he was hearing. "Loud bursts? Like gunshots?"

"I heard the body drop right before I ducked into the stairwell."

"Toxic. What do you think happened?"

"Someone must be stealing something." Lucy punched the powerless elevator buttons with no response.

Jake swung open a cage door leading to a steel ladder running up the shaft. "This might be our best bet."

When they reached the platform at the top they slowly cracked the door open and peered out. There was just enough moonlight from the windows to see the outline of the giant Ferris wheel. They were back in the "Chicago: Then and Now" exhibit. Now, however, instead of a half-assembled exhibit, it looked half-demolished.

"Not good," Lucy whispered as they squinted through the darkness at the open crates scattered around the room.

"I guess we know what the big boom was," Jake said. "I think the nearest exit's at the end of this wall, just past the Ferris wheel. We could crawl along here. Or go back to the stairwell. Two solid options. I propose we—"

Lucy had already slid out of the stairwell and was commando-crawling on her elbows and stomach along the edge of the wall.

"So, crawl it is." Jake slid onto his stomach following her.

As they squirmed past the open crates and debris, the moonlight passing through the occasional window threw an eerie spotlight on the wreckage. Jake noticed something. While many of the cases had been blown open, the contents were still there—the Super Bowl trophy, Michael Jordan's shoes, all the movie props. The more they crawled through the debris the more he realized it was all still here, just tossed around like garbage.

"Curious," Jake whispered.

"What?"

"All this choice stuff, it's got to be worth millions," Jake said. "They left it all."

They were almost to the end of the room when they found something blocking their path. Jake recognized the steel box immediately. The box that looked like it could survive a nuclear explosion—hadn't. The door marked "Lincoln Library" was littered with black scorch marks. Shattered bits of glass, flecks of steel, and scraps of paper were scattered all around. The box itself was empty.

Lucy motioned that she was going to climb around the crate and slowly rose to her feet, leaning against the box.

"I think they got what they wanted," Jake said, joining her.

"Who? What?"

Jake swept around the room with his eyes. "The Lincoln case. It's the only one where things are missing."

"That's interesting but we have bigger problems." Lucy tried to quietly push on the crate next to her. It was about the size of a refrigerator. "Give me a hand."

Jake leaned against the crate and joined her in pushing.

Suddenly the door gave way, and the crate and all its contents came crashing down on them. Jake was knocked to the floor by a pile of old firefighter helmets, antique pickaxes, and display mannequins. He fought his way out and scrambled to his knees, spitting a Styrofoam packing peanut out of his mouth. "That could have killed me."

"Don't panic," Lucy whispered, looking over Jake's shoulder.

"I'm not panicking. But with any potentially lethal situation I think—"

"No, just turn around. But don't panic." Lucy pointed over Jake's shoulder.

Jake slowly turned to see the lifeless eyes of the redheaded security guard staring from the rubble.

8

A SITUATION

JAKE STUMBLED BACK, scraping off the packing peanuts and staring down at the body. "Ahem. Is he—?"

"Definitely," Lucy said, kneeling with her ear to the man's mouth and feeling his wrist.

Jake raised his eyebrows. "You have a lot of experience examining dead people?"

"Just once; our tribal chief ate some unripe popolo berries. Not pretty." She began patting the man's jacket and searching his pockets. "He doesn't seem to have any injuries. Maybe it was a heart attack or something."

"Tribal chief? Wait. What are you doing?"

"Looking for a weapon."

"What? No. No. We're just looking for the exit. We're not stocking up for a counter-assault."

Lucy ignored his protest and finished rifling through the guard's pockets. "Just a penlight and this old handkerchief.

Not exactly combat-ready." She pocketed the penlight and tossed the cloth to Jake. "Use this. Your lip's still bleeding."

Jake caught the cloth and dabbed the trickle of blood from his lip.

"Where did you get this?" Jake asked as he shoved it into his pocket.

"It was in his hand. I had to pry it out."

"Don't stop until you find it." A voice suddenly echoed through the lobby as flashlight beams bounced across the walls and began to move toward them.

Jake and Lucy dropped to the floor and slid toward the stairwell, making it inside just as the lights hit the spot where they had been standing.

They scrambled up the stairs, coming to a dead end at a steel door. Lucy dropped to her knees and edged the door open. As Jake eased onto the balcony, he could see the glow of flashlights fanning out across the lobby below. They slid along the floor until they found themselves nudged up against the entrance to the 727 suspended from the ceiling.

"If we don't find them, you get to be the one to tell him." The voice was followed by the sound of boots kicking through the debris.

Jake and Lucy quietly retreated from the railing and slipped into the plane. The inside of the passenger plane was set up just like it had been when it was still flying. They crept between the rows of seats until they reached an opening where one of the plane's windows had been removed for the exhibit. They slowly rose up and gazed out over the wing. The flashlights were cutting back and forth below, bouncing off the piles of rubble.

"What's the big deal?" This was a new voice, wafting up from the wreckage. "He's got the hat."

"He wants the gloves. So, we get the gloves." The first voice stepped toward the other man into a pocket of moonlight. He had a short military haircut, a triangle-shaped scar on the side of his neck, and some kind of small high-tech rifle slung over his shoulder. "Unless you want to be the one to tell him."

Jake and Lucy backed away from the window. Jake pressed up against the airplane wall and slid down until he was sitting on the floor next to a row of seats. Lucy silently joined him.

"What do you think the chances are . . ." Jake pulled the faded cloth out of his pocket. His blood had already begun to dry on it. As he spread it out on the floor, the stiff cloth cracked and separated into two pieces. ". . . that this old handkerchief has fingers?"

Lucy flicked on the penlight as Jake carefully unfolded one of the pieces, then the other, each revealing the fingers of a glove.

As they leaned in closer, Lucy passed the beam over the gloves, dimly illuminating every wrinkle, crack, and discoloration. As the beam reached the wrist of one of the gloves, two sewn letters were revealed.

"A.L.," Jake whispered. He slumped back against the wall. "I think we found the source of their agitation."

The men continued to rummage below, tossing aside boxes, kicking at whatever was in their way.

"They don't sound like they're leaving." Jake winced as he wiped his lip on his sleeve.

Lucy shone the light on Jake's lip. "You're still bleeding a bit. I'm sorry."

"Yeah, you said that already. I'm OK."

"You need a tissue." Lucy dabbed his lip with part of her sleeve.

"Sure, but how about something that's less than a hundred fifty years old?" Jake carefully folded the gloves and shoved them back into his pocket.

Lucy directed the beam along the aisle until it illuminated the door to the airplane lavatory. "Let's see how realistic they make this exhibit." She scooted softly over to the door. "Maybe there's a tissue in here." She carefully pulled on the door latch. Nothing. She pulled harder. Nothing.

She put both hands on the handle and pulled even harder. At last, the door sprang open. Before Lucy could reach for her penlight, a hand lunged out of the darkness and grabbed her face.

UNACCEPTABLE

LUCY DROPPED THE LIGHT and spun around, snapping her foot into her attacker's forehead. As he fell back, Jake lunged for the door and slammed it shut. They heard a crash as they jammed themselves against the door. No one tried to get out—there was no pushing, no pounding. In fact, there were no sounds coming from the other side at all—only the sounds of the men loudly rustling through the crates below.

Minutes went by. They pressed against the door, hearts pounding. The only noise came from the muffled rustling in the lobby below. Jake and Lucy slipped down to the floor, careful to keep their weight pressed against the door. Jake wiped the sweat off his forehead with his sleeve and stared silently at Lucy. *We can't stay here forever. Sooner or later the goon in the bathroom will wake up. And then there's the guys below. Not exactly a lot of good options.* From the look on Lucy's face, Jake could tell she was thinking the same thing.

After several more minutes of silence, Lucy rose to her

knees and cupped her ear to the door. She shook her head at Jake and slowly stepped back. Jake followed, easing his weight off the door. This time, there was no violence. The door just swung back lazily, dangling on a broken hinge. They took a step closer, squinting through the darkness. Lucy flicked on the penlight. The beam settled on a body slumped on the floor against the toilet seat. The figure was wearing a Captain America T-shirt and a name tag that read: "Hi! My Name is TJ."

Lucy rolled her eyes, stepping over TJ's body to pull a tissue out of the dispenser on the wall. "Look at that. They have tissues." She smiled and handed the tissue to Jake, who pressed it against his lip. He stared at Lucy, then at the unconscious TJ, then back at Lucy. He wasn't sure whether to be impressed or scared. He went with both.

Lucy reached over and tapped TJ's forehead. Nothing. She began softly slapping his cheek. She flicked his ear.

"Whatthewhat?" TJ rose up, protecting his face.

"Shhhhh." Lucy covered his mouth with her hand.

He rubbed his ear.

"Sorry," she said. "Necessary procedure."

"It's us," Jake whispered, turning the penlight on himself so TJ could see him.

"Shhhhh." Lucy pointed out the plane window.

TJ gently rubbed his cheek where he had been kicked and eased into the aisle, joining Jake and Lucy on the floor. "OK, this scavenger hunt has gotten out of hand. I think Greg's out for blood." He pulled the small tube of sanitizing gel out of his pocket.

"It's some sort of heist," Jake said. "Level 3 situation I'd say. We think they blew up something and now they're right down below."

TJ was staring at Jake but seemed distracted. "Your eyes, they're—"

"Yeah, I know. One gray, one blue," Jake said.

"Whoa. Just like the commander in Sonic the Hedgehog. Let me ask you something, do you ever—"

"Guys! Can we focus? How did you get here?" Lucy asked TJ.

"I was coming up to find you." He squirted a dab of gel onto his hands and rubbed them together. "I'd just stepped into the plane when I heard this explosion and all the lights went out. I looked out the window and saw these guys with some kind of laser guns coming down the hallway, storm trooper style. I ducked in the bathroom."

"Was that it?" Lucy asked.

"I hid in here for a while. Sometimes I'd hear voices or someone running past. But then someone came on the plane. They tried to open the bathroom door. The lock doesn't work, but I held it tight. It must have been a few of those big goons though, because I couldn't hold them off. They finally yanked the door open. I took a swing at one of them. I think I tagged him pretty good, but it wasn't a fair fight. He whomped me in the head, felt like the butt of his rifle. Must have knocked me out."

Lucy looked at Jake and rolled her eyes.

"The next thing I know, you guys are waking me up."

"That was quite a fight. The butt of a rifle?" Lucy said.

"Look, I don't like to brag, but you don't reach two million on Super Smash Bros. without picking up a few moves—Tornado Punch, Power Slap, a few combos."

"Well, actually—" Lucy started, but Jake gave her a stare and shook his head.

"What was that?" said TJ.

"Long story. Another time," said Jake.

"What happened to *you*?" TJ pointed to the tissue Jake was holding to his lip.

"Similar situation. Big goon. Worthy fight. Knocked out," Jake said.

Lucy looked up at the ceiling and shook her head.

"These guys are vicious!" TJ said. "What do you think's going on? If this is some kind of hazing thing, my dad's a lawyer."

"Not quite," Jake said. "It looks like they're after the Lincoln artifacts."

"Really? What about Optimus Prime, did they take that?" TJ asked with a look of concern.

"No, just the Lincoln stuff."

"Whewww," TJ said, but after seeing Jake's and Lucy's looks, he quickly added, "But, yeah, the Lincoln stuff. That's awful. It's just that a life-size Optimus Prime . . . I mean . . . never mind. Yeah, Lincoln stuff, terrible."

A door below swung open. Jake, Lucy, and TJ crawled across the aisle and slowly rose to peek out over the lobby. A sharp sound rocketed off the marble walls like a firecracker. The men below jumped to attention.

"Well, gents, what's the good report?" an intimidating voice called out from the shadows.

"Nothing yet, sir," one of the men replied.

The bright crack sounded again as the figure stepped out of the shadows. Jake could make out only the dark outline of a man's back. The shadowed figure took another step, spinning some sort of cane. The moonlight from the window glanced off the silver handle as he twirled it.

He brought the cane down with unexpected force onto one of the crates, smashing a hole through the top. "Unacceptable. I'm afraid that's unacceptable."

"We're looking, sir," said the commando with the crew cut and the triangle scar. "We at least have the hat." This time the sound was cane on flesh as the commando was struck by the man, causing him to drop to the ground, grabbing his shoulder.

By now, a strange rancid smell had started to rise up to the plane. The three kids felt their eyes begin to water and they covered their noses.

"Excuses, Mr. Slate, excuses. The hat is not enough. Highly unacceptable. Shall we try again?"

"We'll . . . we'll find the gloves." Slate stumbled back to his feet.

"We'll find the gloves *quickly*," the voice said.

"Yes. We'll find them quickly."

"Yes. You will." The figure disappeared back into the shadows and the soldiers returned to sifting through the rubble, twice as fast as before.

Jake, Lucy, and TJ eased away from the window and dropped back to the airplane floor.

"OK. First, what is that smell? It's like rotten eggs," TJ asked.

"Maybe it's the explosives they used." Jake wiped his eyes.

"Hey, maybe they'll find the gloves and get out of here," TJ suggested.

Lucy looked at Jake with concern.

"What?" TJ looked at Lucy and then at Jake. "I've seen enough movies to know that look. When there's three people and one guy says something and the second guy looks at the third guy without saying anything, that's never good. What is it?

Jake pulled the gloves from his pocket and smiled sheepishly.

"OK." TJ blinked. "Don't tell me that's the one thing Mr. Happy Cane down there wants for Christmas."

They said nothing.

"Lincoln's gloves?"

Jake waved the gloves. "The source of his agitation."

"Well, OK, I'm out," TJ said.

"You're out?" Lucy asked.

"Right. See, I don't do scavenger hunts where the winner gets a pair of old gloves and the loser gets a date with psycho storm troopers."

"Well, that's nice, but you can't be out."

"Look, just give them the gloves."

"Sure, we'll tell them it was all a misunderstanding," Lucy said.

"We could just drop the gloves over the railing, create some kind of diversion, and run for it," TJ said.

"There's too many of them, and they're between us and the door," Lucy said.

Jake eased back up to the window. He peered through, his lips moving while he quietly muttered to himself before turning back. "It's crucial we get to a phone. Even if someone's already called 911, we may need to hide until they get to us. There's a door on the other balcony. Looks like a stairwell." He slumped down and turned to Lucy. "We should get back to the auditorium, crack open the footlocker, retrieve the phones."

"Our mobiles. Great idea," Lucy said.

"Well, unfortunately I left my jetpack at home." TJ was staring out over the lobby to the opposite balcony.

"We can crawl out over the wing," Lucy said. "And then jump to the balcony."

"Really? Crawl on the wing and jump?" TJ shook his head. "I think there's some confusion. I know I'm wearing a Captain America T-shirt. But I'm not, you know, actually Captain America. And I don't want to be in your crazy action movie! Look, they don't even know we're here. I say we just cram into the bathroom and wait for the police."

"Just hang around like sitting ducks?" asked Lucy.

"I'd rather be a sitting duck than a dead duck," TJ responded.

"Where do you think dead ducks come from?"

At that moment the inside of the plane lit up in a flash of red light. They dove to the floor as a red laser streamed through the windows from below and bounced off the walls. Then it was gone.

Jake peered out the window. The lasers from the guns of a small group of shadowed figures were streaming across the dark lobby.

"They're spreading out," Jake said, ducking back down.

They crawled toward the opening.

"Too late." Lucy pointed through the window to two red beams at the top of the stairs. "It's just a matter of time before they search the plane. We've got to get out of here."

"We can't get out that way, they'll see us," Jake said.

"Maybe there's another way." Lucy crouched onto the seat next to the open window and began to lift herself through.

"What? No way," TJ said.

"Leave the gloves on the floor where they can see them. It's our best bet," Lucy whispered back.

The sound of shuffling boots grew closer.

"I don't know if—" Before TJ could finish his thought, a stream of red light sliced through the back windows.

Lucy dove through the open window and onto the wing. TJ and Jake were right behind her.

They lay silently in the darkness, listening for any movement below. Nothing. The cold steel chilled Jake's face as he clung to the wing. They weren't in flight, but as Jake squinted over at the cement floor three stories below, he figured they might as well be.

Loud banging echoed through the air. The commandos were in the plane. The wing shook. The kids doubled their grips, trying desperately to keep from being thrown off.

There were no voices, just shuffling boots and the rustling of storage compartments as the soldiers searched the plane. An occasional stray laser beam bounced through the window and streamed over the kids' heads, stopping Jake's heart.

Lucy looked at Jake. Jake looked at TJ. TJ closed his eyes.

It was only a matter of time before they were discovered.

Lucy carefully shifted her body so she faced the edge. She began slowly pulling herself along the wing.

Jake tapped TJ's arm and began to follow. The further they scooted toward the edge, the more Jake's hands seemed to tremble.

A red beam shot through one of the windows, passing just in front of TJ's face. As he ducked, his name tag snapped off. The kids froze. There were about three seconds of silence as the name tag dropped through the darkness. Then came the sound of plastic hitting the marble floor.

They pressed their faces into the metal wing as tightly as they could. Jake just barely made out a red beam skittering toward the spot where the name tag had landed. A soldier moved toward the spot, leading with his rifle's laser sight until he was directly below them. A boot crunched over something plastic. Through the dim red glare, Jake could see the man reach down and pick up the name tag. He looked to his left and then to his right, and then tossed the name tag onto a pile of debris. Jake exhaled as the man returned to his work.

Lucy inched herself forward one more time, reaching the wing's end. Jake and TJ followed and were now clinging to the wing just behind her. Small beads of sweat dropped from Jake's forehead, hitting the wing like liquid marbles. Lucy slowly rose to her knees.

"Hopefully they'll just grab the gloves and leave," TJ whispered, his face still smashed against the wing.

"Hey, what are you doing up there?" One of the commando's voices rang out. Lucy ducked and held her breath.

"We're searching the plane," a voice responded over the crackle of a radio. "If you're done down there, we could use some help."

"On our way."

It was now or never.

Lucy rose to her knees, crouching low on the tip of the wing. She counted to three in some language Jake didn't recognize. Then she leapt.

CHICAGO'S FINEST

THE WING BOUNCED as Lucy pushed off. The boys fought to hang on. She landed on the edge of the balcony and hoisted herself over the railing.

TJ was next. "OK. Just like the lava pit in Super Mario," TJ mumbled. The plane rocked again as TJ launched into the air. Jake tightened his sweaty grip as TJ landed on the other side.

A red beam cut through the air and began moving across the wing.

Jake rose to a crouch. His turn. *Not a big jump. Totally manageable. Less than the standing jump in gym class.* This felt different, though. Maybe it was the pitch-black darkness. Maybe it was the thirty-foot drop to certain death. Maybe it was the lunatics with the laser guns. Well, actually it was probably all of the above.

Jake could hear the crackle of the radios and see the laser inching closer across the wing. He took a breath. "I'm OK. I'm

OK," he whispered before swinging his arms and launching from the wing.

However long he was in the air, it was a little too long. In the seconds between the moment his feet left the wing and when they were supposed to land on the overhang, a red laser lit up his face. Jake slammed blindly into the side of the balcony. He lunged for the railing, just barely catching it before he slid off. His eyes burned. All he could see were red spots. He felt his grip slipping. He tried to swing his leg over the railing but missed. On the next try one of his hands slipped off. Just as his other hand was losing its grip, someone latched onto his wrist. TJ had clawed back over the railing and had a hold on Jake's arm.

Jake dangled by one arm and flailed for the railing with the other. Radios across the lobby erupted. "Target East Balcony." Two red beams cut through the air, spraying bullets as they traced across the wing. TJ hoisted Jake over the rail and they dove to the floor as more rounds slammed into the wall above them. The three kids crashed through the door and into the stairwell just as the first commando launched himself out the window and onto the wing.

When they reached the first floor, the one thing they had on their side was the dark. From the moonlight passing through, Jake could just make out the entrance doors across the lobby. They crouched and ran to the middle of the lobby before sliding behind the remains of the tornado exhibit.

"Halfway," Jake whispered. They took a breath and crouched back up, ready to sprint. "Totally doable. Get ready to run," he said. "On three. One, two—" Before Jake reached three, a series of pops exploded through the lobby. Each one brought a flash and another overhead light back to life. Someone had restored the power.

They dove back onto the floor behind the shattered exhibit as the lobby filled with light.

Though they now clearly saw the exit doors just across the lobby, they could also spot commandos gazing down from the balcony. They would never make it with the lights on.

"If anyone has a diversion in mind, this would be a good time," TJ said.

Jake looked across the shattered glass from the destroyed Twister tower. Then he saw it. For such a complicated exhibit, the Twister had a pretty simple control switch. The panel said "Vortex" with a dial reading from "Off" to "10." A green sticker next to the "6" said "Maximum Speed for Public Tours."

Jake glanced up from the panel just in time to see Slate launch himself from the balcony over the railing. The soldier hit the lobby floor only a few yards away, sprang up like a cat, and began to sprint toward the kids. Jake cranked the dial all the way. A blast of air erupted. He had heard tornado survivors on TV describe the sound as a freight train; this sounded more like a jet engine. The kids were blown off their feet and their bodies didn't stop moving once they hit the floor. It was like someone had turned on a giant leaf blower and they were loose scraps of paper.

At least they were on the back side of the explosion. The front side of the blast was even worse. Without the confines of the tower, the twister erupted across the lobby with a fury.

The angry wave of air hit Slate and his comrades full-on, scattering them like rag dolls.

The swirling vortex then slammed into the far wall. With nowhere to go but up, it shot skyward, straight into the 727. The blast propelled the plane's nose up into the ceiling, rocking it off its steel supports. The plane then rebounded, plummeting down into the lobby as the twister exploded out through the glass doors.

The kids rose to their feet and wiped the dust from their eyes. Plane fragments and dust and debris rained down. The sound of electrical sparks and crackling filled the air. Fire alarms began to wail as the sprinklers kicked on. Through the swirling dust cloud, Jake could hardly even see the entrance doors, which were now blocked by the fallen tail section of the plane. There was one dim light flickering next to an unblocked door. The trio dashed through the door and followed the stairwell up.

They passed each floor until they ended at a steel door bearing a "Roof Maintenance Only" sign. They burst through the door and collapsed in a pile on the roof, coughing and sucking in the warm night air. They were on a massive flat rooftop, as big as a football field. Stray ribbons of moonlight glanced off weathered electrical boxes emitting a dull hum. The only other light was a faint glow at the roof's edge, where ancient brass floodlights beamed down to the grounds below.

"It doesn't . . . look like . . ." Jake said to TJ in between breaths, "you've got a choice."

"What? About what?"

"Crazy action movie."

"Yeah, well, that's my only scene," TJ said, stumbling to his feet. "Did you see that freaky jump from the balcony? That's not normal."

Lucy leaned back against a large steel air-conditioning unit. "You read too many comic books. Can we focus?" She coughed. "We need to get out of here."

Jake stood up and walked to the edge of the roof, staring over the night sky across the park and the university campus beyond.

"The good news is I don't think our laser tag friends are going anywhere soon," TJ said, stepping next to Jake.

"We shouldn't count on it," Lucy said, joining the boys at the roof's edge. "Unless they found the gloves before the plane blew up."

"Or," TJ said with a smile, "we can wait for the cavalry." He pointed out toward the boulevard where two police SUVs were streaming into the museum park.

The SUVs screeched to a stop in front of the entrance steps just below the kids. Two police officers jumped out of each one. Jake leaned over the edge to try to get their attention. Before he could yell, one of the officers' radios blared.

"Bravo 8, this is Precinct. Do you read?"

The officer pushed a button on his shoulder and shouted back. "Bravo 8 read, this is Lieutenant Bates."

"Affirmative, Lieutenant Bates. We have a report of an alarm and power surge in Museum Park. Do you need support?"

"Negative, checking on it now. It looks like just a generator fail, no support needed," responded Bates. "Will report back if needed."

"Affirmative, Bravo 8."

The kids exchanged looks of confusion.

No support needed? Jake thought. *What is he talking about? This is definitely a "call every fire truck and a small army" situation.* Jake rose up to yell to the police but was interrupted again, this time by the museum's huge doors clanging open.

A cloud of dust poured out and two dark shadows emerged from the swirl. They were covered in grime, but Jake recognized the guns strapped to their backs.

The kids hit the floor, bracing for a shoot-out. There was nothing—no gunfire, no struggle. Not even an order to "Drop your weapons." Just a calm voice.

"Get a little messy in there?" said the police officer's voice.

"A few complications. It's under control. Two bodies to extract. And one missing piece," said the soldier. "We're doing another sweep. Can you keep the hold?"

"I just bought us some time with the District and we're intercepting all the 911s."

"Well, Lieutenant Bates," the soldier said, laughing as they headed back into the building. "They don't call you Chicago's finest for nothing."

PANIC LIE

THE KIDS' LOOKS OF CONFUSION turned to shock.

"So much for the cavalry," said Lucy, edging toward the back of the roof. "We need a Plan B."

"Have any ideas?" said TJ as he and Jake crossed toward her.

"Rubbish," Lucy said, staring over the edge.

"What?" Jake looked down to a garbage dumpster below. It was about the size of a truck and filled with black plastic bags. Normally Jake would have thought jumping off a three-story building into a pile of garbage to be one of the strangest things he had ever done. Tonight it wouldn't make his top five.

TJ peered over the edge. "Wait. Maybe somebody left a rope or a ladder or a Bat-hook lying around."

"It's not that high." Lucy stepped up on the ledge.

"Right. It's not the height so much as the garb—"

Lucy jumped.

"Of course," TJ said as Lucy hit the garbage below.

Jake went next, plummeting into the sea of stuffed garbage bags before pulling himself up on the side with Lucy. TJ hesitated at the roof's edge, desperately looking around for other options. Finally, he jumped. He hit the garbage like a toddler eating broccoli: eyes clenched and nose pinched.

The three rolled out of the bin and bolted across the museum grounds, slowing only when they reached a grove of trees at the far edge of the park. They collapsed onto the grass, out of breath and smelling like a mix of yesterday's leftovers and dirty mop water.

"Chicago's finest?" TJ said, frantically squirting sanitizer onto his hands and smearing it over his arms, legs and even his face.

Jake rose to his knees, still catching his breath. "I heard it, but I don't believe it."

"What I can't believe is that we made it out," Lucy said. "But what about the other kids, and the teachers?"

"We need to get to a phone," TJ said.

"What if they're intercepting more than just 911 calls?" said Lucy.

"OK, no phone. We need to get to someone in person, someone who can send help, someone we trust," Jake said.

"Are your parents where mine are tonight?" Lucy asked.

"Wolf Island," said TJ. "Seven hours north and no cell phones."

Wolf Island was the Summer's Over Sleepover for seventh grade parents. It was on a remote island the school owned in northern Michigan.

"Ditto," Jake said, his eyes searching the park as if an answer might be hidden somewhere in the towering elm trees. His lips moved silently as he surveyed the bushes and running trails as well as the university bookstores and cafés just beyond. "My place is in the South Loop," he said. "Manageable. Just thirty minutes on the L."

"L?" Lucy asked.

"Elevated train," Jake said. "Chicago's subway, but mostly above ground."

TJ turned to Jake. "Wait, I thought you said your parents were at Wolf Island with ours?"

"They are. Well, not my parents, my Uncle Gabe. He's pretty much my dad. Anyway, we live at the Greystone. Gabe's at the Wolf Island deal, but I think Artie's working tonight. He's our doorman. Top-notch guy. He'll know who to call."

They stepped out from the bushes and hurried across the playground through the back of the woods. The street was empty as they crossed under the bridge. The faint sound of a train whistle rose in the distance. As they eased out from under the bridge, they saw a small flickering light. It grew larger.

"This one is going our way. I've got extra tickets. We'll take it to the Van Buren stop." After another minute the train was blasting its horn and rolling into the station.

"The stops are quick this late at night. We'll have to hurry," Jake said, turning back around to find Lucy and TJ already sprinting up the stairs.

Lucy and TJ made it onto the platform, jumped over the turnstile, and ducked through the open doors onto the last train car.

Jake followed close behind but paused at the entrance sign.

"Please stand clear of the doors. The doors are closing," the automated warning blared from the train.

Lucy stuck her leg back into the opening and the doors bounced off her and reopened.

"Do not block doors. Train departure is being delayed."

Jake finished scanning the sign, jumped through the gate, and squeezed through the doors just as they closed.

They collapsed onto the plastic bench seats as the train jerked to life. At least they had the car to themselves.

"What was the holdup?" Lucy asked.

"I was just checking to make sure my ride tickets were good for you guys."

"Seriously?" said TJ. "You know, I think you get a free pass if you're running from evil goons."

At the next stop, a train worker wearing a Chicago Transit Authority shirt and a loosened tie stepped onto the train.

Great, thought Jake. *We don't want to see anyone official right now. No questions. We don't need anyone trying to call the police.*

The man settled into a seat directly across from them, lightly drumming his fingers along the edge of his lunch box. He looked at TJ, then Jake, then Lucy, and then back at TJ, who quickly dropped his head and pretended to tie his shoelaces.

Jake glanced at the map on the wall. *We just have to make it one more stop.*

TJ was on his fourth round tying and untying his shoes when the man nodded to him.

"A little late for you kids, isn't it?"

"Hmmm?" TJ was trying to act normal.

"It's a little late for you kids to be out by yourselves, isn't it?" the man repeated.

"Yeah," TJ said. He laughed nervously, trying to act cool, but doing the exact opposite. The man didn't break his stare. TJ cracked. "So, we're, uhh . . . doing research for a school project," he blurted out in a loud voice of fake confidence. "Yes, late night traffic patterns of urban train customers."

Jake raised his eyebrows. Lucy shook her head and looked at the ceiling.

"Documenting the number of riders—when they get on, when they get off, manners and hygiene, the usual stuff."

The man gazed at him skeptically, but said nothing. There was more awkward silence, with only the sound of the train bouncing along the tracks.

"As a matter of fact . . ." For some reason TJ couldn't stop talking. "It's part of a study analyzing Chicago's potential for the 2028 Summer Olympics. Yep. We're looking at all the variables across the board: transportation, signage, you know the drill. We can get you the full report once it's been—"

The ceiling speaker crackled to life. "Next stop Van Buren. Next stop Van Buren."

The man stood up and so did TJ. Lucy quickly yanked him down. "Not our stop," she said.

"No, I think it was Van Buren," TJ said, looking to Jake, who didn't know what to say.

"It's . . . not . . . our . . . stop," Lucy repeated, giving TJ an intense look and pulling him back into his seat.

THE GRAY LADY

THE TRAIN SLOWED TO A STOP at Van Buren and the man stepped off, glancing back at the kids with a confused look before walking away.

"What was that?" TJ said as the train doors zipped shut and they sped off. "I thought you said Van Buren."

"Not with your new friend getting off there. Traffic patterns? Summer Olympics? Hygiene?"

"Look, I was just trying to throw him off our trail."

"You were doing the exact opposite. How about, 'We're on our way home from a friend's house?'" Lucy said.

"OK. Well that's another way to go, I guess," TJ said.

Lucy turned to Jake as they approached the next stop. "How far?"

"Not drastic. Totally manageable. Maybe fifteen minutes," Jake said as they bounded off the train.

Towering skyscrapers loomed against the night sky as they crossed into the park. With the exception of a few late-night taxis crawling along Michigan Avenue, everything was still and quiet as they moved past a giant mirrored bean sculpture and onto the sidewalk. As they passed a pair of imposing stone lion statues framing the art museum's entrance, a siren's cry pierced the air. They ducked behind one of the lions as a police car screamed past, emerging only when the vehicle had moved blocks away. They hurried on without talking for several minutes until Jake came to a stop. He always knew he was home when he could see the towering spray of Buckingham Fountain lit up through the park trees, its rain cascading across the night air.

Jake took a deep breath. "OK," he gestured across the street. "This is it."

Lucy and TJ gazed up at the impressive stone building and massive pillars. Two crimson flags announced "The Greystone" in shimmering gold letters. Marble steps rose to an entrance guarded by two mischievous-looking stone gargoyles.

"This is it?" Lucy asked. "You live at this hotel?"

"Yeah," Jake said.

"Well, Richie Rich," TJ said. "I think I'll go ahead and let you pay my subway fare from now on."

"It's not like that. It's kind of a fixer-upper on the inside. My Uncle Gabe runs the building maintenance, so we live in the old servants' quarters. It's just an apartment by the mechanical room in the attic. But it's good."

Jake had begun to step off the curb when Lucy grabbed his arm.

"Maybe walking in through the front door isn't the best thing," she said.

Jake considered this and nodded. "This way."

They crossed the street, but instead of heading up the steps, Jake continued down the sidewalk and turned into a small alley behind the hotel. "There's a delivery entrance." He stepped up to a steel door next to a loading ramp and inserted a key.

They walked into a dark hallway. Even from the back entrance, entering the Greystone was like stepping through a time machine. The smell of old wood and polished brass seemed to come straight from a hundred years ago. They got a quick peek at the lobby as they passed a doorway—massive, three stories tall, with wood panels and old crystal chandeliers. Reporters used to call it "The Lakeside Princess," but that was a long time ago. The Greystone had definitely seen better days. It wasn't easy keeping up with the old building's demands, not to mention all the competition from the newer hotels along the lakeshore. Lately, most just called her "The Gray Lady."

They came to the end of the hallway and a bronze cage door. The chains rattled as they stepped into the service elevator and Jake slid the accordion door closed. "We'll call Artie from the intercom in our apartment and have him come up." He punched a code into a small touch screen that was patched with duct tape, causing the elevator to jolt to life.

TJ rubbed the old door. "So this ancient elevator has a plasma screen?"

"Yeah. Gabe tries to step-up the tech whenever he can," said Jake, fixing the duct tape on one corner of the screen. "This one needs a few repairs." The elevator shook to life with a series of jolts and the sounds of a chain grinding.

"So you and your Uncle Gabe live here?" said Lucy. "I don't mean to be nosy, but it's just you two?"

"Just us. He's the caretaker of the hotel and helps out at the museum when he can. He says 'caretaker' is a fancy word for handyman, but I think it's more than that."

"How long have you lived here?"

"Gabe's been here forever, about fifty years. They call him the Greystone Mayor. His wife died about forty years ago. He surprised everyone when he adopted me when I was just a baby."

"Sounds like an awesome guy," Lucy said. "So, he's your uncle?"

"Not literally. He says he's too old to be called Dad, but he feels too young to be Grandpa. We settled on Uncle Gabe."

The elevator lurched to a stop with a loud clack as the "21" button lit up. Jake slid the door open and stepped onto a beaten-up plank floor stretching across the cavernous loft space. Raw wooden beams rose to a ceiling of angled rafters, exposed ductwork and jumbled cables. The steady hum of electrical equipment and generators filled the air.

"The mechanical room is kind of the hotel's guts." Jake walked to an oversized steel door with peeling dark green paint and "Maintenance" stenciled in gold letters. He stepped to a small screen and punched in a few numbers. There was a beep and the screen flashed "Invalid Code." He tried again. Same thing. On the third try there was a zap and the Greystone logo on the screen was replaced by two words: Bragg's Bodyguards.

"Ughhh," Jake groaned.

"What?" said Lucy and TJ at the same time.

"Gabe's idea of a joke. Sometimes he resets the password and leaves a clue for me to solve."

"A clue?" TJ asked. "Like some kind of riddle?"

"Sometimes. Sometimes more like trivia. Something about the Civil War or *Lord of the Rings* or Sherlock Holmes. He says it's to prove my worthiness, but I think it's just for his amusement."

"What's the clue?" Lucy stepped past TJ to see the screen.

"OK, hold on there, Miss Tibetan village," TJ said, lifting his hand to block her. "If this has anything to do with pop culture, I don't think the 'Who is Willy Wonka?' girl is our best bet. Better let the A-team have a look."

TJ leaned over and read the clue. "I'm out," he said with his hands in the air.

Lucy stepped back to the screen. "Bragg's Bodyguards?" She turned to Jake. "Do you have any idea?"

Jake stood silent, his hand across his eyes. He stared at the floor mumbling quietly to himself before breaking into a smile. "He's getting soft," he said, stepping back to the keypad. Jake typed the letters L-I-C-E. The screen beeped and flashed green followed by the click of the door lock.

"Lice?" Lucy asked.

"We watched a show last month about how nasty the Civil War army camps were. Bugs everywhere," said Jake as he pushed the door open. "The Confederate Army nicknamed the lice after their general, Braxton Bragg. They called them Bragg's bodyguards."

"OK, I guess I need to brush up on my Civil War hygiene trivia," TJ said, following Jake and Lucy into the room.

Jake closed the door behind them, shutting out the drone of the generators and maintenance equipment. He flicked on the light switch.

The plank floors and exposed rafters were the same as in the mechanical room. The rest was very different. The walls were lined with industrial bookshelves stuffed with everything from *To Kill a Mockingbird* to *Calvin and Hobbes*. A beat-up claw-foot table, crammed with half-assembled Lego creations, an Xbox, subway coupons (both the train and the sandwich kind), and more books, dominated the center of the room. A Darth Vader helmet crowned a medieval knight's armor in the corner. At the far end a giant antique globe sat on a wooden pedestal in front of three huge windows that looked out past stone gargoyles to the park and Lake Michigan.

"Kind of 'Indiana Jones garage sale,' but I can go with it." TJ paused and then he swooped down on a DVD on the table. "Now *that's* what I'm talking about," he said as he picked up *The Princess Bride*.

"What's that?" Lucy asked.

"*The Princess Bride*? Oh, it's just heroes. And giants. And villains. And wizards. Quite possibly the perfect movie," said TJ.

"Definitely on my Mount Rushmore of greatest movies ever made," Jake said.

Lucy paused at a mishmash of photos and papers pasted to the wall. There was a younger Jake with an old man, both of them in Cubs hats and jerseys at a baseball game. In the next photo, Jake and the same man were riding a roller coaster with their hands in the air. In yet another photo, Jake was in full wrestling gear with a medal around his neck, and the man was lifting him into the air. There must have been thirty more photos just like them. Lucy turned back to the door, reading the gold script letters painted on the trim. "'Malice toward none, charity for all.'"

"Gabe's favorite quote. It's from one of Lincoln's last speeches. It's about healing the country after the war." Jake stepped over to an open kitchen area. An old-fashioned black phone sat on a counter next to a sloppy stack of mail and bills, some of them stamped with "Overdue: Final Notice."

"I'll call down to Artie." Jake picked up the receiver but then set it back down. "That's weird," Jake said, staring at a backpack on the kitchen table. "This is Gabe's bag for the retreat." He opened the bag, pulling out clothes, pajamas, a small shower kit, and a whoopee cushion. "He left all his stuff."

TJ raised his eyebrow. "A whoopee cushion?"

"He thinks people take themselves too seriously at events like this," Jake said.

TJ nodded. "I like this guy."

"His directions to the retreat are in here too," Jake said, emptying the rest of the bag. "He couldn't have gone far without that."

"Maybe something came up and he couldn't go," Lucy said.

Jake walked to a sliding wood door and peeked in. "Nope, his room's empty. He's never out this late." He walked back to the phone. "Maybe Artie knows."

"Hey. It looks like you've got messages," Lucy said, noticing a flashing red light blinking through a strip of duct tape on an answering machine.

"Answering machine? You got a horse and buggy downstairs too?" TJ asked.

"Gabe doesn't like to throw things out if they work," Jake said, pressing Play.

"You have three new messages," said the automated voice.

"*Beeeep* . . . Message one, 10:00 a.m. Mr. Herndon, this is your third notice on your past-due insurance payment. Please call us to avoid—"

Jake hit the fast-forward button. "Gabe sometimes juggles which bills we pay. I'm sure he'll get to that one," he said, blushing.

"*Beeeep* . . . Message two, 2:15 p.m. "Gabe to Jakester. Gabe to Jakester. I know tonight's the Big Do-Over. You'll do great. And remember, if I could line up all the boys in the world and just pick one, it would be you. And don't worry about the armpit thing. It's perfectly normal at your age. Just keep your shirt on and whatever you do—"

Jake lunged forward and hit the delete button. "That's, uh, not really relevant."

"Message two deleted."

"Big Do-Over?" Lucy mouthed to TJ.

"Armpit thing?" TJ mouthed to Lucy.

"*Beeeep* . . . Message three, 8:00 p.m. Good evening, this is Club Thirty confirming your dinner reservation tomorrow for five o'clock. We look forward to seeing you."

"*Beeeep* . . . End of messages."

"What's Club Thirty?" Lucy asked.

"Never mind that. What's the Big Do-Over?" asked TJ.

"Nothing, just . . ." Jake turned to Lucy. "Anyway, what were you saying?"

"Club Thirty?"

"I've never heard of it. We don't belong to any clubs," said Jake leafing through the rest of the backpack.

"Do you have a computer here?" TJ asked.

"My laptop is in my bedroom." Jake motioned to a sliding door on the other side of the room. "Can you grab it?" he asked TJ. "I'm going to see if there's anything else in Gabe's room."

Jake had barely set foot in Gabe's room when TJ yelled, "Jake, you better come here!"

Jake bolted across the loft to where TJ and Lucy were standing.

"What is it?" asked Jake.

TJ moved aside so Jake could step into the room. It looked like the twister from the museum had passed through. Dresser drawers had been pulled out and thrown to the floor. Half the contents of the shelves lay on top of them. Old Hardy Boys books, video games, and clothes were scattered around the room.

"It looks like someone wanted to find something real bad," TJ said.

PLAN X

JAKE BROKE INTO A LAUGH. "Yeah," he said, "and I know what they were looking for: clean underwear."

"OK. I think you're losing it," TJ said.

"No, I'm serious. It was a crucial exercise; a quest for clean underwear when I packed this morning."

"You did this?" Lucy asked.

"Not all this morning, but yeah. Gabe says I'm organizationally challenged."

"Disgusting," said Lucy.

"Sorry. I wasn't expecting visitors. I would have stepped up my game, made it more respectable. Here we go." Jake grabbed a small laptop from the top of the pile of papers on the cluttered desk.

When he flipped it open, the screen was already on. "And Gabe thinks I'm the one who's bad at turning stuff off. What was the name?"

"Club Thirty," Lucy said.

Jake typed it into Google and clicked on the first link.

TJ leaned over and read from the screen. "Atop the Capital Hotel, Club Thirty offers incredible gourmet meals set against a magnificent view from the thirtieth floor of downtown Springfield's tallest building."

"It's a fancy restaurant in Springfield," Jake said.

"Springfield?" asked Lucy.

"State capital," said Jake. "A couple hundred miles downstate. We went there in fifth grade to see Abraham Lincoln's home and tomb and stuff."

"Why would he be going so far away?" Lucy asked.

"And without telling you?" TJ added.

"I don't know. We don't eat at places like that." Jake closed the laptop.

"Wait a minute. Why did you say, 'And Gabe thinks I'm bad at turning stuff off?'" asked TJ.

"Failure to disengage. He never remembers to turn the laptop off. He just closes it up."

"So he uses your laptop?" TJ asked.

"Sometimes. He says he doesn't need one. I think it's more because we can't afford it, but he would never admit that."

"And he didn't shut if off?"

"Yeah, I guess not, so—?"

"So let's see if he searched for anything before he left," TJ said, pulling up the online search history.

"Club Thirty. That's the link we just checked. What's before it?" Lucy leaned over TJ's shoulder with Jake.

"Here we go: an Amtrak schedule, a news story, a couple of museum websites, Marvel.com, and some article: 'From

Picked-On to He-Man: How to Add Muscle in All the Right Places.'"

Jake's face turned red. "Ummm, OK. Well, I think the important ones are those first three. I'll print those out." He hit Print and quickly clicked away the search history.

"The Capital Express." Lucy pulled the first sheet off the printer. "It's all the train times from Chicago to Springfield." She read the next sheet. "This is a news story. Illinois governor to officially announce campaign for president at the State Fair."

"Which is in Springfield," TJ said.

Lucy grabbed the next sheet and turned to Jake. "Did you do any research on the museum before you came tonight?"

"Negative. Why?"

"This one is about the Lincoln artifacts in the new museum exhibit."

"Gabe was going to take me there next week. Probably just getting the details."

"And this last one is the home page for some other museum, the Grand Army of the Republic Memorial Museum in Philadelphia."

"OK. So your Uncle Gabe decided to take a last-minute trip to Springfield for a fancy dinner without telling anyone. A little weird, but we just blew up a 727 in order to get away from agents of the evil empire, so who's to say?" said TJ.

"Curious. Doesn't make sense." Jake grabbed the papers. "He would have told me."

"Whatever the reason, it doesn't look like your Uncle Gabe is going to be much help right now," Lucy said. "We need to go to Plan B."

"Plan B?" said TJ. "I think we're up to Plan D. Plan A was unleash the killer tornado. Plan B was the cavalry. Plan C was Uncle Gabe."

"OK, but we need to do something. And I don't think we can assume it's a coincidence that Jake's Uncle Gabe has mysteriously left," Lucy said.

"He didn't mysteriously leave," Jake said defensively. "He just . . . took some sort of . . . last-minute trip."

"Right. So the hotel maintenance guy had a surprise business trip to a fancy restaurant hundreds of miles away," TJ said.

"I didn't say it made sense," Jake snapped. "But there's got to be a reason."

"I'm not saying there's not a reason," Lucy said. "Just that if two of the strangest things that have ever happened to you both occurred in the last twelve hours, they might be connected."

"Acknowledged. We need to find Artie."

"Hold on," Lucy said, grabbing Jake's hand on the phone. "Do you trust him?"

"Definitely. He's like family, a straight-up guy. If we can't trust him, we can't trust anybody. He's probably at the front desk or in the lobby." Jake shoved the printouts into his pocket and picked up a rumpled gray T-shirt off the floor. "I'll change my shirt and go find him."

"You shouldn't go alone," Lucy called to Jake as she followed TJ back to the living room. "We should stick together until we figure out what's going on."

"Sure. All for one and one for all, and all that good stuff," said TJ.

Lucy didn't respond.

TJ turned back to Lucy as he headed for the door. "The Three Musketeers?"

"Got it. Nineteenth-century novel. Alexandre Dumas."

"Right. Actually, I meant the movie and the candy bar," TJ said, "but if there's a book, great."

"Ready?" Jake rejoined them wearing a gray University of Chicago Summer Camp T-shirt.

"Was that the shirt off the floor?" said Lucy.

Jake sniffed it. "Acceptable. I've only worn it once this week."

The hum of generators filled the air as they opened the door. They stepped inside the elevator and Jake pulled the cage screen door shut. "We'll get off on the balcony level and take the back staircase to the office."

The elevator lurched to life and they descended in silence.

Jake slid the door open as the elevator came to a stop on the second floor. They stepped into a hallway that looked very different from the maintenance floor. Elegant globes mounted on brass eagles gave off a soft golden glow. The smell of old wood rose from polished oak floors while antique paintings of serious-looking men peered out from fancy gold frames lining the dark paneled walls.

"Whoa," said TJ, spinning around. "It's like the Old White Guy Hall of Fame."

They had just passed from the overlook to the lobby when a noise rose from below. "Probably a group getting back from a late night out," said Jake as he continued toward the end of the hall. TJ paused and leaned back to get a good view of the lobby.

"Uhhh, guys," TJ called out. "Unless they're coming from a costume party, we might have a problem."

Jake and Lucy stepped back to join TJ at the overlook. A trail of police officers poured through the revolving doors into the lobby.

"I know it was dark when we were on the roof," Lucy said, pulling the boys back. "But I'm pretty sure that's Lieutenant Bates."

"So much for Plan D," TJ said, backing away from the railing.

"Escalation," Jake said, turning and looking down the hall. "Time to improvise, adjust the plan. I suggest Plan X."

"Which is?" asked Lucy.

"RUN."

JUST WALK AND ACT NATURAL

THEY HIT THE BACK STAIRWELL and took the steps two at a time. When they reached the first floor, they burst into the dark alley at full speed, barely dodging a stack of trash cans before dashing into the empty street.

Jake was leading, although he had no idea where he was going. He just wanted to put as much distance between them and the Greystone as possible. They bolted through an empty plaza and cut through the courtyard of an old church. A few patrons at an all-night diner glanced up with mild curiosity as the kids tore past.

Jake was in decent shape from wrestling, but he knew they couldn't just keep running. They were crossing a stone bridge over the river when sirens filled the air. A convoy of police cars and fire trucks turned onto the street and screamed toward them. Jake spotted a set of steps next to the bridge, made a quick turn, and plunged down the stairway with Lucy and

TJ following. They huddled underneath the bridge while the sirens shrieked past them above.

"Wait. I need . . . to catch . . . my breath," TJ panted.

"We can't . . . stay out here, in the open," Jake said, trying not to show how winded (or scared) he was.

"Down here." Lucy motioned to a small dock next to the riverside walkway.

They collapsed onto a bench in the darkness. After the sirens faded into the distance, the only sounds left were the kids' gasping for air and the lapping of the river against the bridge.

TJ was the first to speak, still catching his breath. "Look . . . my parents, they made me pick a sport. I chose fencing, because of the cool swords, and because there's no running."

"Why are they following us?" Lucy asked. "*How* are they following us? Do they know who we are? What do they want?"

"And how can they intercept 911 calls and pretend to be the police?" asked TJ. "Unless they are the police."

"I don't know, but we need to get somewhere safe," Jake said, turning to Lucy. "What about your house?"

"Our stuff is still in storage. Our house won't be ready until Sunday."

"We're in Evanston, about forty-five minutes north," TJ said. "There's no one there, but we could hide out."

"I think I'd feel safer getting to someone we can trust. Especially if we want to be any help to the kids still at the museum," Lucy said, turning to Jake. "How far did you say it is to Wolf Island?"

"About a seven-hour drive. And then a ferry boat."

"Sounds good, your car or mine?" TJ said. "Oh yeah, that's right, we're twelve years old!"

"I can drive," Lucy said.

"Of course you can," said TJ. "Let me guess—you drove a tank through the jungle to rescue endangered snow monkeys."

"We had an old pickup in Nepal. When I turned twelve, my dad taught me so I could take supplies to the villages."

"Sure. You've been driving since you turned twelve."

"Actually, eleven. But that's another story."

"OK, so we've got a driver, sort of."

"Sort of?" Lucy asked.

"Not plausible anyway," Jake said. "We don't even know where they're camping on the island."

"We do know exactly where one person will be," Lucy said.

"Club Thirty," Jake affirmed, pulling the printouts from his pocket. "We can get to Springfield. I'll bet there's an early morning train."

"But what about the kids at the museum?" asked Lucy.

"Good question. I've given that some thought," Jake said. "All those police cars and fire trucks swarming past us weren't coming from the hotel. They were headed in the direction of the museum. That's got to be a good thing, right? I mean, if they were the good guys. If not, then things are even more wacked than we thought and it's even more important to get to someone we can trust."

"Someone like Uncle Gabe," Lucy said.

"My parents are going to freak," said TJ.

"Well, since they're without cell coverage in the middle of nowhere, at least they won't freak until later tomorrow. Gabe will know how to contact them. We just need to stay positive. Totally doable."

"OK, not to go all Eeyore on you," TJ said, "but how far is the station? And we'd have to buy tickets, from an adult in the middle of the night."

"It's right here, downtown," Jake said. "We can walk. At this time of night you just buy from a machine. But we need money."

"Ba-BAM!" TJ slapped a platinum American Express card onto the bench. "Emergency card from the parents. Don't leave home without it. I think they were thinking more if I forgot my toothbrush, but I guess running for your life from stormtrooper goons qualifies."

"Stellar. Train station, TJ's magic money card, Springfield, Gabe." Jake stood up. "The station's about five blocks."

They stood and entered the river walk.

"And yes, I caught the Eeyore reference," Lucy said to TJ.

"Great. Pooh. At least we've got that to work with," TJ said.

They followed the stone walk, passing under more bridges as the glow of the full moon cut through the gaps in the buildings and reflected off the river.

When they reached the base of the next bridge, they climbed back up to the street. At the top of the stairs, Jake paused and looked across to a huge stone building with massive Greek columns—Union Station.

"Wow," Lucy said, taking in the titanic building that stretched for an entire block.

TJ stepped onto the sidewalk. "It looks like someone dropped an ancient temple down in the middle of Chicago."

"'Make no little plans; they have no magic to stir men's blood,'" Jake whispered.

"Huh?" TJ said, straining to see where the building ended.

"The guy who designed it did a lot of stuff in Chicago. He said, 'Make no little plans; they have no magic to stir men's blood. Remember that our sons and grandsons are going to do things that would stagger us.'"

"Cool," TJ said.

"He didn't think anyone's daughters or granddaughters would do great things?" asked Lucy.

"I think it was just a saying," TJ said.

"Well, it's a saying I'd revise," Lucy responded, stepping into the street.

"Anyhooo," Jake continued. "I've used the ticket machine before. We'll just go in. There's a whole wall of them. Probably won't be many people at this time. We'll use the card."

"Ba-BAM!" TJ interrupted, a bit too loudly, flashing the credit card. "Sorry. Please continue."

"We'll buy the tickets and then just hang back and wait."

They passed through the arched doors and into a lobby that seemed as big as a football field. Statues rose from the marble floors. Skylights soared the length of the room a hundred feet overhead. There were a handful of tired business types scattered on benches and a few college students sleeping on overstuffed backpacks.

Jake led the way to a row of ticket machines against the far wall.

"It says the next train to Springfield doesn't leave until seven o'clock."

Lucy tensed as she noticed a security guard enter the far side of the lobby. "Anything sooner? I don't think we want to hang around here."

Jake studied the screen. The next train south went straight to St. Louis. He looked down at the floor, squinting and mumbling under his breath.

The security guard stared directly at Jake. He glanced down at his watch and then back at the kids.

"Wait," Jake said, nervously avoiding the guard's eyes and looking back at the screen. "If we took the express to St. Louis, I'll bet we could—yes—brilliance! We can catch a connection from St. Louis back to Springfield. We'd have to wait in St. Louis for a while, but we could still get to Springfield before Gabe's dinner."

The security guard spoke into his hand radio and began crossing the lobby toward them.

"What time does the St. Louis train leave?" Lucy asked, watching the guard over Jake's shoulder.

"It's already boarding. There's a sleeper compartment still available. Costs more but we could have a private room."

"Great. A little sleepy time. That's what the Ba-BAM's for!" TJ said, pulling the card back out.

"I agree. Let's get out of here," Lucy said. An older man in a suit stopped the guard in the middle of the lobby. It looked like he was asking for directions.

"OK, do your thing." Jake stepped back from the screen.

The guard answered the man's question and then continued toward the kids.

TJ stepped up to the machine and jammed his card in. Jake tried to stay calm, casually glancing over his shoulder at the approaching guard while he pulled the tickets from the machine. The guard was now three steps away, then two, then one. The stale air grew thicker. Jake froze. TJ dropped down to re-tie his shoelaces. The guard brushed past them and entered the men's restroom. They all exhaled and quickly moved away from the ticket machine.

"Gateway Express to St. Louis. Train number 222. Final call for boarding on Gate Twelve."

"That's us," Jake said.

"Just walk and act natural," Lucy whispered out of the corner of her mouth. "If anyone asks, we're visiting our grandparents in Springfield."

"Our grandparents?" TJ whispered. "I guess my Denzel looks blend at least a little with your J.Lo vibe, but . . ." he nodded to Jake, who was looking particularly pale, ". . . not so much with Casper the Ghost here."

"Adoption. Blended family," Lucy said as they approached the boarding line. "No, let's make it simpler. We're students coming home from camp."

A uniformed man stood at the gate sipping from a Big Gulp Slurpee while checking tickets. The line inched forward. As they reached the front, the ticket taker put his hand out for TJ's ticket. "Together?"

TJ looked silently at the ticket taker, then at his shoelaces, and finally back at the ticket taker. "What? No, uh, yes," TJ said. "We're, uh, students, exchange students," he stuttered. "No, I mean we're meeting exchange students, in Springfield. But they're not from Springfield. They're from . . . Kazakhstan. The glorious Republic of Kazakhstan. But we're meeting them in Springfield. It's all part of—"

"Sorry," Lucy said, stepping in between TJ and the ticket taker. "He has a strange sense of humor. We're headed back to Springfield after camp."

"Whatever," the ticket taker said, taking another slurp. "Just confirming you're in the same compartment. Car number seven."

"Oh. Yeah. Great, thanks," TJ said as the attendant handed their tickets back to them.

They passed through the turnstile—TJ sweating bullets, Lucy looking like her head was going to explode, and Jake walking awkwardly, trying not to do any more damage to the priceless fragile gloves still hidden in his back pocket.

SWIRLING

LUCY WAS SEETHING. They walked from car to car until at last they reached their compartment. "Here we are," Jake said, sliding the door open and stepping inside. It was small, barely enough room for the three padded bunks that folded out of the wall, but that somehow made it feel safer.

"Home sweet home," TJ said, crashing onto one of the bunks.

Lucy flipped the lock shut and erupted. "What was that all about? Kazakhstan? Exchange students?"

Jake quickly lowered the door shade.

"I don't know, it just kind of popped into my head," TJ said. "I guess when the guy started grilling me—"

"Grilling you? You mean when he turned his evil Slurpee toward you?" Lucy was pacing the small compartment. "First with the traffic patterns and the 2026 Olympics, and now Kazakhstan. Your crazy panic lies are going to kill us!"

"Hey, have a seat," Jake said, moving in between them and

guiding Lucy to sit on the other bunk. "It's late. Fatigue makes cowards of us all, right? Who said that anyway?"

"2028," TJ mumbled.

"What?"

"2028. I said the 2028 Summer Olympics. There won't be a Summer Olympics in 2026. I chose 2028 because the site hasn't been selected yet."

"That's not the point!" Lucy was back on her feet.

"OK. So what's your point?"

"My point is, whenever anyone asks us anything, you launch into some crazy story that draws even more attention to us. How about until we get to Uncle Gabe, you don't talk to anyone? Just don't talk."

Jake winced. He could tell that stung.

TJ pursed his lips tight as if trying to keep from exploding. "You know, you're not the only one who can handle themselves. I was doing just fine before you came along."

"Oh yeah. Knocked out in the airplane bathroom, you were definitely doing just fine."

"What? Hey, I don't know how many of those freaks I took out first, but yeah, one of them whomped me with a mean roundhouse. I'd like to see how you would have done."

"It wasn't a roundhouse," Lucy muttered.

"Ahem." Jake jumped up. "I think if we endeavor to—"

"What do you mean 'It wasn't a roundhouse'?" asked TJ.

"Wow," Jake said. "Look at the time! I vote we get some sleep before things—"

"It was a butterfly kick. And I barely snapped it," Lucy said.

"What?" TJ said. "Wait. *Whaaaat?*"

"—escalate." Jake sighed and dropped his head into his hands.

"We opened the bathroom door and you freaked out. I didn't know it was you. It was just a reaction," said Lucy.

"You?" TJ rubbed the purple welt under his eye. He turned to Jake. "Can you, can you believe this?"

"Uhhh, yeah," Jake said, smiling meekly. "It's, uhh, kind of how we met too. Down in the mine."

"You whomped him too?" TJ turned to Lucy. "Like me?"

"Well, not exactly. That one actually was a roundhouse."

"Well, this definitely changes my psycho diagnosis of you."

"Look, I didn't know either time that it was you guys. I thought it was one of those lunatics with the guns and I reacted."

"How exactly was that your reaction? How about just slam the door shut?"

"You lunged. It was reflex."

TJ just looked at her.

"It's called Budokai-do. Nepalese martial arts."

"Oh, right. Nepalese martial arts."

"The monks in the village taught us."

"Sure. The monks in the village taught you. I get it. We played dodgeball in gym class, sometimes a little badminton. You did no-rules street fighting with the ninja monks."

"Look, I'm sorry I beat you guys up," Lucy said.

"Well, I wouldn't say—" Jake started.

"Yeah, I don't think you'd call it—" TJ interrupted.

"I mean it was dark and—"

"I kind of sensed you were a girl so—"

"Yeah, and it was dark—"

"But no one actually got beat—"

"OK. Whatever." Lucy sat back down, "Can we just figure out a plan?"

Jake grabbed a seat as the train began to lurch out of the station. They sat in silence for several minutes. Lucy stared out the window. TJ stared at Jake. Jake stared at the floor, his lips silently moving.

TJ leaned over to Jake. "Hey, if you're talking to us, you should know you're not making any actual sound."

"Sorry, just thinking," Jake said. "Our plan's still tight. It holds water you know, it's workable: Get to Gabe, figure it out, right?"

"The dinner reservation," Lucy said. "We should have written that down."

"Five o'clock, Club Thirty, thirtieth floor atop the Capital Hotel, 800 East Adams Street," said TJ.

Jake and Lucy looked impressed.

TJ smiled. "Hyper memory. Some people say photographic memory, but researchers don't believe that really exists. That's more eidetic memory, although that's just images. But I kind of have that too."

Jake and Lucy were just staring at TJ. He didn't seem to notice.

"My doctor just calls it hyper memory. Comes in handy with school. Boy genius and all. But I've got to be careful because people can get annoyed when I—" He paused as he looked up to see Jake and Lucy. "Anyway, hyper memory."

"I can respect that. A superpower of sorts," Jake said. "Five o'clock. 800 East Adams. I'd write it down, but that's probably not necessary, huh?" He smiled at TJ. "We might need some cash to take a cab or a bus when we get there." He emptied out the rest of his pockets onto the small table.

"Impressive." TJ sorted through the pile. In addition to the papers he had printed out, there was Jake's name tag, two hard pieces of Bubble Yum, a five-dollar bill, two ones, a library card, a packet of Frank's RedHot sauce and enough lint balls to make a small sweater.

"OK," TJ said, standing up and pulling out his wallet. "I'll see your seven dollars, stale Bubble Yum and hot sauce packet and raise you five, six, seven, eight, nine dollars and . . ." He tossed five GameStop gift cards onto the bench. "What can I say? I'm an easy person to buy for. But most important, don't forget Ba-*BAM!*" He added his American Express card to the pile.

The boys turned to Lucy.

"O . . . K?" TJ asked.

"OK . . . what?" asked Lucy.

"Let's have it," TJ said. "All for one, one for all? What are you bringing to the party?"

Lucy pulled a small copper lion charm out of her pocket and placed it on the table.

"Great. Helpful if we're starting a souvenir bracelet for the trip," TJ said. "What else?"

"That's it. The rest was in my backpack. Sorry to disappoint. Just the lion. Gift from my dad."

"So we've got sixteen dollars," Jake said.

"And the lucky lion charm," TJ added. "Don't forget the lucky lion."

"Oh, like five video-game gift cards are going to be a lot of help."

"Hey, you'd be surprised. And don't forget the Ba-BAM!" TJ slapped the credit card. "Maybe I should do that louder for full effect?"

"Well, hopefully it's enough to get us to Uncle Gabe. You keep the card." Jake tossed the credit card back to TJ. "Why don't you hold the cash?" He scooped the bills up and handed them to Lucy.

Lucy slipped the money and the lion charm back in her pocket. "Sounds like a plan. We've got a few hours. We should try to get some sleep."

"Agreed," Jake said, shoving the papers back in his pocket. He reached up and pulled down the third bunk, which folded out of the ceiling. "I can take the top if you want." He unfolded the blanket and laid it across the bunk. "You know, it's not the perfect plan, but knowing what we've survived already, not bad. I think it's plausible, you know, a manageable scenario, a worthy—" As he turned back, he found both TJ and Lucy fast asleep on their cots.

Jake checked the door lock and flipped off the light. A small opening in the window shade allowed just enough light for him to fumble his way back to the bunk. As he stepped onto the ladder, he noticed that both TJ and Lucy had fallen asleep in awkward positions. One of TJ's legs was dangling off his bunk, while Lucy had fallen asleep half sitting up. He stepped down and carefully pushed TJ's leg back onto the cot. Then he put one arm around Lucy's neck and the other around her waist and turned her onto her back. He unfolded their blankets and covered them both before climbing up to his bunk.

Jake lay there for a while staring into the darkness as the train rumbled across the countryside. He was exhausted but couldn't sleep. His mind was swirling with questions. Who were those maniacs at the museum? Why did they want the gloves so badly? And then there were the questions he was too confused to even share with TJ and Lucy. Like why did the driver's license in Gabe's backpack have Gabe's face but the name Caleb Smith?

GOOD NEWS AND BAD NEWS

ZHAAAWWW-HHHHHH-ZHAAAWWW . . .

Jake woke with a start. Where was he? What had happened? That's right, the train. Still dark. The middle of the night. How long had he been asleep?

Zhaawwww . . .

That noise. It sounded like a drill or a saw. Someone was trying to get in the room.

Hhhhhhh . . .

No, wait. Someone was already in the room. They were breathing. Just standing and breathing.

Zhaawwww . . .

Jake dropped from his bunk. He hit the floor and jumped up swinging. Light from passing streetlights bounced through the curtain with a quick flash. He finally caught sight of the source of the hideous noise: Lucy.

Zhaaawww-Hhhhhh-Zhaaawww . . .

A few more seconds of light shot through the curtain. She

was snoring. But this wasn't a normal snore. Jake was used to Gabe snoring. This was different, unlike anything he had ever heard. Like Darth Vader choking on a hairball. He didn't know how to process what he was seeing—the combination of Lucy's peaceful face with the disturbing buzz-saw sound was quite unsettling.

Jake's jumping must have awakened TJ because he was now staring back at Jake from his lower bunk.

"I think there's some kind of wounded animal trapped in the wall," he whispered.

"Negative," Jake whispered back. "It's just Lucy. She's snoring."

"Well, of course," TJ said, burying his head in his pillow.

Jake crawled back into his bunk. He tried to get his pounding heart to slow down. Gradually, his breathing returned to normal and Lucy's snoring blended in with the rest of the train's rumble, allowing him to fall back asleep.

* * *

"Fifteen minutes to arrival in St. Louis. Fifteen minutes to arrival," the speaker blurted out. It felt like it had been only a few minutes but the late morning sun told Jake otherwise. He rubbed the sleep from his eyes and dropped to the floor, sliding the shade up to reveal the St. Louis skyline and its giant arch.

"We're almost there. Time to get up." Jake shook TJ's foot and then reached over to tap Lucy's shoulder.

Lucy sat up, squinting at the sunlight streaming through the window.

"We're almost in St Louis," Jake said.

"Not exactly sweet dreams," TJ said, rubbing his eyes and yawning.

"I slept great," Lucy said.

"I'm sure you did," said TJ.

"What's that mean?" Lucy asked, leaning over the small sink and splashing her face with water.

"Nothing," Jake said, giving TJ a stern look and shaking his head. "You just fell asleep right away."

They took turns freshening up in the sink as the train slowed to a stop. They stepped off the train into a crowded terminal. Jake paused in front of a large screen listing the schedules. "We've got quite a while before our Springfield train leaves."

"Sounds like breakfast time to me," TJ said, walking toward the food court. "Or would it be lunch?" He glanced at his watch. "Ten thirty," he said with a huge smile on his face. "I think we all know what that means." Jake and Lucy shook their heads.

"McMashups!" TJ said.

Jake and Lucy shook their heads again.

"Are you kidding me? Well, you're in for a treat, my friends. Ten thirty is the perfect time for. . ." He paused for effect. "The cheeseburger combined with an egg muffin sandwich: the McMashup. That's right—beef patty, double cheese, Canadian bacon and fried egg, all on a delicious English muffin."

Lucy looked nauseated. Jake was intrigued.

"Yes! Proud to be an American! And all possible because I didn't leave home without Ba-BAM!" He pulled the American Express card out. "My treat."

"You know, I've been thinking about your card . . . I don't think it's a good idea to use it anymore," Lucy said.

"What? Wait a second. No, it's not a good idea. It's a great idea! Food your parents are paying for—always a good choice. And did I mention . . . yes, I believe I did. We're talking about McMashups!" TJ walked toward the counter.

"We still don't know who these guys are," Lucy said. "If they can intercept police calls, if they can track us to the Greystone, maybe they can trace a credit card."

TJ didn't like where this was going. "How would they even know who to trace?"

"Name tag," Lucy said. "Your name tag dropped when we were on the wing."

"What?" TJ had to catch his breath. "The guy barely looked at it. It's probably buried under the rubble. I don't think a few McMashups are going to—"

"Until we know what's going on, I think it would be better not to leave a trail. They might already know we used the card for these tickets."

"Sorry, I think she's right," Jake said. "Too risky. Seems like the unfriendlies might have extreme resources."

TJ exhaled. "Great. How much cash do we have?"

"Sixteen dollars." Lucy counted the bills from her pocket. "But I don't think we should spend it all. We might need bus fare or something."

"OK, how much is a bus? Maybe a dollar or two. Let's see what we can get over there." Jake motioned to a convenience store.

After looking around the small store and finding nothing

but eight-dollar muffins and bags of gummy bears, Lucy pulled three breakfast bars out of a discount basket on the counter.

"What kind of deal can you do on these?" Lucy asked.

"The discount price is on them. A dollar each," the clerk responded.

"Too much. I can go fifty cents each," Lucy said.

"Ahem." Jake nudged Lucy and whispered. "That's not really how they do it here in the States. You just pay what the tag says."

"Look, they're a dollar each. Do you want them or not?"

"OK, tell you what," Lucy said. "I'll go to two dollars for three of them. Last and final."

The clerk looked around. "Boss did say to get rid of them."

"That's a cash offer, good for the next five seconds." Lucy turned as if she was going to leave.

The clerk looked around. "OK."

Lucy smiled, and before TJ could protest, she grabbed three of the bars and handed the clerk the money.

"Lumberjack Raisin and Date Bar," TJ said, making a disgusted face. "From the discount basket. We're getting the food even the health nuts rejected."

"It's protein. More than a lot of kids in Haiti or Rwanda get in a whole day," Lucy said.

"All this and a life lesson too," TJ said, taking a bite out of his bar. "This is turning into a bad field trip."

They found seats on the floor against the wall, where they sat and ate their granola bars while watching the passengers rush by.

Lucy turned to Jake. "You know, you never answered the question about the Big Do-Over."

Jake squirmed uncomfortably. "Not interesting or really relevant. Just a thing."

"Not buying it," Lucy said.

"Come on," TJ added. "We've been blown up, shot at, and made to eat squirrel food. How bad can it be?"

"Not a big deal. Sixth grade was just a bit of a debacle, a calamity on most fronts. But hey, I'm not alone on that, right? I mean Abe Lincoln lost what, five or six elections before he became president? Benjamin Franklin failed math. I mean, all the greats had epic fails. No such thing as an undefeated life, right? Not that I'm one of the greats, but you never know, maybe I just haven't found my thing. I could be on the verge. Poised for greatness, you know."

TJ gave up on his granola bar. "So what happened?"

"It wasn't just one thing. Or maybe it was. Actually, I guess it was. Toward the end of the year I started to fall asleep at weird times, even when I wasn't tired."

"Like in class?"

"Sometimes. Not that I wanted to. It just kind of happened. Anyway, at the spring dance I was hanging by the punch bowl. It was a big one, obscenely large actually. Colossal. I still contend there was no reason for its scale. If you saw it, I think you would . . . anyway, I must have . . . kind of . . . you know."

"You fell asleep in the punch bowl?" TJ asked.

"It was a spectacle. I pulled the whole table down—lots of ruined dresses, yelling, classic overreaction, people rankled."

"People what?" TJ said.

"Rankled. Chafed, annoyed, ticked off. Anyway, afterwards

the nicknames started swirling. It's like there was a contest or something."

"Kids can be such jerks," Lucy said.

"It really wasn't that big of a deal. Just kind of one more bad thing in a less than stellar year. When the Uni Prep scholarship opened up, Gabe felt like it could be time for a reboot. A Big Do-Over. Which it will be, as long as we don't, you know, get shot or blown up or something. . . . So, hyper memory, huh?" Jake said, turning to TJ and wanting to change the subject. "I bet that comes in handy."

"Sure. School, trivia, party tricks, you name it," TJ said.

"In that case I challenge you to a battle of wits," said Jake. "A test of your *Princess Bride* hyper memory."

TJ grinned. "*Princess Bride* trivia? You're on."

Round one. "What does not become a man of action?"

"Lies."

"Excellent. What does the most famous blunder involve?"

"A land war in Asia!"

"Impressive. What kind of sandwich is better than true love?"

"An MLT—a mutton, lettuce, and tomato sandwich where the mutton is lean and the tomato is thick."

"Wrong! He says the tomato is ripe."

"I don't think so. I know my *Princess Bride*."

By this point, Lucy was leaning against the wall and snoring.

"Agree to disagree for now," Jake said. "But when we get Google action again and we confirm I'm right, I want acknowledgment of the limitations of hyper memory."

"Won't happen," TJ said, yawning.

102

Eventually TJ also dozed off. Jake fought the impulse. He told himself it was so they wouldn't miss their train, but he also wondered if maybe Lucy was right about someone being able to trace their tickets.

When the speaker announced, "Prairie Star Limited, Train 244 to Springfield now boarding, Gate 3," it seemed like half the crowd stirred from their seats and crammed near the gate.

Jake nudged the others as he hopped to his feet. "That's us, we're boarding."

It was a smaller train this time, one without sleeper cars, so they grabbed a small booth with seats facing each other. As they settled in, Jake pulled out his ticket. "We should get there about four thirty. What time was that reservation?"

"Five o'clock, Club Thirty, thirtieth floor, Capital Hotel, 800 East Adams Street," TJ said. "Hyper memory. Which is how I know the tomato is thick, not ripe!"

As TJ and Jake launched into a new *Princess Bride* debate, Lucy picked up a Chicago newspaper that had been left behind on the seat.

"Guys!" Lucy said as soon as she scanned the front page.

Jake and TJ were in the thick of it. "Even if your hypothesis is plausible, and I'm not admitting that it is, I think the difference between mostly dead and all dead is more—"

"*Guys,*" Lucy said louder, holding up the newspaper.

TJ stopped and turned to Lucy. He read from her paper. "'Navy Pier hosts clogging festival.'"

"Not that one. This one." Lucy pointed to another story on the page.

"'Museum closure,'" TJ read. "'An early morning electrical

fire occurred at the Museum of Science and Industry. No one was injured but the facility will be closed until further notice.'"

"What?" Jake grabbed the paper.

He read out loud. "'The fire happened overnight in the main lobby. The only occupants at the time were a school group on a sleepover and the night watch staff. The group was evacuated to the University Prep campus without incident.'"

"Sure. I guess a huge explosion and the destruction of a 727 aren't worth mentioning," TJ said.

"And the dead guard situation doesn't count as an injury," Jake said. "'Of related interest,'" Jake continued to read, "'during the relocation, three University Prep students left without authorization and are wanted for questioning related to the fire. The police have not released the names of the minors, but they are actively searching for them.'"

"So good news and bad news," said TJ. "Good news is the kids are safe. The bad news is psycho killers apparently control the police, the newspaper, and the city, and they're all hunting for us."

"Good thing we didn't use that credit card," Lucy said, giving TJ a fake smile.

TJ started to make an argument and then held back. Jake continued to read the paper.

"Is there something else?" Lucy asked.

"No, uhmmm . . . no." Jake dropped his head and rubbed his temples.

"This doesn't really change anything. Our best shot is still to get to your Uncle Gabe," said TJ.

"I think that's right," Lucy said, turning to Jake. "Don't you agree?"

Jake's eyes were glued to the newspaper.

"Jake? Isn't that right? Our best bet is still Uncle Gabe?"

"Oh, yeah, right," Jake said.

The train rumbled onto the bridge and crossed the Mississippi River, leaving the arch and the city in the background.

TJ and Lucy squirmed in their seats for nap positions. Jake closed his eyes but once again found it hard to rest. He gazed back at the newspaper on the seat next to him. His head was clouded with the same questions as last night. But now there was a new cloud: the other article he had just read—the one at the bottom of the page, about the break-in last night at the Grand Army of the Republic museum in Philadelphia.

CLUB THIRTY

THE REST OF THE RIDE WENT QUICKLY. Jake pretended to nap, but he mostly just stared out the window at the passing farmland and looked for answers to questions that were getting stranger by the minute.

They pulled into the Springfield station under a brilliant blue sky as the late afternoon sun glistened off the state capitol's silver dome.

"Let's see if there's a map inside," Jake said as they stepped onto the platform.

The depot was a one-room lobby filled with wooden benches and a single ticket window. Jake saw a rack of tourist brochures and coupon books at the far end. He searched the rack, flipping past brochures for "Haunted Springfield Night Walks," "See the Lincoln Sites," and "Mary Todd's Miniature Golf."

"Bam!" TJ reached over Jake's shoulder and grabbed a tourist map of downtown Springfield. "Done!"

Jake examined the map. "The hotel is only about five blocks away. We can walk. No bus fare needed!"

"And I consider this a sign." TJ pointed to a coupon on the map. "Dangerous Delbert's Donuts. Top Secret Recipe. Coupon good for six donuts for five dollars. How much do we have left?"

"Fourteen dollars. We should just head to the restaurant. We might still need the cash," Lucy said.

"What are you, some kind of robot? I'm all about getting to Gabe and getting this over with, but it's on the way. See, they marked it on the map with this little spy donut. And I really don't think any doctor would advise going to our big meeting on an empty stomach."

"Didn't you eat your granola bar?" Lucy asked.

"OK. That was not eating. Chewing, yes. But hardly edible. I'm a growing boy. You don't get all this Chocolate-Thunder, Boy-Wonder by eating hippie rabbit food. And it's a coupon. It seems almost un-American not to use it."

"I guess we've got time for a quick stop on the way," Jake said.

"Exactly," said TJ.

"But I agree with Lucy on the money. Let's hold onto at least ten dollars."

"Better than nothing," TJ said, already heading out the door.

After they walked two blocks, they saw an old sign protruding from a corner shop. It was a giant donut wearing sunglasses and a black hat and read, "Dangerous Delbert's. Top Secret Recipe since 1935."

"See? It's so good the recipe is top secret," TJ said, pushing open the glass doors. They were met by the unmistakable smell of freshly baked donuts and coffee. An older lady in a hairnet and apron was wiping the counter behind a line of padded stools next to the cash register. "You're just in time. We close at five on Saturdays," she called out as she adjusted her "Beverly" name tag and stepped behind a glass display counter.

"Life is all timing, my friends," TJ said, stepping up to the counter. Most of the case was empty but there were two shelves with a couple dozen donuts of mixed varieties. TJ browsed the selection. "Hmmm. Just a moment, Beverly. I'll have to confer with my associates." He turned to Jake and Lucy.

"I'm good," Jake said. "Not really a donut guy. I'll hold for the fancy dinner."

"Me too," Lucy said. "Get whatever you want but no more than four dollars."

TJ shook his head. "Donut-hating robots."

"Why don't you let this lady order while you decide?" Lucy motioned to an older woman who had just entered.

TJ gave Lucy a slightly annoyed look but stepped to the side of the cash register to gaze into the glass case while the woman ordered.

"What is that?" He pointed to a large chocolate donut topped with a massive lump of white. It looked like a small volcano had erupted with whipped cream.

"That's the Honest Abe," Beverly said while continuing to fill a box for the older woman. "It's a glazed donut filled with whipped cream, covered in chocolate icing and topped with more whipped cream."

"Wow," Lucy said. "How could anyone ever eat a whole one of—"

"Bam! I'll take two," TJ said, raising his head from the case to Lucy's shocked face. "Hey. No judgment, please."

The older woman finished her order. "And six of those. I've got a big group of hungry soccer players."

"Nothing wrong with that," Beverly said as she handed three boxes to the woman.

"OK." TJ stepped back to the register. "After that, mine's going to be easy. Just two of those Honest Abes."

"Sorry," the counter lady said, gesturing to the case. "All gone."

TJ was horrified. "What?"

"She bought the last two."

"OK, I'll take whatever other cream-filled goodness you have left in the back."

"Sorry, son, we put it all out. It's the end of the day. We do have a few of these left." She placed an open box of packaged bars on the counter. Each bar had a smiling lumberjack on it. "Boss thinks we need to offer a healthy option. It's kind of a granola thing, with raisins and dates. Haven't sold a single one. I told him, 'Why would anyone want that at a donut shop?' But they don't listen to me. I can give you three for the price of one."

"Uhh, no, thanks, I think I'll pass," TJ said, giving Lucy the evil eye. Lucy returned his glance with a "Why are you blaming me?" look.

"OK, how about six for the price of one?" said Beverly.

"No thanks." TJ shook his head and joined Jake and Lucy at the door.

"All twelve for a dollar!" she called out as the door closed behind them.

"'Why don't you let her in front of you?'" TJ repeated in a whiny voice as they turned back onto the sidewalk.

"I don't sound like that. And you did a good thing for that nice lady," Lucy said.

"Yeah, well that nice little lady cleaned the place out. Would it have hurt her to leave one behind?"

After another few blocks, they rounded the corner and found themselves staring up at a large streamlined tower shadowing the surrounding buildings.

"Completed in 1973 at 352 feet, the thirty-story Capital Hotel is the tallest high-rise building in Illinois outside of Chicago," TJ said, making a tour guide gesture with his hand. He continued his spiel. "Located in the heart of downtown Springfield, the Capital is close to many of the Abraham Lincoln historic sites."

"OK, enough with the hyper-memory tour guide. Let's get up there," Jake said.

"Great. Hyper memory is hyper hungry."

"Hold on," Lucy said, grabbing Jake's and TJ's arms before they could cross the street. "What's our plan?"

"I thought the plan was to tell Uncle Gabe what happened, have him call the good guys, and then order a bunch of food," TJ said.

"But what if Gabe isn't there?"

"If he's not there, I say we give up, take our chances with the police, and then order a bunch of food," said TJ.

"Hopefully it won't come to that," Jake said. "We'll scope

it out first, just slip in, low key. We won't ask for Gabe, just see who's in there."

They crossed to a crowded sidewalk where swarms of kids were unloading from a string of tour buses. At the far end of the walkway, a group of Girl Scouts was collecting money for charity.

"Must be a bunch of school groups in town for the parade," Jake said. They cut a path through the crowd, past the Girl Scouts, and pushed through the revolving door. It was more of the same inside; the building was crammed with late-season tourists, band members, and cheerleaders. Frazzled-looking adults in several corners were holding up clipboards with names like "Pleasant Hill Summer Camp" and "St. Louis Kennedy Academy." This was definitely not the Greystone with its antiques and old statues. The glass atrium was filled with brightly colored sofas and a chrome staircase curving up to the second level.

"Looks like the elevators are over there." Jake pointed just past the staircase. Seeing the elevators and getting to the elevators, however, proved to be two different things. They made it about halfway when they were cut off by a large group of kids wearing blue "Future Farmers of America" T-shirts. Jake almost tripped over a bellhop pushing a cart stacked high with luggage.

"Careful," the bellhop said, putting his hand out to steady Jake. He smiled and yelled above the noise. "It's a jungle in here today. The State Fair's opening and the Twilight Parade is tonight."

"We just need to get to the elevator," Jake said.

"You're in luck," the man said. "I'm going your way. Just follow me." Jake, Lucy, and TJ hunched closely behind the bellhop as he cut a path with his cart across the lobby to the elevators. The bellman eased the loaded cart onto the elevator and pushed the button for 26. "What floor do you guys need?"

"Club Thirty," Jake said.

"Fancy." He pushed the "30" button.

It was only as the elevator doors swooshed shut that Jake realized just how noisy the lobby had been. Unlike the jerky clanking of the old cage elevator at the Greystone, this was smooth and quiet. Jake silently counted off the floor numbers as they clicked in lights above the door.

"Thanks for being our snowplow back there," Jake said.

"No problem. Welcome to the Capital. My name's Jeff." He squeezed in tight between TJ and his cart. "Sorry for the craziness. It's the same every year. Seems like everyone shows up a couple of hours before the parade." He turned to TJ. "You guys here for the fair?"

TJ looked up from his shoes with a bit of surprise.

"So. We're uhmmm, we're—"

"Visiting family," Lucy interrupted.

They came to a stop and the doors opened on the twenty-sixth floor. "Enjoy." Jeff eased the cart off the elevator and the doors closed behind him.

The elevator zipped up the final four floors and the "30" button lit up.

"OK, this is it," Jake said. "No incidents. Under the radar. If anyone asks, we're just meeting my dad."

It felt like they were floating in the clouds as they stepped off the elevator. The walls were nothing but windows slanting slightly outward from the floor all the way to the ceiling. The entire city of Springfield stretched out below. Black leather chairs were clustered around a modern fireplace with glowing glass beads instead of logs. At the far end of the lobby a young woman stood next to a hostess desk. As they stepped closer to the windows, they could look down on all of downtown. The silver dome of the capitol shimmered outside the window like a dramatic painting. Further out, the neighborhoods gave way to the edge of the prairie.

"Sweet," TJ said, pressing his head lightly against the glass and gazing down at the dome reflecting the late afternoon sun.

"So if that's the state capitol, what's that?" Lucy pointed to a smaller red-domed building several blocks away.

"That's the old state capitol where Lincoln worked as a young lawyer and state congressman. It's where he gave his famous speech about slavery, 'A house divided against itself cannot stand.'"

"'This government cannot endure, permanently half slave and half free,'" Lucy said.

Jake looked at her, impressed.

Lucy smiled. "We studied more than Budokai."

"Yeah, well I'm especially glad the half-free side won the day," said TJ. "My great-great-grandfather was one of those freed during the war." The kids stood in silence absorbing the fact that only a few generations before, it was legal to own another person.

"Can I help you?" The woman from the desk approached

Jake, but then paused and turned her head slightly sideways when she noticed his eyes.

"Uhh, we're just meeting my dad here," Jake said, trying his best to smooth out his bed head from the train sleep.

"Certainly. If you'll give me his name, you can wait in the lounge and I'll let you know when he arrives."

Ughh. Jake didn't think it was a good idea to give them Gabe's name.

"Reed Richards," TJ piped in, leaning against the counter. "Dr. Reed Richards."

Lucy stomped on TJ's foot and gave him the evil eye.

"No reservation, ma'am," Jake said, stepping back in front of TJ. "He's a bit of a free spirit, seat-of-the-pants, go-with-the-flow gentleman. Appreciate the offer, though. We'll just wait in the lounge until he gets here."

The lounge was empty except for an elegant woman in a dress sitting alone in a corner booth and a bartender stacking glasses at a curved bar. They took a seat in a group of black leather chairs next to a window overlooking the city.

Jake looked at TJ. "Reed Richards, really? Mr. Fantastic?"

"Just kind of popped into my head," TJ said.

Jake smiled. "Well, he's definitely my favorite of the Fantastic Four. Top-notch scientist. Mad combat skills. What's not to like? It's just a good thing she's not a fan."

"You gave the lady a superhero name?" Lucy asked in a whisper. "What if she'd recognized it?"

"Come on, did she look like the Fantastic Four type?" TJ said before turning to Jake. Your favorite, really? What about the Human Torch?"

"Come on. Mr. Fantastic. Super-elasticity, plus he's an engineering and chemistry genius," Jake said.

Lucy shook her head and gazed out the window while Jake and TJ launched into a debate about which superpowers would be more useful in seventh grade.

"I'm not saying that the flames wouldn't help with bullies; it's just in gym class I think I'd rather—" Jake suddenly stopped mid sentence, his mouth slightly open. He stared dumbstruck at the front of the lounge where a short, stocky man with a beard slid into the booth next to the elegant woman.

"Artie?"

APPETIZERS

ARTIE LOOKED UP AT JAKE WITH SURPRISE. Jake wasn't used to seeing Artie out of his usual Greystone doorman garb.

"Jake. Wow, uhhh, I mean, hey! What are you doing here?"

"I'm . . ." He cleared his throat. "I'm looking for Gabe. Is he with you?"

Artie stood up and took several steps away from the booth, drawing Jake with him. "No. Why would you think that?"

"He has a dinner reservation here. That's why we came."

"Oh, yeah, right . . . dinner reservation," Artie said, glancing back toward the door. "Well, he did have one, but he sent me instead. Hotel business."

"There's some mad-crazy stuff going on. We need your help."

"Sure. Sure. Sit down." He stepped back toward the booth and motioned for the kids to join him. "This is Miss Michaels. Bridget Michaels."

The woman smiled and slid over as they all squeezed into

the booth. "She's working on a project with us for the Greystone."

Artie turned to Lucy and TJ. "So you're Jake's friends? I don't think we've met."

"We just met last night at the museum; Lucy and TJ," Jake said.

"Ahh, yes, the new school. Wait a minute. Aren't you supposed to be at that school thing right now?"

"Yeah," Jake said. "That's what I wanted to tell you." Jake glanced at the lady. "Can we talk somewhere private?"

"Bridget is an old friend. You can say anything."

Jake paused a second and then let it spill.

"You won't believe what's going on."

Jake told them about the sleepover and what happened at the museum, the police officer and their trip to Springfield. He still didn't know what to make of the name on Gabe's driver's license and the museum articles, so he left that part out.

The whole time Jake was talking, Artie kept glancing over Jake's shoulder to the lobby. When Artie would return his attention, it was almost as if he was trying too hard to stay focused on Jake.

"Wow," Artie said, putting his hand on Jake's shoulder. "I thought you looked a little ragged. Are you guys OK? Wait a minute." He leaned in closer to look at Jake's lip. "Did you get hit?"

"No, I'm fine. Just an accident," said Jake as Lucy looked away uncomfortably.

"Well, good." Artie caught a glimpse of the lobby. "I mean, not good that this happened, but good you're OK."

"We didn't know what to do. When I found Gabe's reservation, we came here."

"Well, that was smart. Gabe knows everyone. I'm sure he knows someone on the state police. We'll track him down and turn this over to the right people." Artie stood up. "First, though, I've got to, well, I'll just be a minute. Be right back." Artie scooted out of the booth and disappeared into the lobby.

"He'll be right back," Miss Michaels said awkwardly. "So you've basically been on the run since last night. Have you eaten?"

"Well, as a matter of fact, we haven't," TJ said. "We were led to believe," he glanced at Jake, "that dinner would be part of the evening."

"Sure." Miss Michaels waved to the bartender. "A few menus, please and perhaps a platter of appetizers?"

"Nice. Finally a voice of reason," TJ said, pulling the sanitizer from his pocket and squeezing the last drops onto his hands as he rubbed them.

Lucy stood up, excusing herself from the table. "I need to use the restroom." She headed back into the lobby as the bartender brought water and menus to the table.

Jake and TJ took a few minutes to make their choices. They had just finished ordering when Lucy slid back into the booth.

"And anything for you, miss?" the waiter asked.

"No, I'm not hungry, thanks," Lucy said, staring directly at Jake when she said it.

"Really?" TJ looked shocked. "Did you live on granola bars in Naples?"

"Nepal," Lucy said. "Naples isn't even a country, and no,

I'm just not hungry." Even though she was talking to TJ, she continued to stare straight at Jake.

"So, how'd you get the black eye?" Miss Michaels asked TJ.

"Right. Well, it wasn't pretty. Goons on all sides. But sometimes a man's got to do what a man's got to do. I had to make my stand . . ."

As TJ spoke, Jake's mind wandered. He couldn't stop thinking about the Gabe stuff—the fake name on the driver's license, the Philadelphia museum article. There had to be a good explanation.

Lucy now seemed to be squinting at him. No, not squinting. She was winking. No, not winking—blinking. Did she have something in her eye?

"And where were you during this battle?" Miss Michaels asked Jake.

"Uh, sorry, what were you asking?" Jake was distracted, trying to decode Lucy's look.

"Is that where you got your bloody nose, during the firefight with the twenty goons on the plane?"

"Firefight with twenty goons?" Jake asked.

"He came in a bit later," TJ said, cutting Jake off. "Anyway, so I yelled, 'For God and Country' and came out swinging."

Jake flinched. Something rubbed his leg. He glanced down. Lucy was tapping his ankle with her foot. Jake remembered an old black-and-white movie he'd watched with Gabe. *That was how this lady flirted with this guy. Hmmm. Maybe the Old Spice is working. Maybe she's—*

"Excuse me, TJ, that really is an incredible story," Lucy said.

"But Miss Michaels, would you mind checking on Artie? We really need to talk with Jake's Uncle Gabe as soon as possible."

"Absolutely. He probably got a call. I'll see what's up." She excused herself and left the lounge.

As soon as she disappeared from view, Lucy leaned in.

"I've got to talk fast. I didn't go to the restroom. I was looking to see what Artie was doing. Something didn't feel right. I saw him in the restaurant leaning over a table talking to two guys."

"What?" TJ said. "You're too nosy. It's a good thing he didn't—"

"One of them was Bates," Lucy said with a troubled face.

"Are you serious?" Jake said. "That can't be."

"I know what I saw. He wasn't in a police uniform this time, but it was Bates. And they looked like old pals."

"I don't get it," Jake said. "I mean, I know Artie seemed a little weird, but that's kind of normal for him."

"Look, we can debate what it means later, but if we wait until they get back we might not have a choice."

Jake's mind was racing. *There must be an explanation.* His eyes roamed across the lounge. The bartender disappeared through the swinging doors into the kitchen. Jake didn't know what to do. Lucy was right. They needed time to think.

A noise grew from the lobby. A group had left the restaurant and was approaching the lounge. Jake looked back to the kitchen doors behind the bar.

Lucy looked at the doors and then at Jake.

"Back to Plan X!" Jake sprang from the booth and headed for the kitchen door. Lucy was next, then TJ, who barely missed snatching a mozzarella stick as they dashed by the bar. They burst into the kitchen, passing a large grill sizzling with steaks. As they swerved around a steel counter, TJ made a grab for a basket of chicken strips but came up empty. They reached the back of the kitchen, only to be engulfed in a cloud of steam as a worker slid open a dishwasher and pulled out a rack of hot dishes. They choked and waved the steam away, still fumbling forward. As the cloud thinned, Jake could make out a red glow at the far end of the room. The red letters "E" and "X" came into focus. Just before he reached the exit, a huge sweaty hand reached out and latched onto his neck from behind.

"Not so fast!" the dishwasher yelled. "No dining and dashing today." In one quick motion Jake reached back, grabbed the man's massive hand and dropped to his knees, flipping the man onto his back. Jake popped back up as Lucy stepped over the stunned worker and pushed through the door. Jake and TJ rushed behind her as TJ made a final desperate grab off a food tray next to the door.

They burst into a hallway lined with boxes and empty wine crates that led to a small service elevator. TJ looked down to see that he had grabbed a fistful of carrots and celery. He tossed the vegetables and ran to help Jake slide open the steel elevator door. A worker was inside, hunched over a load of laundry bags. Jake almost knocked the man down as he jumped in and punched the first-floor button.

"Sorry, sir. Emergency situation," Jake said.

"Yeah, I know." Jeff the bellhop stood and turned to Jake. "We need to talk."

HERO SANDWICH

THE ELEVATOR HAD DROPPED only a few floors when Jeff flipped the emergency stop switch. They came to a jarring halt, with the elevator suspended between floors. An alarm bell pierced the small compartment with an obnoxious clang as a red light flashed on the panel. The bellhop reached into his jacket. Jake saw the flash of a gun and flinched, but Jeff simply pulled out a wallet, flipping it open to reveal a badge and photo ID.

"Special Agent Matt Blair. FBI," he yelled over the blaring alarm. "This has to be quick. How do you know Ed Chase?"

They gave him a confused look.

"Sorry, sir. We're not familiar with that particular individual," Jake said, yelling in between clangs of the bell.

"Nice try. You just spent ten minutes with him in the lounge, and from the looks of the hug he gave you," he motioned to Jake, "I'd say you do."

"You mean Artie? He's a doorman where I live in Chicago.

I think there's some sort of misunderstanding, a mix-up, a case of—"

"Interesting. You told me earlier you're visiting family. What are you really doing here?"

"We *are* visiting family! We thought my Uncle Gabe was having dinner here but then we saw Artie."

"Well, your friend's name isn't Artie. It's Ed Chase and he's a problem. We're not exactly sure what kind of problem, but he's definitely a problem. At the least he's involved with some bad people. Did he mention anything to you about Caleb Smith?"

Jake hid his surprise at hearing that name and just shook his head no. He felt like he was being tortured by the still-clanging bell.

"What about this man?" He showed them a small photo. It was an out-of-focus, grainy image, like ones that Jake had seen of criminals taken from a security video. Jake flinched slightly. It was of an older man with graying black hair and a full beard and mustache. He looked just like Gabe after two weeks of camping.

Again, they said no.

"Look, kids. I know this is all hard to believe, but sometimes people get desperate and in over their heads. Two museums were broken into last night. Right now, we need to get you to a safe place." He flipped the emergency switch off. The ringing stopped and the elevator resumed its descent.

"When you get to the lobby, go straight to the front desk and ask them where you can get a good hero sandwich. Go straight there. Don't talk to anyone else and don't trust anyone."

"OK, but where are you—" TJ didn't get a chance to finish before Blair pushed open a panel in the ceiling and hoisted himself up. "Hero sandwich," he called out and slammed the panel shut behind him.

The elevator continued its descent as the screen ticked off the passing floors. At the twenty-fifth floor they felt the elevator car lurch downward a bit, as if someone had jumped off the roof.

24, 23, 22 . . . Jake, Lucy, and TJ stared at each other in silence. Just past the twentieth floor Jake reached up and flipped the emergency stop switch.

The annoying alarm bounced off the walls again.

"I'm not sure what to do. This is flat-out crazy!" Jake yelled.

"Well, since Artie might be a criminal mastermind," TJ yelled over the alarm, "I say we do what the guy with the badge and gun says. Hero sandwich!"

"I don't know," Jake said. "I don't know about him."

"Look," Lucy said, "if he was one of the bad guys, I don't think he would have just let us go." The ringing seemed to be getting louder, if that was possible.

"Maybe they're getting Artie mixed up with someone else," Jake said.

"If you're right—" Lucy said.

"I *am* right," Jake said, pressing his lips together.

"OK. If you're right, the best thing we can do is get to someone who can clear up all the confusion. And we're out of options," Lucy said.

Jake stared at the panel, saying nothing. Lucy reached

over and flipped the emergency switch off. "This alarm is going to trigger someone downstairs, and it might not be who we want."

The elevator began to descend again. 19, 18, 17 . . .

"Our best shot is to do what he said," Lucy said.

16, 15, 14, 13, 12, 11 . . .

Jake exhaled. *Stay positive. Keep a clear head.* "OK. Front desk. Hero sandwich."

Lucy and TJ nodded.

10, 9, 8, 7 . . .

When the elevator doors slid open, the sounds of the packed lobby poured in. They could barely step out without getting swept into a swollen stream of people. They paused as a line of kids carrying trombones, tubas, and drums snaked past them. When the band had cleared, Jake looked across to the registration desk. A man was leaning over the counter talking to the clerk. The man had a military crew cut and a triangle scar on the side of his neck.

NO BIG DEAL

JAKE LUNGED BACK FOR THE ELEVATOR, but the door closed before he could reach it. He ducked behind a woman holding up a sign that read "ACES GROUP" and pulled TJ and Lucy with him.

"It's that guy, Slate, from last night," Jake whispered as they inched behind the stream of kids. "He's at the front desk."

The ACES woman began leading her kids away from the lobby. Jake, Lucy, and TJ went with the flow of the group, hiding behind them as they passed through a hallway into a large conference room.

As they entered the room, a muscular boy in a T-shirt with rolled-up sleeves and a cowboy hat was handing out brochures.

"Welcome ma'am," the teen cowboy said, flashing Lucy a bright smile. "If there's anything you need, just let me know." He gave Lucy a wink and handed her a brochure, completely ignoring Jake and TJ. A whole room of kids entered after them. It was your basic large hotel meeting room, except that someone had stacked all the chairs to the side. This left a large empty space in the middle and a few folding tables lining the wall.

"Everyone grab a seat," the lady barked into a megaphone, causing the kids to flinch. "We'll get rolling in a minute." All of the kids spread out on the floor, their conversation and laughter echoing off the walls.

Jake, Lucy, and TJ ducked to the back of the room, taking seats on the floor behind one of the folding tables.

"Well, Plan Z? Not so good," TJ said. "Especially since Artie is apparently hanging with the goons."

"Look, he's not . . . he's not a criminal." Jake was obviously shaken.

"Maybe he doesn't know what he's involved in," Lucy said.

Jake rubbed his temples. "I don't know . . . I don't know."

The room continued buzzing with noise. Several kids carried large boxes into the room and set them on the table.

"Well, the hero sandwich isn't a whole lot of help if the goon squad is guarding the front desk," TJ said, looking back toward the door. "Maybe we should take our chances with 911."

"Are you forgetting what you saw last night? And what Agent Blair said?" Lucy asked.

"Yeah, well 'Don't trust anybody' doesn't leave us with a lot of options, does it?" TJ turned to Jake. "What do you think?"

Jake was staring at the floor.

"Jake? Earth to Jake."

"Sorry, I just . . . what were you saying?"

"Lucy doesn't think we should call the police," TJ repeated. "But I think we've got to call someone."

"I, I don't know. I . . ." Jake kept staring, his eyes slowly moving from the floor to the brochure Lucy had put in front of her. It was a State Fair program. Although he was staring at it, he wasn't really focusing on anything.

"Hey, if we can't trust the police, let's go over their heads. CIA, the Marines, the president, I don't care," TJ said.

"Sure, let's just call the White House. I'm sure they'll patch us through," Lucy said.

A slightly older girl, with 'Tina' sewn on her shirt, stepped up to the table with a large box. "Excuse me, kiddos, but we need to do a little prep here."

"Kiddos?" TJ whispered as they moved away from the table.

Jake continued to stare at the program, his lips slowly moving as he read. "I think . . . that's it! TJ's right!"

"I am? Sure. I mean, yeah, I know. About what?" TJ asked.

"The president. Well, not the *president*, but the idea," said Jake. "Look who's in the parade tonight!" He held up the program.

"The 4-H Racing Pigs," TJ said, reading from an ad in the paper. "I don't think so. You see, I've got like this sensitive, almost-superhero sense of smell. Ever since—"

"Not that, *this*." Jake pointed to the top of the page.

"Presidential front-runner Governor Amanda Haven will close out this year's Twilight Parade."

"Brilliant!" Lucy said.

Jake blushed. "Not bad, right? Actually it was TJ's president idea that made me think of it."

"Sure. I'll take a little slice of the brilliant cred," TJ said, moving to fist-bump Lucy.

Lucy looked down at TJ's fist. "Is this that paper-rock-scissors thing?"

"What the . . . ? It's a fist bump," TJ said.

Lucy gave him a questioning look.

"A fist bump, it's a . . . a thing," TJ said.

"It's a form of congratulations or respect," Jake explained. "You make a fist and tap them together. I'm not a big fan of it myself but I've heard it's more hygienic than a handshake or high five. It's very common in sports."

"Actually I think the Wonder Twins were first," TJ said.

"Wonder Twins," Jake explained. "Extraterrestrial siblings from *Super Friends*."

"Well, that certainly clears that up," Lucy said, shaking her head. "You think we can just go up to the governor in the middle of the parade?"

"Well, maybe. She'll be doing the politician thing where she rides in a convertible, jumps out, shakes hands, kisses babies, stuff like that."

"So, this parade—will there be candy thrown?" asked TJ.

"It's worth a shot," Lucy said, ignoring TJ's question.

"We can just hang back in the crowd and wait until she comes by," Jake said. "It starts at six thirty, so we don't have a lot of time. We just need to find a way to get there."

"Listen up, kids," the megaphone lady blared. "The buses are here. We're ready to roll. Pick up your hat from Tina on the way out. And remember, we've got a lot of new kids this year, so sit next to someone you don't know. It's only ten minutes to the parade."

"You were saying?" Lucy said with a smile.

The kids all stood and began making their way to the table where Tina and the boy in the cowboy hat were unpacking various colored ball caps.

"What?" TJ said. "We're just going to stow away on their bus? We don't even know who these people are."

"ACES—some kind of summer camp," Lucy said. "I think I need to make a new friend." She headed over to the hat table.

"So how about that kid in the cowboy hat?" TJ said after Lucy was out of earshot. "Do girls really go for that cowboy thing?"

"It's plausible," Jake said. "I think they like feats of strength. You know, like lifting and throwing stuff."

"Really? Even more than clever banter? I thought they liked clever banter."

"I think maybe it's both; the feats of strength and the clever banter. I hear hygiene also comes into play."

"What's that?" Lucy said, returning from the table.

"Uhh, nothing," Jake said, straightening up.

"I told Tina we were first-timers," Lucy said. "She was very helpful. She gave me these." Lucy handed white ACES ball caps to Jake and TJ and popped one on her head.

"See, no big deal," Lucy said, joining the line heading out the back door. "We're in."

As they passed the hat table, Tina smiled and waved to them. Lucy tipped her hat. "Looking good!" Tina yelled.

"See what you get when you make a new friend?" Lucy said while smiling and waving back.

They left the hotel and lined up to board the bus.

"This does not feel good," TJ said.

"Stop worrying," Lucy said. "It's just a ten-minute ride. Not a big deal. And no crazy panic lies."

They crammed into one of the last seats in the back.

"OK, so what happens when we get there?" TJ whispered, fighting for more space from the middle of the seat.

"When we get off the bus and they head to watch the parade, we'll just hang back and slip away. There's so many kids, no one will notice," Lucy said.

"Howdy, ma'am. I don't remember seeing you around these parts before." The cowboy kid who had greeted them earlier moved into the empty seat in front of Lucy and turned and offered his hand to her.

Lucy smiled and shook his hand. "Lucy, first time."

"Well, welcome, Miss Lucy." He tipped his hat. "My name's Brad and I've been around the horn a few times. If there's anything I can do to help a pretty lady, you just let me know. I'm at your service."

Lucy blushed. "Thanks, I uhhh . . ."

"We're good, thank you," TJ said, leaning in between Lucy and the boy. "We're together." He motioned to Lucy, Jake, and himself.

"Yeah," Jake joined in. "She's, uhh, with us. We're together. We're good."

TJ gave the boy a tense smile.

"Well OK, then," the boy said. "Didn't mean to intrude."

He stepped back in the aisle and leaned over to Lucy before heading back to the front. "Here if you need anything."

"Five minutes away," the lady with the bullhorn said.

"Can you believe that guy?' TJ asked.

"He was just offering to help," Lucy said.

"Yeah, just offering to help. Please. Jake, some support here," said TJ.

"Well, I did find his cowboy swagger a bit thick maybe. I mean, how did he know we weren't, you know," Jake said.

"Yeah, my point exactly," said TJ.

"How did he know what?" Lucy asked.

"It's just, well, what if this was a dating situation? If you were my, I mean, one of our, together, you know, girlfriend," Jake said.

"Oh, please! I thought he was nice," Lucy said.

"Yeah. Well, Cowboy Brad can take his nice act somewhere else," TJ said.

"OK, ACES!" The bullhorn lady stood up at the front, struggling to keep her balance while the bus pulled into a parking lot. "We're running a little late, so move quickly. You know the drill."

"The drill? There's a drill?" TJ whispered intensely out of the side of his mouth. "No . . . we definitely do not know the drill."

"Relax," Lucy said as they put on their hats. "Not a big deal. Just go with the flow."

They pulled to a stop behind a group of other school buses. Before they knew what was happening, the megaphone lady was rushing them off the bus and into a parking lot next to an office building. The lot was jammed full of school buses, parade floats, and marching bands. "OK, you know the drill," megaphone lady called out. "Line up by hat color." As they lined up, Jake noticed a lot of blue, green, and red hats, but no one else was wearing a white one. They tried to drift to the back but bumped into the megaphone lady.

"All right, let's go. No time for lollygagging," she blared into the megaphone while nudging them back toward the line, "especially you white hats."

"What does she mean by 'especially you white hats?'" TJ whispered as they reluctantly stepped back toward the rest of the group.

"OK," said the lady. "Take your marks. We're right between a high school band and the 4-H float."

TJ's eyes grew big. "We're not *going* to the parade . . . we're *in* the parade!"

"Relax," Lucy said. "We'll just march a little and then cut away. It's no big deal."

"And remember everyone," the lady called out. "You're the Adams County Equestrian Society. So show your ACES Pride!"

TJ stopped in his tracks. "Did she say equest—"

Neighhhhhh. Hmphh-CHOOO!

TJ jumped as something sprayed the back of his neck. He slowly turned to find he was the victim of a horse sneeze.

"Make way for the ladies. Make way for the ladies." Tina was leading two large horses by the reins. Brad was right behind her leading another. Each horse was draped with a saddle and an Adams County Equestrian Society banner. They led the horses to their places three wide, directly in front of Jake, Lucy, and TJ. Tina and two other girls with blue ACES hats mounted them. These weren't just large horses—they were giant Clydesdales, like the ones Jake had seen pulling wagons in Super Bowl commercials.

"White hats, meet Bessie, Claire, and Daisy," the megaphone lady said. "And remember, stay close, but not too close. You don't want to get kicked while they're marching."

TJ was standing perfectly still, staring ahead, almost in a trance.

Jake tried to get his attention, but TJ just stared ahead, not exactly at the horses—more past them, out into nothingness.

"ACES," TJ said softly. "Adams County Equestrian Society."

"Yeah," Jake said.

"Right. Horses, Jake, horses."

"I know, it's a bit of a situation, but I think it's manageable if—"

"Smells." A glazed look had settled across TJ's eyes. He was talking like a zombie. "And I think that's horse snot on my neck. I'm all out of gel, Jake. All out of gel."

"Look, I get the aroma issue and the Level 2 germ potential. We'll get a towel and—"

"C'mon," Lucy said. "Like I said, we'll march a few blocks and then we'll cut and run. No big deal."

"Here you go, white hat crew." The megaphone lady handed each of them a shovel. "You know the drill. Keep it clean. Let the horse finish her business and then scoop it into the bin in the back of the wagon. And remember, they keep walking while they do their business, so you've got to be quick."

WHITE HAT GET BACK

TJ SLOWLY TURNED TO JAKE. "So. We're not watching the parade. We're *in* the parade."

"Yes" Jake said, "but I think we can accommodate—"

"Right. And we're not just in the parade, we're following three mega-butt horse behinds." TJ continued patting his pocket for the hand sanitizer that wasn't there.

"Yes, but I don't think it has to go toxic. If we're careful not to agitate the beasts, we can—"

"Sure. And we're eye to butt level with the giant horses. Eye to butt level."

"It'll only be for a few minutes," Lucy said. "Not a big—"

"Stop. Don't say it. Do *not* say it. It *is* a big deal. Everything about it is a big deal. Especially what we have to scoop up."

"Yeah, but—"

"And Tina? Not our friend. Tina is definitely not our friend."

"OK, team, move 'em out," megaphone lady yelled as the

band in front cranked up. Tina gave a forced smile and waved to Lucy and TJ from atop her horse as they moved out.

They moved at slow parade speed, stopping every several blocks for small performances when the riders did maneuvers with the horses and the crowd cheered. Fortunately, Jake and Lucy were able to handle the cleanup without TJ's help. Each time they scooped up after one of the horses, the crowd chanted, "White Hat Crew! White Hat Crew!" At one stop Jake noticed TJ's eyes were watering.

"I'm having trouble breathing!" TJ wheezed.

"Here's a tip. Un-pinch your nose," Lucy said, shoveling another scoop into the bin.

"It's the stink. I think he's allergic to the stink!" Jake yelled over the crowd cheering Lucy's latest scooping efforts. He turned back to TJ. "Hang back a bit more. Try to get some fresh air." TJ slowly drifted back, turning his head to the side and sucking in air.

"White Hat, Get Back! White Hat, Get Back!" The crowd erupted, turning on TJ as if he had broken some sacred trust. TJ scrambled to catch back up with Jake and Lucy, even half-helping with one hand on a shovel and the other firmly pinched on his nose.

"So much for cutting and running," TJ said while glaring at Lucy.

"Relax, how long can it be? Maybe another fifteen or twenty minutes," Lucy said.

After two more hours the parade finally turned onto the home stretch. Jake could see the lights of the fair's grand entrance archway. The sun was beginning to set and roving spotlights were swinging back and forth across the sky. Flags fluttered from the archway as the parade began moving through the entrance into the fairgrounds.

This was their chance. Jake motioned for Lucy and TJ to follow him to the back of the wagon. They tossed their shovels and made a break for it just as they were passing under the arch.

"Hey! White hats, get back!" Tina yelled, turning her horse to face them.

"Shut it, Tina!" yelled TJ over his shoulder as he ran away. They slipped in between the crowds lining the sidewalk along the fair's main street and the rows of souvenir stands behind them.

"OK, no more 'Not a big deal,'" TJ said, yanking off his hat and tossing it in a garbage can. "Whenever you say, 'Not a big deal,' it always is."

"We get it. You've got a dirt thing," Lucy said, tossing her hat along with Jake's into the can. "And a smell thing. And a food thing," Lucy said.

"Hey, guys," Jake interrupted. "We're here. We made it. That's worth something, right? This is salvageable." He pulled the wrinkled program from his pocket with the fairgrounds map. "We just need to find a place to hang out. Somewhere that's not in the open, somewhere we can wait for the governor."

They walked behind the massive crowd watching the parade. They could just barely make out the lights of the Ferris wheel and the other rides illuminating the sky in the distance. They passed rows and rows of food stands, the smells of corn dogs, french fries, and saltwater taffy filling the air.

Jake realized that TJ had fallen behind and turned back to see him in front of a food stand.

"So, while we're waiting, we should get a little nourishment," TJ called out. "How much do we have left?"

Lucy and Jake joined him at the stand—Frank's Fried Fantasies On a Stick. The posted menu included fried corn dogs, fried pickles, fried Snickers and fried Oreos. "Are you serious?" Lucy asked. "I hardly think the word 'nourishment' applies."

"Hey, it's better than nothing. And it's on a stick! How can you argue with that? They've taken a Snickers bar, dipped it in batter, and fried it!" TJ said. "And put it on a stick! Genius!"

"How can you even think of eating that?"

"Wait," TJ said, moving to the food stand next door. "I can't believe it." He broke into a huge smile as he walked up to the counter. He was standing under a giant bacon balloon and a banner reading, "Bill's Bacon Bonanza."

TJ read from the sign. "'Chocolate-covered bacon baked in maple syrup on a stick.' They've done it! These beautiful mad scientists have done it!" He was talking as if he'd seen a flying car.

"Chocolate-covered bacon, in maple syrup and, wait for it . . . on a stick! On a stick! Only in America!" TJ was fumbling in his pockets.

"I'm getting sick just hearing you say it," Lucy said.

TJ's face turned to shock. "What? What's not to like? Chocolate? Maple syrup? Bacon? And it's on a stick! Come on, Lucy! The perfect snack for three busy kids on the run. If these guys don't win the Nobel Prize for Food—"

"There's no Nobel Prize for food. And no, thank you," Lucy said.

"Well, suit yourself. I'm getting one. What do we have left, fourteen dollars?"

"We can't," Lucy said.

"We can't? No, we can. Or at least I can. You keep your dollars for the granola stand, but I'm cashing out here."

"No, I mean we can't. We don't have it," Lucy said.

"What do you mean? We piled it all together on the train. One for all, all for one? Sixteen dollars. The rabbit food at the St. Louis station was what, two dollars? That leaves us fourteen. They're only five bucks. We could even just get one and split it."

"Remember the hotel? The Girl Scouts collecting for charity?"

TJ stared at her.

"I thought we were getting ready to meet Gabe. I thought this was over," Lucy said.

"You didn't—" TJ said.

"I gave them ten," Lucy said. "We only have four dollars left."

SPLITTAHHHSSSS

JAKE WINCED. "Ohhhh, not good."

"Like I said, it looked like we were heading up for dinner with Gabe and we wouldn't need it anymore."

"How could you just—" TJ started, in shock.

"I was almost right. We almost did get dinner, didn't we?" Lucy said.

"Well, yeah, but the key word there is 'almost.' Tell that to my stomach," said TJ.

"Not that it wasn't for a good cause, but you should have asked us first," Jake said.

"You know what? You don't get to lead anymore," TJ said. "You have bad ideas. And you're so sure you're right. Dangerous combination: high confidence and bad ideas. I'm pretty sure that's how Watergate happened."

Jake couldn't tell if Lucy was hurt or just irritated.

"You're right," Lucy said. "I'm sorry. I should have asked first. But the fact is we only have four dollars left. And we probably shouldn't spend that on junk food. We might need it."

They found a spot back from the sidewalk behind a thirty-foot statue of Abraham Lincoln holding an axe. They sat on the ground at the base of his boots.

"It sounds like the governor is at the end of the parade. Probably walking and shaking hands and stuff. We'll try to get close and tell her we need help."

"Won't she just think we're kooks and have her bodyguards whisk us away?" TJ asked.

"I think that's a chance we'll have to take, unless anyone has a better idea."

They stood up to watch the rest of the parade.

"They sure like their Abe Lincoln here, don't they?" Lucy said as a Lincoln High School band marched by.

"Land of Lincoln—his house, his presidential library, his tomb, the whole shindig. It's all here," Jake said.

"Shindig? Where do you get these words? Do you have some 'Word of the Day' app from the 1920s?"

"Old movies with Gabe. Three Stooges. That kind of stuff. I guess some of it sticks."

"Well, all this Lincoln stuff definitely gives me a different picture of our sixteenth president," Lucy said as a group of little kids marched by wearing Lincoln stovepipe hats.

"Wait until you see the Rail Splitters," TJ said with a big grin.

"The what?" said Lucy.

"They're legendary," TJ said as he stretched to catch a piece of candy thrown from an antique fire truck. A little girl cut in front of him and intercepted it.

"They're kind of hard to describe," Jake said.

Next came a group of BMX bikers, all wearing Lincoln beards and stovepipe hats. They raced in circles and performed wheelies and flips for the crowd. They were followed by a group of assorted old men in tasseled caps, driving go-karts. Each man's knees were pushed up around the steering wheel. The tight squeeze didn't seem to bother them as they zipped in loops and figure eights along the parade route and squealed their tires for the crowd.

"Shriners," Jake said. "They raise money for sick kids and hospitals."

"And drive little cars in parades," TJ said.

"Part of their deal," Jake said. "They like to make kids laugh."

Each time a float passed by that was throwing candy, TJ stepped out from behind the statue to battle a group of little kids scrambling for it. Every time he came up short.

Just after another marching band passed by, Jake heard a cheer go up from the crowd at the entrance arch. Everyone sitting along the curb rose to their feet and began pressing in tighter. Jake, Lucy, and TJ ventured out from behind the statue to see what was going on.

An imitation steam engine was pulling a large float styled like a wrestling ring, a "History In Your Face!" banner draped along its side. A black van emblazoned with the same logo followed closely behind.

"Wow. They really get excited about history here," Lucy said. "What's with the boxing ring?"

"It's not exactly a boxing ring," Jake said as the crowd roared.

"Splittahhhssss!!!"

Lucy flinched as a man behind her screamed and pumped his fists in the air.

"Railsplittahhhssss!!!"

As the caravan came to a stop, a deep voice blasted from the van's speakers. "Ladies and gentlemen, children and lovers of freedom: *History In Your Face!* presents your Rail Splitters and 'A House Divided'!"

"It's their new show. I haven't seen this one," TJ said, craning to see over the crowd.

An old rock song swelled up over the speakers.

"Bum-bum-bum-bum-bum-bum-bum . . .

BAMMM! The music exploded. Some woman was singing about needing a hero.

The doors of the van burst open and three tall, wiry men emerged, each a spitting image of Abraham Lincoln. The crowd went wild.

"Splitters! Splitters!" the crowd chanted.

The men were so similar they could have been clones. Each had shaggy, short black hair and a matching beard. Each wore a black stovepipe hat and an overcoat with long coattails, their only other clothes being black one-piece wrestling tights, the kind that looked like a pair of biking shorts with a tank top attached. They finished off their outfits with shiny black army boots.

The crowd cheered as the three skinny Abes ran a lap around the float, their bony elbows and knees pumping like pistons. They jumped onto the ropes and into the ring, meeting in the middle for a three-way high five.

They pumped their fists in the air and ran around the ring, following each other. When they'd completed their lap, two of the Abes climbed out and took their places on the outside of the ring, leaning on the ropes while the music faded out.

Another figure stepped into the ring, a smaller man with thick wavy hair flowing over his ears and a gray silk bow tie to go with his fancy black overcoat and wrestling tights. He motioned for cheers but was met only with hisses and boos.

"The election of 1860," the speaker blared.

He turned and spread out his coat like a cape to reveal the words "Little Big Man" in large white letters across the back.

"It's Stephen Douglas," Jake said, "Lincoln's opponent the first time he ran for president."

Douglas ran a tight lap around the ring as Abe #1 stood in a corner stretching and doing deep knee bends. When he reached the far corner, Douglas climbed up and balanced on the top rope. He reached into his coat and pulled out a white sign that read "Popular Sovereignty." The boos increased. He threw the sign at the crowd, dropped into the ring, and trotted to its center, where Abe #1 offered a handshake. Douglas refused.

It was on. In fact, the gangly Abe said as much. He withdrew his hand and looked down on the much shorter man, saying, "My dear sir, it is on. It is most certainly ON!"

The referee stepped between them. "OK, let's keep it clean, gentlemen. Go to your corners and come out with the bell!"

Douglas returned to his corner and took off his coat, laying it carefully over the ropes. Abe #1 tossed his hat to the other Abes and began running in place.

"Isn't he going to take off his coat?" Lucy asked.

"A Rail Splitter never removes his coat," TJ said. "It's a dignity thing. It wouldn't be presidential."

"Of course! Dignity," Lucy said as Abe did a series of deep knee bends that evolved into a kind of Russian dance, hunched down, arms folded, squatting and kicking around the ring as the crowd clapped in rhythm with his kicks.

The bell sounded and the two wrestlers met in the center of the ring. Abe immediately went on the offensive, lunging for Douglas. The smaller, more nimble Douglas ducked and went low, sliding under Abe and jumping up behind him. Douglas latched onto Abe's throat but Abe reached back for Douglas's hand, dropped to his knees, and spun to the ground, flipping Douglas onto his back and popping up.

"Bam! Looks like your move with the dishwasher, Jake," TJ said.

"Coach says it's my secret weapon. They call it the Beast Boy," Jake said.

The fight went back and forth, each wrestler gaining a temporary advantage only to have the tables turned. After escaping once again from one of Abe's chokeholds, a winded Douglas stumbled to the edge of the ring where another figure appeared—a Confederate soldier wearing a gray army jacket. Douglas tagged the man's hand and the Confederate jumped over the ropes into the action.

"It's a tag-team match. He's coming in for Douglas," TJ said.

"That doesn't make sense." Lucy looked confused. "Douglas wasn't with the Confederacy. He ran against Lincoln, but he was for the Union."

"I guess it's more of a metaphorical thing—you know, the story of Lincoln's various opponents." Jake shrugged.

"Yeah," TJ yelled over the crowd as one Abe tagged the other. "It's a metaphorical thing."

The announcer came back on. "1860, Lincoln defeats Douglas and wins the presidency . . . but that was only the beginning."

The music swelled back up as Abe #2 traded places with Abe #1.

"Railsplittahhhhhhs!" the man behind Lucy screamed again.

Abe #2 wasted no time. He spun behind the man and began crazy-slapping him across the back of the head. He then jumped in the air and brought his elbow down on the soldier's shoulder.

"Bionic elbow with a cobra clutch. Now we're talking," TJ said. "Pro wrestling move."

Lucy turned to Jake as Abe grabbed the man's nose and twisted it. "Pro wrestling? So that's a professional version of what you do?"

"Not exactly," Jake said. "Actually not at all. It's, well, different."

Abe #2 kept fighting dirty. He kicked, scratched, and even covered the soldier's eyes from behind with one hand while grabbing one of his victim's ears with the other.

"Atomic Stink Face!" TJ yelled.

The soldier twisted free, then stumbled across the ring and slipped out. Abe chased after him, but stopped short of jumping over the ropes. He prowled the ring, putting his hand above his eyes as if scanning the horizon for another opponent. There apparently was no one who wanted what he was dishing out. He walked to the center of the ring, raised his fists in the air, and high-stepped triumphantly.

"The rebellion is vanquished!" the announcer proclaimed as the music swelled back up.

Abe #2 ran to the corner and high-fived Abe #1 and Abe #3 over the ropes.

The music, however, suddenly screeched to a stop. Smoke poured from the van, covering it in fog. A hush fell over the crowd. A figure emerged through the haze, standing on the van's roof. Someone shrieked. An old woman put her hands to her face in horror. Children wailed. Everyone felt it. Something evil had arrived. As the smoke cleared, Jake could see a man dressed in all black twirling a dark cane.

"Loser!" the man behind Lucy screamed.

"Coward!" a grandmother yelled and then hissed.

The man's beady eyes were like steel. His neatly trimmed mustache matched his wavy black locks. Like the other wrestlers, he was wearing a long black jacket and tights. His clothes were a bit more dapper, however, as he completed his outfit with a pocket handkerchief and a gold watch chain that matched the tip of his walking cane.

Lucy squinted. "Is that supposed to be—"

"The assassin," TJ said.

"John Wilkes Booth," Jake said as the man twirled his cane in the air.

"Traitahhhhh!!" the man behind Lucy screamed, causing her to flinch again.

The Booth look-alike leapt from the van in a single bound and landed in the ring. He charged Abe #2, who still had his back turned, catching him off guard with a sharp crack of his cane across the back.

Abe #2 staggered and fell to his knees. Booth took another swing but Abe was able to roll to his left and then pounce to his feet with fists up.

The two men slowly circled the ring, sizing each other up.

A new beat of music began slowly rising over the speakers.

Da-da-da-da-da . . .

Da-da-da-da-da . . .

A burst of electronic drums kicked in.

DUN!

DUN DUN DUN!

DUN!

DUN DUN DUNNNNNNNNNNN . . .

The beat made Jake want to jump into the ring and defend his country.

Abe made a fake thrust toward Booth, who flinched but held his place. They continued to circle each other. Booth twirled his cane in one hand while faking a jab at Abe with the other. They kept circling, faking lunges and then withdrawing. The music grew louder as a singer kicked in, singing something about the eye of a tiger. Booth pounced, swinging wildly with his cane, but Abe was too fast. He ducked and darted, dodged and dove. During a particularly big swing and miss, Abe ducked and slid between Booth's legs. It was quite a sight given Abe's tall frame and lanky limbs, but somehow he managed to slip through and pop up behind Booth.

Booth tried to spin around to face Abe, but it was too late. Abe grabbed the smaller man from behind and lifted him off the ground. Booth flailed like a cat that didn't want a bath. The crowd erupted as the music swelled again. Abe locked his hands behind Booth's head.

"The Double-Lock Frankensteiner!" TJ yelled.

Abe slowly forced Booth to his knees and then to the floor of the ring. Booth flailed with no success. He released his grip on his cane and dropped it to the mat. Just when Abe was ready to complete his victory, the Confederate soldier leapt back into the ring, jumping onto Abe's back and grabbing his ears. Abe staggered forward, releasing Booth as he fell to the ground. Booth saw his opening, snatched his cane, and turned to face his fallen opponent.

"This isn't looking good," TJ said.

"I don't think historians believe Booth had help from the Confederate Army," said Lucy, but no one was listening.

"Somebody do something!" a woman screamed.

At that exact moment, Abe #2 and Abe #3 leapt over the ring and into the mix.

The first song about needing a hero came back on.

Arms and legs and jackets with long tails seemed to fly everywhere as the five wrestlers engaged in a battle for the ages.

TJ was calling out the moves as fast as possible, but even he couldn't keep up. "Romanian Butt-Hammer! No, wait, Detroit Clown Bite!"

Finally, Abe #1 emerged from the pile with Booth's cane, raised it in the air, and snapped it in two. The crowd went wild. Booth ran for his life. He was halfway over the ropes when Abe #1 caught him, pulled him back in, and proceeded to pummel him mercilessly against the ropes. The other two Abes dished out the same to the soldier.

"I guess the 'malice toward none and charity for all' doesn't apply here," Lucy said.

"Do the Double Eagle!" TJ yelled. Abe #1 apparently heard TJ. He forced Booth into a headlock with one arm and the soldier with his other arm. It was an awe-inspiring show of strength as Abe lifted the two men off their feet in matching headlocks.

The music shifted. It became slower, more somber, a lone snare drum and trumpet. A powerful choir of deep men's voices slowly rose over the instruments.

"Mine eyes have seen the glory of the coming of the Lord;

He is trampling out the vintage where the grapes of wrath are stored."

" 'The Battle Hymn of the Republic'?" asked Lucy in disbelief as Abe proceeded to parade his two prisoners around the ring.

"Nice touch," TJ said.

"His truth is marching on.

Glory, glory, hallelujah!

Glory, glory, hallelujah!"

Abe finally dropped the men to the ground and they scurried out of the ring.

The three Abes met in the middle and joined hands. They raised their hands triumphantly as a mash-up of the hero song, the tiger song, and "The Battle Hymn of the Republic" played to thunderous applause.

"Ladies and gentlemen, these are your Rail Splitters," the speaker announced. "Brought to you by Bill's Chocolate Bacon Bonanza. And don't forget to join us for our water show, 'Showdown at Fort Sumter' at the High Dive Pavilion. See your program for show times."

"Wow. Wow. Wow!" TJ said as the float drove away. "They do not disappoint, do they?"

"You know, I don't think their new show is completely accurate," said Jake.

"You mean the part where Stephen Douglas teams up with the Confederacy, or the part where Lincoln beats Booth mercilessly against the ropes?" said Lucy.

"I think it's what they call a homage. Kind of history lesson meets the Marx Brothers," TJ said.

"Yeah, well, I think I actually know less history after watching it," Lucy said.

There were a few more marching bands, floats, and antique tractors, but nothing that matched the excitement of the Rail Splitters. After a line of fire trucks passed by, a cheer went up as a small army of people came marching through the gate. There must have been at least fifty, all wearing matching blue T-shirts.

TJ was the first to make out the writing on their shirts. "Haven for America. Bam!"

"Governor Haven. That's her!" Jake shouted.

The marchers were followed by a large antique convertible with a "Haven for America" banner draped on the side. The car stopped as the crowd swarmed toward it, hoping for a handshake or at least a closer look at the woman who might become president. A distinguished-looking lady jumped from the back seat and waded into the crowd, shaking hands. A half-dozen serious-looking men in dark suits and sunglasses moved in a circle around her.

Jake, Lucy, and TJ hurried into the street and began pressing toward the governor, who had worked her way to the other sidewalk. The convertible kept creeping along, moving just fast enough to keep up with the governor's pace.

"We'll never get through this crowd," Lucy said. "Let's go back by her car. If we plant ourselves there, we'll have a better shot."

After a bit more jostling, the three of them were able to get within arm's reach of the car. Several minutes passed as the governor shook more hands before she began making her way back.

The three kids fought to hold their own against the increasingly powerful pull of the crowd. Jake knew this was their best chance for help, maybe their only chance.

"Governor Haven!" Jake yelled, squeezing forward, trying to reach the car. Jake was only a few feet away when he was knocked down from behind.

"Watch it!" Jake yelled at the man who had bumped him, but the guy didn't even look back. The man reached the governor and put his arm around her. That was when Jake saw he was a Secret Service agent, dressed in the same blue suit and black sunglasses as the others. Still, that was no reason to be rude. By the time Jake regained his footing, the crowd had pushed in, separating him further from the car.

"Governor Haven!" It was no use. Not only was everyone

else yelling for the governor, but the agent was now leaning in, whispering in her ear. Haven nodded and said something to the agent. As the governor climbed back into the car, the agent turned.

"Flat-out obnoxious," Jake said. "I know he's security, but that guy almost—"

"Right. Uh, Jake," TJ said, his face becoming very serious.

"—knocked me down. What?" said Jake.

"The guy in the suit."

"Yeah, he's a Secret Service agent, but still."

"No, I mean he just took his glasses off. Look."

Jake turned back to look. That's when he saw the triangle scar.

That's also when Slate turned and stared directly at Jake.

GREEN APPLE

SLATE LOCKED EYES WITH JAKE. The kids hit the ground. The last thing Jake saw before he ducked was Slate yelling a command into his watch and lurching toward them. This time, however, the push of the crowd worked in their favor, the tightly packed bodies creating a sea of people pushing Slate away from the kids. They scrambled on their hands and knees against the current of the crowd. Someone's knee caught Jake in the back of the head. A boot came down on his hand. From the grunts and groans next to him, he could tell that TJ and Lucy were getting the same treatment. They made their way to the sidewalk and ducked into a dark alley behind the food stands. After they had all caught their breath, Lucy was the first to talk.

"Slate is with the governor?"

"Which means Miss Presidential Candidate is in on this," TJ said.

"We don't know for sure. It just looks like—I don't know. It's murky, maybe some of her guys are," Jake said.

"Sure, and some of her guys are the Chicago police, the Secret Service, and everybody in between. Other than that, I think we're OK," TJ said.

"We need to think," Jake said. "But somewhere else. Fast."

They gazed out over Main Street from where crowds had continued to spill into the fairgrounds after the end of the parade. Both the street and the sidewalks were jammed.

Jake looked out past the trees to a ticket booth next to a row of chairlifts rising up on a cable. It looked like something you'd find at a ski resort. The brightly colored chairs were moving along a cable from tower to tower about fifty feet in the air, crisscrossing the fairgrounds.

They made their way through the shadows behind the food stands, quickly reaching a booth with a Sky Tram sign.

"Uncle Gabe took me on this once. It goes all the way to the other end of the fairgrounds. You can go round-trip but we'll get off at the other end."

Lucy stepped up to the ticket counter. "How much are one-way tickets?"

"Opening night special. Only a dollar each for one-way," replied the lady inside the booth.

"I can go two dollars for three," Lucy said. "That's a cash offer."

"Sorry. A dollar each."

"I'll tell you what I can do—"

"Just give her the three dollars," TJ said, glancing over his shoulder.

Lucy paid and they grabbed the tickets and stepped into line.

"OK, folks," the man working the loading zone said. "The cable doesn't stop and neither do the seats. First, step onto this spot here. When the seat hits the back of your legs, just sit down and I'll pull the lap bar down."

The lift climbed quickly, rising over the food booths and souvenir stands as the last of the evening turned into night. The Lincoln statue was lit up behind them. They passed over a giant yellow slide, about thirty feet high, filled with riders zipping down on small mats. Off to the right, spotlights bounced off the spray of a towering fountain.

The return cable with chairlifts coming from the other direction was about ten feet off to their left. Most of the lifts were still empty, but a few had laughing kids messing around or a couple on a date sitting much closer than Jake figured was necessary.

As they rose higher, an amazing kaleidoscope of light emerged ahead.

"That's the midway," Jake said, leaning out and pointing to a Ferris wheel, roller coaster, and other rides bathed in a sea of neon. "Gabe loves roller coasters, but hates any ride that spins around. He says that the 'Tilt-A-Whirl will make you hurl.' He still goes on it, but he's always faking like he's going to get sick."

The chairlift bounced a bit as they passed along one of the support towers.

"Whoa, seems a little unstable," TJ said.

"Nah, that's just what happens when you pass along one of the support towers. I've seen kids bounce them."

"You mean—" Lucy rose up in the seat and sat down quickly, bouncing the chair on its cable. "Like this?"

TJ grabbed for the handrail. "OK, got it. No further demonstration needed."

As they glided closer to the midway, they could hear the screams of roller-coaster riders in the distance as music filled the air.

"There's a concert every night in the grandstand and then fireworks. Gabe even talked our way in so we could see the fireworks up close once." Jake pointed far ahead to the back of what looked like a football stadium. The glow of floodlights was washing over from the other side.

"Sounds like you have some good memories here with Gabe," Lucy said.

"Yeah, I wish he was . . . I just wish—" Jake turned away and wiped something from his eye.

"Hey, you all right?" Lucy put her hand on his shoulder.

"What? Hey, no, I'm OK. Just allergies or something." He sat up straight and quickly changed the subject. Anyway, when we get off, I think we'll be close to the grandstand. There's a park on the other side. It shouldn't be very crowded at night."

"What's going on over there?" Lucy pointed up ahead to a tall thin tower lit up by spotlights.

"That's the Rail Splitters' high-dive show. At the end of the show, the Abes climb to the top. Somebody lights them on fire and they do a high dive into the pool. Completely gigantic."

"History in your face again?" asked Lucy.

"Something like that," Jake said. "We'll pass right by. Maybe we'll get to see them jump."

"Looks like someone is doing their own light show." Lucy pointed to the beam of a flashlight shining from a chair approaching them in the distance.

"Somebody's probably trying to bust couples kissing as they pass," Jake said.

The chair with the flashlight bounced slightly as it passed under one of the support towers. The light from the tower illuminated the passengers for little more than two seconds, but it was enough to outline two men in blue suits. The chair quickly disappeared into the darkness.

"It's them," Jake said, pulling Lucy and TJ down into their seat as far as possible. "Cover your heads."

The approaching chair was only a short distance away and was closing fast.

"Get down!" Lucy pushed TJ's head down to his knees.

"What about you guys?" TJ said, twisting to look over at Lucy and Jake still sitting upright.

"Shhhhh!" Lucy said, turning to Jake. "Don't get any ideas." She grabbed Jake by the collar and pulled him close. They were squished into the far side of the bench, with Jake's face buried in Lucy's hair. All you could see from the other side was the back of Jake's head. Anyone passing by would simply think it was another couple out for a romantic ride.

Lucy's hair reminded Jake of his favorite Jolly Rancher.

"And don't sniff my hair. I can hear you sniffing my hair."

"Mmmpphhh. Trying to breathe," Jake mumbled.

"Sorry, sure. Go ahead and breathe," Lucy whispered.

"I don't know what's going on up there but I definitely got the short end of this," TJ mumbled.

"Shhh, here they come," Lucy said.

The cable hummed as the two chairs drew closer. Jake started to look up but caught the reflection of a flashlight beam.

It seemed like the next few seconds went on for an hour. Finally, Lucy peeked out from around Jake's head and saw the other car had passed by.

"Coast is clear," Lucy said, moving back to her end of the seat.

"That was close," Jake said. "Good thinking."

"Thanks," Lucy said. "Sorry about the sniffing comment."

"No problem. But it's Green Apple, right?" asked Jake.

"I knew it. You were sniffing."

"I wasn't sniffing. I was trying to stay alive while being suffocated by hair."

"Uh, hello?" TJ said, still doubled under the lap bar. "A little help?"

"Oh, sorry. Sure," Jake said, helping TJ back up.

Just as TJ sat straight, a light illuminated his face. They looked up to see another blue suit in a chair coming their way. There was only one this time, but it was too late to hide. As the lift passed under the light pole, they could see it was Slate stepping up onto his seat.

"He's gonna jump!" TJ said.

"Hold on," Jake said. Lucy and TJ grabbed for the handrail as Jake jumped up and began bouncing the sky chair. The chair bounced on the cable. It seemed as if it was going to disconnect, but then it recoiled and began to sway wildly from side to side. On the second bounce, the chain reaction caused the empty lift in front of them to bounce sideways so that it swung directly into Slate's chair. By the time Slate scrambled back up, he had already passed the kids.

"Nice job," TJ exhaled.

The next moment was a violent blur as the chair snapped upward, nearly throwing them out. If the safety bar hadn't stopped them, they would have been thrown clear. Jake couldn't believe his eyes. Slate had recovered and somehow had managed to leap from his side to theirs, landing two chairs behind them.

BIZARRO BATMAN

THE CHAIRLIFT JOLTED WILDLY UPWARD as Slate launched off his chair. He latched onto the cable and began swinging himself hand over hand toward them. When he reached the chair directly behind the kids, he heaved himself up onto the seat. He stood and turned toward them. His eyes seemed to glow white.

Jake looked down—a thirty-foot drop to asphalt and a crowded street. He looked behind. Slate locked in on Jake, and two white laser beams streamed out of his eyes toward the kids. Jake looked ahead to the Ferris wheel, the roller coaster, and the water show. *The water show.*

Jake pointed to the approaching pool. "Five seconds. Then we take a plunge."

"What . . . ? I don't think—" TJ started.

"Feet first, keep your hands at your sides," Jake yelled.

"No way," TJ yelled back. "We can't—"

Slate's white lasers locked onto TJ.

TJ jumped.

Jake and Lucy went right after him, launching into the darkness. Jake felt suspended above the noise, hovering as if he were in some kind of video game. He felt the warm night air. He saw the blur of the midway neon below. Then gravity took over and he plummeted toward the pool.

He hit the surface with less than perfect form, the water stinging as he crashed in. He plunged down through a sea of bubbles. For a second, everything was quiet, as if someone had just hit mute. He pushed off as his feet hit the bottom of the pool, springing back upward. His lungs burned for air. He flailed, trying to propel himself up toward the light shimmering on the surface.

Jake broke through first, gulping a mix of oxygen and heavily chlorinated pool water. TJ erupted from the depths a second later, followed by Lucy. They swam for the side of the pool, gasping for air. They reached the pool's edge and hoisted themselves onto the deck, splashing waves onto the Rail Splitters who had rushed over to help them up. The crowd jumped to their feet. They must have thought it was a new twist to the act.

As one of the Abes helped Jake to his feet, Slate hit the pool, sending another tower of water into the air. The fans erupted again. They loved this stuff. Lucy and TJ leapt off the stage, hitting the ground just in front of the bleachers. Jake went to follow but felt a jolt from behind as Slate latched onto his neck. Jake dropped to his knees and spun around, flipping his attacker and causing him to tumble forward as Jake popped back up.

Jake raced toward the edge of the stage but suddenly pulled up. He grabbed one of the Abes and pointed to Slate, who was scrambling to his feet. "That guy said Lincoln spit on the Constitution. Called him a bearded baboon."

Abe got a look of fire in his eyes. He rose up and stepped toward Slate, blocking him. "Now see here, young man. If you're referring to Mr. Lincoln's suspension of habeas corpus in 1861, I must take issue—"

Slate smashed his forearm into Abe #1's chest, knocking him to the deck. It was on! Abes #2 and #3 pounced on Slate before he could take another step. The last thing Jake saw as he jumped from the stage was Abe #2 hoisting Slate over his head and spinning him like a helicopter before throwing him into the pool. The fans exploded in applause. Jake hit the ground next to TJ and Lucy.

Their soaked shoes sloshed a trail of water and mud as they sprinted past the bleachers into a dark alley beyond the stands. They cut behind a row of horse barns and onto a wide boulevard and began weaving in between more horse stalls and trailers until they came to an alley just across from the concert grandstand. On one side was a group of large garbage dumpsters and an alley leading further to their left. On the other was a small tractor and some landscaping equipment. They could hear the roar of the concert crowd coming from the grandstand ahead.

"Dude," TJ said, kneeling on his hands and knees. They were all gasping for air and dripping with water. "Beast Boy mode, again, total action hero. When we . . . get back, I'm giving you . . . one of my capes."

"Wait, *one* of your capes?" Lucy said.

"Don't . . . judge me," said TJ.

They sat on the ground for a few minutes.

"But how did you get Abe so worked up?" Lucy asked. "Did you yell something about the Constitution?"

"It just popped into my head," Jake said, finally regaining his breath. "It's something that Lincoln's critics said. I figured it would be fighting words to the Abes."

"Literally," TJ said with a laugh.

Jake rose up to peek out over the garbage bins. The boulevard was packed but there was no sign of Slate or any other of the blue suits. "Looks like we lost him for now."

"Lost him or lost it!" TJ said. "And again with the jumping? And the freaky eyes. I think Bizarro Batman's after us."

"Bizarre what?" Lucy asked, standing up and wringing water out of her shirt.

"Bizarro Batman," Jake explained. "A replicant from Planetoid Bizarro. Result of blue sun radiation."

"Well, he's technically not a replicant," TJ said. "I mean if you compare, say, Bizarro III to Batman I think—"

"Never mind. What about his eyes?" asked Lucy.

"What? You didn't see it? It's like they were shooting white lasers at us," TJ said.

"Just a reflection of the tower lights," Lucy said, glancing back toward the street.

"I don't know. I saw something too," Jake said. "Weird. And no one can jump like that."

"Shhh." Lucy grabbed Jake and TJ and ducked back to the ground.

"*Crrrrrr. Crrrrrr.* All blue units, all blue units." A radio crackled from the sidewalk.

They slowly rose and looked out over the dumpster. A group of police officers was fanning out across the boulevard, led by another blue suit.

OUT OF OPTIONS

THEY WAITED QUIETLY ON THE GROUND for a few minutes, catching their breath as the police moved past. Jake removed his shoes and began to wring the water out of his socks. Lucy emptied the contents of her soaked pockets onto the lid of the recycling bin. TJ frantically patted his pockets for the hand gel that wasn't there anymore.

"Sure, we can't let our precious dollar get all soggy," TJ said as Lucy flattened out the dollar next to her lion pendant.

Jake did the same, emptying his pockets onto the lid. Everything was soaked—the train schedule, the other papers, the glove.

"Is that . . . ? The gloves!" TJ yelled.

"Wait! You didn't toss them in the airplane?" Lucy asked in disbelief.

"I gave it some thought, considered it, but it didn't seem right. They were coming anyway; it wouldn't have mattered."

"It wouldn't have mattered?" TJ said. "Maybe they would

have found them and, I don't know, not shot at us? Or not chased us to Springfield? Or not sent Bizarro Batman to hunt us down? But other than that, yeah, it wouldn't have mattered."

Jake knew TJ was right. "I'm sorry. It happened so fast. I just thought, I don't know, maybe I was supposed to protect them or something."

TJ turned his back and walked to the wall. Jake didn't want to look at Lucy.

"You should at least have told us," Lucy said. "Like I should have asked you guys before giving the money away. We're either in this together or we're not."

"Yeah," Jake said. "I know. I just thought maybe it was a quest I was supposed to—wait! Ahhh, no, no, NO!"

Jake frantically rustled through the pile: wet papers, train schedule, news articles, and a glove. A single glove. "There's only one glove here!"

"Are you sure?" Lucy sorted through the pile.

Jake turned his pockets inside out. "It must have come out when we jumped. We've got to find it."

"Are you kidding? How about we get away from Bizarro Boy first, find someone we can trust second, get some real food third, and then maybe worry about the ratty old glove?" TJ said.

Lucy stood up and began pacing. "We're running out of options. Who can we trust?"

"I don't know, but I know who we can't: The police, the Secret Service, Governor Haven, Artie the Bellhop, and Tina the Weasel in the blue hat," TJ said.

"We don't know about the governor," Jake said. "And we don't know about Gabe either. He would never—"

"No one said anything about your Uncle Gabe," Lucy said. "But as far as Artie goes, I know what I saw."

"I know he was there and acting weird and you saw him with Bates, but that doesn't mean he's—it could just be a coincidence. There could be a—" Jake stopped his thought, realizing he wasn't even convincing himself.

"Either way, I don't think we should trust him right now," Lucy said.

Jake just stared at the ground, rubbing his hands on his temples.

"Wait. What about Agent Blair?" TJ asked. "If we can get back to the hotel, you know—hero sandwich."

"But what about what he said about Artie?" Jake said. "I don't buy it."

"If he wasn't a good guy, I don't think he would have just let us go. You saw his gun," Lucy said.

Jake looked at TJ, who shrugged. "I'm with her this time. It's either that, or just grab one of the police officers out there and hope he's one of the good guys."

Jake kept rubbing his temples and moving his lips silently. "Thinking, thinking, thinking," he mumbled.

"I know you don't like what Blair said, but if you've got a better idea, now would be the time." Lucy rifled through the pile on the bin.

"OK. OK. I'm not saying I believe everything he said, but OK." Jake began pulling his socks and shoes on.

"Right. So hero sandwich it is," TJ said.

Lucy scooped up the dollar bill and the lion charm, but paused as she began to grab Jake's papers.

"What's this?" She picked up the driver's license for a closer look.

"Nothing," Jake said, scrambling to his feet, snatching the license out of her hand.

"Caleb Smith?" she asked, looking at Jake with disbelief.

"Caleb Smith," TJ said. "The guy Agent Blair asked about?"

"Jake," Lucy said. "Why do you have Caleb Smith's driver's license?"

OK?

LUCY LUNGED FOR THE PAPERS ON THE BIN. This time she was a split second faster than Jake. She turned her back to block his reach.

"Museum home page, Governor Haven article, Gabe's train schedule." She stopped reading and turned to Jake. "This train schedule. The one you printed out. It says Caleb Smith." Lucy stepped back, away from Jake. "Jake, what's going on?"

Lucy's question hung in the air. Jake stood silent, his lips tight. She glanced around as if maybe there would be an answer on the walls and then turned back to Jake. "The picture Blair showed us in the elevator, the look on your face. Was that—"

"Uncle Gabe," Jake said. "He doesn't have that beard and mustache, but it looked just like him." Jake stared at the floor.

"Your Uncle Gabe . . . ?" TJ jumped up.

"And," Lucy said, "there's something else. Isn't there, Jake?" Jake looked up but didn't respond.

"This article from Gabe's search, about the Grand Army museum in Philadelphia. That's—"

"That's the other museum that was broken into." Jake dropped his head. "I read it on the train."

"What? So you knew that on the train. Why didn't you say something?" TJ asked.

"I wasn't sure," Jake said.

"You weren't sure? How could you not be sure?"

"It wouldn't have mattered. We still needed to find Gabe. I thought, I mean, I think there must be some explanation."

"Really? It wouldn't have mattered? How about we decide not to walk into a restaurant that might be a trap?"

Jake continued to stare at the ground.

"Jake, not to rub it in, but the gloves, these other things— you should have told us," Lucy said.

"I know," Jake said softly.

TJ and Lucy sat back down.

"The fake driver's license," Jake said, "the schedule and everything. I didn't know. I don't know what to think. Look, he's not . . . he's . . . he's just not . . ."

"All I know is this makes it even more important that we do what Agent Blair told us to do," Lucy said.

"Hero sandwich," TJ said.

"Hero sandwich," repeated Lucy.

They sat in silence. Lucy quietly folded up the papers and handed them back to Jake.

"Hey, man, I'm sorry I got worked up," TJ said. "That's a lot of heavy stuff."

"Yeah," Jake said, rubbing his face and standing up. "I'm OK. I'm OK."

"You sure?" Lucy asked.

"Yeah, I said I'm OK," Jake responded without looking at her.

"All right," Lucy said. "It's just . . . Nothing. OK, what's our plan?"

"Well, I think Tina the Weasel and her ACES bus are off the list," TJ said.

"I saw some taxis outside the main gate," Lucy said. "But no cash. And the credit card is definitely out." She looked back toward the alley. "What about the other group buses we saw out front? We can tell them we missed our bus and get a ride back downtown."

"It's worth a shot," Jake said. "The concert should get out pretty soon. We should find a good spot to slip into the crowd when they leave. I'll see what it looks like down this way." He motioned to his left. "TJ can check out that way," he said, pointing to his right. "Meet back here in five."

"Sounds good," said TJ as he headed toward the end of the alley.

Jake turned to leave but Lucy grabbed his arm.

"I know this is crazy, Artie and Gabe and everything."

"I'm OK."

"We don't really know how Gabe's mixed up in this, or even if he is. Maybe he doesn't really know what's going on. Maybe he's—"

"I'm OK," Jake said.

Lucy put her hand on his shoulder. He brushed it off. "I don't want to talk about it," he said.

"We're on your side, TJ and I. We're on your side," Lucy said.

"OK. Let's just get to the hotel."

Lucy looked at Jake as if she didn't know what to say.

"I said I'm OK," Jake said. "Let's just go."

"I know," Lucy said, standing up, but then paused. "You keep saying that."

"Saying what?"

"OK. You keep saying you're OK."

She took another step and stopped.

"Maybe you are. But I don't know. I think maybe you think you're supposed to say that. Like you have to. Even if you're not."

Jake looked away.

"It's kind of weird, being back in the States," Lucy said. "Kids act like they're cool and fine and everything, but . . . I don't know."

Jake just stared at the ground.

"My dad calls it looking real good and hurting real bad. Maybe it was just our little village, but it felt different in Nepal. Not all the faking."

"I need to go."

"I guess I just want you to know it's OK. Whether it's missing Gabe or whatever it is, it's OK if you're not OK. No one is all the time. I guess I just wanted you to know that."

Jake nodded without looking up and started back for the entrance.

He'd taken two steps when the walls of the surrounding buildings began shaking.

BREAKING AND ENTERING

IT FELT LIKE A HERD OF ELEPHANTS had invaded the nearby grandstand.

"That would be two thousand people stomping their feet," Jake said. "It must be encore time. I'll grab TJ."

Jake broke into a run, passing more garbage dumpsters and lawn equipment before finally reaching the end of the long alley as the cheers of the crowd grew louder. "TJ," he called out. Nothing.

On the other side of the road he could just make out a dirt track encircling the lit-up stage. No TJ that way either.

A voice screamed over the speakers. "Thank you, Springfield! You've been great."

Jake stepped further into the path. "TJ."

"Shhhh!" A hand pulled him back into the alley.

Jake spun to find TJ standing in the shadows pointing back toward the street. "This way's no good. There's a whole bunch of police swarming." They were about a third of the way back down the alley when they heard a rumble. Two lights appeared ahead of them. Whatever it was, it was headed straight toward them . . . and closing fast.

Jake scanned the tight corridor. There was nowhere to move. The headlights grew bigger, picking up speed. Jake and TJ broke into a run. The roar of the engine closed in on them just as they dove into a row of trash cans against the wall.

The automobile caught the side of one of the cans, dragging it under its front wheel before spinning sideways and slamming into the other cans. Jake and TJ were thrown clear as the vehicle screeched to a stop.

Jake lay on the ground, shielding his eyes from the headlights. He gazed through the glare to see a white Jeep with its top down. He could just make out a State of Illinois seal on the hood.

The Jeep's door flew open.

"Get in!" a voice called out.

"Lucy?"

Jake and TJ pushed the cans aside and jumped into the back.

Lucy slammed the Jeep into gear, squealing its tires as they tore down the alley.

They clung to the roll bar and the back of Lucy's seat, without seat belts or even seats to hold them in.

"You almost killed us!" TJ said.

"Sorry. Still getting the hang of this thing."

"You stole a Jeep! A government Jeep!" TJ yelled.

"Borrowed. I borrowed a government Jeep," Lucy called back over her shoulder as she shifted into another gear.

A jumble of loose red, yellow, and black wires stuck out from the base of the steering wheel, some torn apart and others twisted back together.

"No. You did not hot-wire a government vehicle!" said TJ.

"You're welcome," Lucy called back.

"She hot-wired a government vehicle," TJ said to Jake.

Jake broke into a big smile.

TJ shook his head. "Are there different prison sentences for 'breaking and entering' and just 'entering'? She's the one that broke. I just entered."

When they reached the end of the corridor, Lucy skidded to a stop in the alley and killed the lights.

"The street we came from is swarming with police. I found this parked next to the gate."

Two flashlights emerged in the alley behind them and began moving toward them. Lucy jammed the stick shift forward and slammed her foot on the gas. They screamed toward the grandstand.

"I don't think there's a road this way," TJ yelled, struggling to hold on as Lucy swerved around a parked golf cart.

The alley was illuminated every few yards by a lamp hanging off the grandstand. This was clearly not a path designed for a Jeep going fifty miles per hour, with its lights off.

She swerved again and skidded to a stop in front of a concrete barrier. On the left, the stands were still filled with concertgoers. On the right, another fence separated the alley from a dirt track circling the infield stage. Worst of all, the bouncing flashlights of the running officers kept growing closer behind them.

Lucy pulled up on a lever that said "4 Wheel Drive." She jammed the Jeep into gear and spun the steering wheel. They took a hard right, plowing through the fence across the path and onto a dirt track.

"Bad news!" Jake yelled, pointing ahead. Two headlights were on the track heading toward them.

Lucy banked the Jeep off the track and into the grass infield.

"Where are we going?" TJ yelled.

"I don't know," Lucy yelled back, picking up speed.

The Jeep lurched downward, hitting a pothole and almost bouncing the boys out.

"How about some lights?" hollered TJ, regaining his grip on the roll bar and leaning forward over Lucy's shoulder.

"No way," said Lucy. "Hold on!"

They crunched into another hole. This time the Jeep dipped to the side and skidded across the grass. They were about halfway into the infield when a second set of headlights emerged from the opposite direction. An explosion of sparks erupted underneath them, sending the Jeep heaving forward. Lucy regained control but overcorrected, sending them fishtailing back and forth. Another flash and explosion rocked the Jeep, sending it sideways across the grass, before spinning to a stop.

"Fire in the hole!" TJ screamed.

They took off again, only to have another explosion erupt right in front of them, then another as a tower of brilliant red and blue sparks shot upward.

"It's fireworks," Jake yelled as another exploded overhead.

"We're in the launch field. That's what all the holes are. We're on top of the firing pods."

Lucy flipped the headlights on. They were in the middle of a grid the size of a football field. There were wooden boxes buried in the ground about every ten yards on every side of them, each with plastic pipes and fuses sticking out. Another rocket shot out of the ground next to them.

"We're not sticking around for the grand finale," Lucy said, jamming the Jeep back into gear. They launched into full speed. Even when they were able to dodge the boxes, the explosions shot up next to them, showering them with sparks and the smell of gunpowder. Jake's ears were ringing.

The second set of headlights now left the track and began cutting across the infield toward them. Another rocket shot out of the ground, causing Lucy to swerve over a launch box just as it exploded beneath them. An explosion of sparks rained down on the Jeep, as if they had plunged into a cloud of fiery green confetti. The Jeep ground to a stop. The tires groaned as they spun against the sides of the hole. The Jeep didn't budge. Lucy threw it in reverse. More grinding. No moving. They were stuck.

They jumped from the back of the Jeep just as a spray of white sparks erupted under them and knocked them to the ground. As the shower cleared, two headlights came slicing through the smoke. A black van swerved to a stop directly in front of them. A new barrage of fireworks rocketed out of the ground.

The back door of the van burst open and a soldier in black gear jumped out. He rolled a small can under the Jeep as three more soldiers spilled out and grabbed Jake, Lucy, and TJ. Jake flailed but they grabbed ahold of him and threw him into the van. The last thing he saw was the Jeep exploding into a fiery ball.

Jake hit the floor hard, but quickly sprang to his feet. Just as the first soldier lunged for him, Jake spun out of the way, sending his attacker into the wall. Suddenly a second soldier grabbed him from behind. Jake grabbed the man's arm and spun, only to be met by a small tablet screen shoved to his face. A brilliant blue strobe flashed in his eyes and Jake crumpled to the floor.

GHOST ENTRANCE

JAKE TRIED TO STAND but only managed to stumble backward, blue spots bursting in his eyes. He dropped to the floor with his back against the wall. The spots began to fade, as if he were recovering from a camera flash. The van was moving at a very high speed. He could make out the fuzzy outlines of TJ and Lucy seated next to him, rubbing their eyes. Several dark figures leaned over them. Each of the figures was in full military gear—black padded jackets, small assault rifles, and combat helmets.

The one closest to Jake leaned forward and removed his helmet.

"*Artie?*"

Jake lunged for the door handle. The handle didn't budge and Artie's men quickly pulled him back.

"Whoa. Take it easy," Artie said.

Artie turned to the man holding a tablet. "Are we good yet?"

"Affirmative," he replied.

"OK," Artie said, turning back to face the kids. "Sorry about the rude introduction. But we have to take certain precautions. For your safety and ours. Now, hold on!"

The van jolted upward as they jumped a curb and accelerated.

"Jake, I need you to trust me," Artie said.

"Trust you? You tried to kill us, and you just kidnapped us!"

It felt like the van had moved onto a smooth road. There weren't any windows, so Jake couldn't see, but they were definitely accelerating.

"Someone is definitely after you. But it's not us, and we didn't kidnap you. We saved you."

"You tried to blow us up."

"We had to blow up your Jeep. It was the only way to throw them off so we could get away."

Jake wasn't buying it.

Neither was Lucy. "I saw you with one of the men from the museum at the restaurant."

"Yes, you did. I was undercover and you almost blew it."

"Nice try," TJ said. "We know about the museum robberies and we know you're really Ed Chase."

"Pull over," Artie called out to the driver.

He reached into his jacket and pulled out a small revolver.

"We've got to make this quick."

The kids froze against the van wall.

Artie handed the gun to Jake. "Take it," he said. "I need your trust. Not all of it. Just enough for us to get somewhere

181

safe. It's complicated. I can and will explain, but that's Step Number Two. Step Number One is we've got to get out of here. Otherwise, there won't be a Step Number Two. I need you to trust us. Just for the next ten minutes. Or we can let you out right here and you can take your chances with the guys in the blue suits. You can keep the gun either way, but you've got five seconds to decide."

Jake kept the gun pointed at Artie. He looked over to Lucy and TJ.

"OK," said Artie and the van accelerated, pushing them all back against the wall.

They came to a stop and Jake could hear a metal gate being pulled open. They accelerated again and it felt like they had pulled onto a smooth road. It sounded like every fire truck and police car in town was rushing past them into the fairgrounds.

Jake shifted the gun from his sweaty right hand to his slightly less sweaty left hand. After about five minutes, he broke the silence.

"Where's Uncle Gabe? Do you have him? Is he in trouble?"

"I told you that this is, uhh, complicated. Let's get to a safe place first."

After another five minutes, the van slowed to a stop.

Artie tapped his earpiece. "We're coming in Ghost Entrance and we've got three guests. They're clean."

The van went down a short incline and came to a stop. Jake heard something big and heavy slide open outside. He felt the van pull forward and then stop again. The back doors opened. They were in some kind of garage.

"After you," Artie motioned.

Jake shook his head, keeping the gun trained on Artie. "No. We're not going any further until we get some answers." Jake tightened his grip on the gun.

"OK, fair enough. Step Number Two: You can put down the gun. It's not loaded."

Jake glanced at the gun and then at Lucy and TJ. He threw the gun at Artie and lunged for the door along with his friends. The men grabbed Jake and Lucy but TJ made it out, hitting the floor in a roll and sprinting away.

"No one ever likes Step Number Two," Artie said, rolling his eyes. "We've got to work on that. Hey," he called after TJ. "There's no way out." He turned back to Jake and Lucy who were now being restrained. "It's a secure room. Navy SEALs couldn't get you out of here." Two of the guards gave Artie a dirty look. "OK, poor choice of words. SEALs, maybe, but everyone else? No." He yelled to TJ who was at the far end of the room pounding on a steel door. "The point is, kid, you can't get out!"

Artie hopped out of the van and motioned for Jake and Lucy to join him. Jake could see they were in some kind of a warehouse or indoor loading dock as his eyes slowly adjusted.

"I hope you understand I couldn't really hand you a loaded gun. Accidents happen: loss of limbs, bleeding out, terrible laundry charges, and paperwork. But think about it. We could have just blown you up right there if that's what we wanted. Simple headline: 'Teens steal car. Joyride ends in tragedy.' Fake up some gruesome photos. A sad but simple story easily sold. Everyone moves on."

"Agent Blair said you're one of them. Wanted for the robberies and murder."

"Oh yeah, about that."

TJ had moved on to another wall and was trying to stack metal barrels to reach a high window.

"Those windows are blastproof from both sides," Artie called out. "I'm not saying this isn't complicated, but there are answers."

TJ finally managed to get a second barrel stacked but it fell over, barely missing him.

"Can you come back over here?" Artie turned to Jake and Lucy. "I'm afraid he's going to hurt himself. Have you ever had an open fracture? I did once. Bone sticks right through the skin. If you've ever seen a half-eaten buffalo wing, it kind of looks—"

Lucy looked like she was getting nauseous.

"Well, anyway," Artie said. "It's not pretty. Someone get him down."

Two of the soldiers grabbed TJ and dragged him over.

"I can give you answers. I just don't think you're going to like all of them. Well, to the Batcave." Artie slid open an old, beaten steel door to reveal a freight elevator they all barely managed to squeeze into.

A few seconds later, the doors opened and they stepped out behind what looked like an old dresser. They were in a one-room log cabin lit only by the glow of a fake fireplace. Without saying a word, Artie led them out through the cabin's front door. They emerged from behind a large oak tree and walked into a dark rotunda with beams rising to meet a domed ceiling high overhead. Through the shadows Jake could see a large replica of the entrance to the White House. What most drew Jake's eyes, however, were the shadowed figures standing in the middle. As they crossed the lobby, Jake realized they weren't people, but rather incredibly real, life-size figures of President Lincoln and his family. He had seen pictures of this somewhere.

TJ did a double take as they passed another life-size figure. Its steely dark eyes and dark mustache identified it as John Wilkes Booth.

"Useless," Jake muttered.

"What was that?" TJ asked.

"Booth's dying words," said Jake. "After he was shot, he looked at his hands and said, 'Useless.'"

They entered a large cylindrical room lined with wood-framed glass cases holding old documents and other items. Jake leaned in closer to one of the displays. "Wait? Is that—"

"The Gettysburg Address. Welcome to the Abraham Lincoln Presidential Library and Museum," said Artie. "My name is actually Artie. It's just not my only name. And the Greystone isn't my only job. I'm an agent with a deep cover organization."

"CIA, NSA, something like that?" TJ asked.

"No. More invisible, and we're not government. But I can assure you we're the good guys. Those guys after you back there? They think I'm something different. They know me as Ed Chase. So do most government agents."

"I don't buy it," Lucy said. "If this was such a big secret, why would you tell us? For all you know, we're with them. Other than Jake, you don't know us at all."

Artie smiled and reached into his jacket. He drew out a small tablet with a blue screen and tapped it.

"Lucille Marie García. Twelve years, two months, and five days old. Born Veracruz, Mexico. Parents are doctors Eduardo James García and Grace Marie Kendall. Homeschooled in Mexico, Kenya, and India. Attended fifth and sixth grade in Nepal. Speaks Spanish, English, Swahili, Hindi, Nepalese, and a little Arabic. Self-starter. Has issues with authority. Likes her pizza with no cheese. Pretends not to like Taylor Swift even though fifteen of the top twenty most-played songs on her iTunes are all *by* Ms. Swift."

"That's not—"

Artie continued. "Thelonious Uriah Jordan McDonald."

"Thelonious Uriah?" Jake and Lucy looked at each other.

"Twelve years, ten months, and nine days old. Born Evanston, Illinois, to James and Hope. Attended North Shore Preparatory Academy until this year. Likes to show off his semi-hyper memory by solving a Rubik's Cube behind his back."

"Semi?" TJ said.

Artie continued. "Third Place at the World Junior Fencing Championships."

"It was really second—"

Artie kept going. "A real Renaissance man. Perfect test scores, advanced classes. Doesn't like his different foods to touch on his plate, has issues with dirt and barnyard animals, hates being asked if he plays basketball. And interestingly enough, the top ten most-played songs on his playlist are *also* by Ms.—"

"OK, OK," TJ said, cutting him off. "We get it."

"And then, of course, Jacob Herndon. Twelve years, two months, and twenty-four days old. Adopted at the age of six months by Gabriel Herndon. Report says he's a genius when he wants to be. Scored only 50 percent on his sixth-grade achievement tests but only because he fell asleep halfway through. Perfect score on the first half. Likes Civil War history and puzzles. Sixth-grade, seventy-seven pound weight class conference wrestling, first place. Hates being called scrappy, but he is. Favorite snack: graham crackers in milk, eaten like cereal. Needs to wipe his feet better when entering the hotel. I just threw that last one in from personal experience. Those little blue wands we flashed in your eyes—retinal scans. The gloves we wore when we grabbed you took skin samples. We ran the information. When they said you were clean, they weren't talking about your underwear."

OFF THE BOOKS

ARTIE WALKED TO THE GLASS CASE in the center. He stared at the Gettysburg Address and exhaled. "I guess 1864 is the best place to start. It was near the end of the Civil War, and Union agents had just uncovered a plot to break into federal arsenals around Chicago."

"The Great Northwestern Conspiracy," Jake said. "Gabe gave me a book about that."

"Exactly. The agents foiled it, which was critical, because it would have split the Union in half. For most people, even historians, that was the end of it. President Lincoln, however, wasn't so sure. He asked his close friend Allan Pinkerton to do more digging."

"Pinkerton? The spy that started the Pinkerton detective agency?" TJ said.

"Exactly," Artie said.

"History Channel!" TJ said with a pleased look.

"Well, Pinkerton found more. A lot more." Artie's gaze

traveled from Jake to Lucy to TJ. "This is where we go off the history books," he said as he walked out into the hall. "Pinkerton uncovered an array of groups working to overthrow the government. Names like Knights of the Golden Circle, the Order of American Knights, the Sons of Liberty, and others."

"Sure, but that's not a secret. I've read about them," Jake said.

"Yes. But what you haven't read, because no one has, is what he uncovered sitting behind all of them. He found they were all just code names for different parts of a single massive organization, a secret group that goes all the way back to the Revolutionary War. They called themselves the Order of the Dark Lantern, and some believed they had even infiltrated Lincoln's White House. The president didn't know who to trust, so he and Pinkerton set up their own internal secret group with a handful of agents."

They walked into a dimly lit chamber that had a glowing domed ceiling. White temple columns ringed the room, draped in black cloth. A large square frame in the center rose high into the air and was draped with black velvet and white silk curtains. In the middle was a casket. Soft, mournful music rose from behind the walls.

"O . . . K . . ." TJ said.

"They were just starting to make progress when a Lantern operative assassinated the president in April 1865."

"Booth," Jake whispered.

They left the display of Lincoln's funeral, passed down the hall and walked into a dark theater. As they entered the room, a man walked out onto the stage.

He looked to be about the age of a college student, but there were two things strange about him. One, he didn't appear to notice them. Two, and even stranger, he was putting on an old Civil War army jacket. He approached the front of the stage but still didn't acknowledge them. He stopped and buttoned up the large brass coat buttons and placed a soldier's cap on his head. At first, Jake figured he must be an actor in a play here. But then he straightened up stiffly, saluted . . . and began disappearing. Starting with his feet, the soldier faded in front of their eyes. It was like his body was turning to steam and drifting away.

"Whatthewhat?" TJ tapped Jake's arm.

"Oh," Artie said, looking up. "Don't mind Captain Miller. He's a hologram. Pretty real though, huh? He's part of the 'Ghosts of the Museum' show. They're making some adjustments to the technology and he's running on a loop."

Sure enough, the soldier appeared again, walked to the edge of the stage, fastened his coat and cap, and saluted before disappearing a second time.

"Nice. When does he come out on Xbox?" TJ said.

"That's nothing. Wait until you see—" Artie paused, seeming to catch himself. "Anyway, with Lincoln's death, Pinkerton was more committed than ever. Funded by a secret stash of gold seized from the Confederates, he launched an underground spy and counter-terrorism group working under the cover of his detective agency. They took the code name the Union Defense League. Over time, they became known simply as the League. Their motto: Preserve and Protect."

"OK, this is great history stuff," TJ said, "and I like the

freaky ghost soldier, but what does it have to do with people shooting at us?"

"Well, the thing is, it's not just history. You see, the Order of the Dark Lantern didn't end with the Civil War. If anything, it grew stronger, with tentacles reaching around the world. Fortunately, the League survived as well."

"What are you saying?" Lucy asked.

"I'm saying that for the last one hundred and fifty years, there's been a secret war raging in the shadows around the world. A war between the Lantern, who want power and wealth at all costs, and the League, which fights to protect freedom. I'm saying that tonight at 2200 hours, you were rescued from the claws of the Dark Lantern by League Rangers led by yours truly."

"You're crazy," said TJ.

"I think what you meant to say was 'Thank you.'"

TJ turned to Jake. "You're a Civil War geek. Any of this make sense?"

"Some of it, sort of. There's some plausible parts, but I've never heard of any League or Lantern."

Artie leaned over and waved the kids close to his face. "That's what we mean by secret." He stood up and walked toward the stage, which Jake could now see had a transparent glass wall around the front. "We fight best from the shadows. Of course, there are always a few rumors floating around, but we have a team that makes sure the stories get lumped in with the Bigfoot and Area 51 crowd. Since the end of World War II, we've made quite a dent in the Lantern. In fact, we think they're down to just one splinter cell left. I've been undercover, getting close to their leader for five years now. My doorman cover at the Greystone has been part of monitoring their work. We're close to snuffing them out for good. That's why we think they're getting desperate."

"Even if this is true—and I'm not saying I believe it—where's Gabe? You said you'd tell me," Jake said.

Artie looked to one of the Rangers and then back to Jake. "We should get somewhere we can sit down." Artie turned to the Ranger in the hall.

"How much longer?"

"We're clear," he called back.

"Follow me." Artie pushed through a wall panel and up steps to the stage where an antique floor lamp lit up. The stage was decorated to look like an old library. He walked to a bookshelf at the back. When he reached it, he walked right through, disappearing straight into the bookshelf.

"Hologram," he called out, poking his head back through. "Follow me."

Jake, Lucy, and TJ cautiously passed through the screen of light pixels and found themselves in a concrete-block room surrounded by large metal cabinets.

"This is what runs the holograms," Artie said. "But . . ." He pulled open one of the cabinet doors, revealing a rack of computer hard drives, lights, and wires. "It's a little more than that." He tapped a screen. A blue light scanned across his eyes and there was a loud click.

"Stand back," Artie said, just before the cabinet swung open, revealing a small elevator behind it. "Your carriage awaits." Artie, the three kids, and two of the guards squeezed into the small compartment.

Their short ride came to a stop and they stepped out into a wood-paneled room about the size of a tennis court. Built-in bookcases lined the walls, rising two stories to a skylight overhead. About halfway up the wall was a narrow wooden walkway with a brass railing stretching around the room. Antique lamps hung from the walls, spreading a golden glow over ancient statues anchoring each corner. Several large wooden tables in the center were cluttered with old documents, pieces of old war uniforms, and a few antique weapons.

"Welcome to League Field Operational Unit 22. It's actually the museum archivist room, but last year we commandeered it and made a few adjustments."

Artie led them past two Rangers dressed in assault gear to a cluster of weathered leather chairs patched with duct tape and a sofa facing a large stone fireplace. As they approached, a figure rose from one of the chairs and turned to face them. Jake didn't need to see the police uniform to recognize the weathered face. "Well, this is a pleasant surprise," said Lieutenant Bates.

NEED TO KNOW

JAKE SPUN ON HIS HEELS but the Rangers blocked them from both sides. With nowhere to run, the kids froze.

"Jake," Artie said, motioning to the sofa, "have a seat."

Jake recoiled. "Where do you have Uncle Gabe?" he shouted.

"Please, let's talk," Bates said. "Have a seat."

The kids stayed standing.

"Look, Jake, sometimes things aren't as they seem, some-times people—"

Jake lunged for one of the Ranger's pistols but the man caught him and wrapped his arms up.

"Please, sit. I know this is a lot to process," Bates said.

"Yeah. A lot to process," Jake said as the Ranger released him. "A small army invades our sleepover."

"And tries to kill us," TJ added.

"The police show up but are in on it."

"And try to kill us," TJ added.

"Some superhuman freak stalks us on the sky glider."

"And tries to kill us," TJ added.

"And Artie shows up, says he's some kind of secret agent."

"And tries to—" TJ paused. "Well, he throws us down really hard," TJ said.

Jake rubbed his hands on his temples and looked down. Finally, he returned his gaze to Bates. "I know those guys broke into the museum," he said through clenched teeth. "I know they tried to kill us. And I know you helped them."

"You need answers. I understand that." Bates took his seat and again motioned for them to sit down.

"And you won't tell me anything about Gabe!" Jake said, ignoring his offer. His voice shook. "You might be the ones who kidnapped him. If you're the good guys, then I want to know where you've got Gabe."

Bates looked at Artie. Both were silent. Finally Bates nodded. Artie turned to the two Rangers. "Guys, I think we're good for now. Regroup with the team downstairs." The two men crossed the room and slipped into the elevator.

Jake's legs felt like Jell-O. Maybe it was the last twenty-four hours catching up with him, or maybe he just needed something solid around him, but he finally sat down. TJ and Lucy followed, settling on either side of him.

Bates nodded slowly. "It's only right. It's not easy, but you need to know. You need to know." He stood up, turning his back as if to leave. He took a step, but stopped. Bates dropped his head and ran his fingers through his hair. He scratched his scalp and pulled his hair, making a pained noise, almost a groan.

Jake felt his body tense. Lucy jumped up. TJ reached for a vase off the side table. Bates tugged again on his hair. He dug his fingers deep into his scalp and pulled down. There was a sizzling static sound followed by blue sparks. His skin ripped away, followed by his hair. When he turned back, he was holding his face in his hands. The sheer mesh mask crackled with blue sparks and thin computer chips on one side, and Lieutenant Bates's face on the other. And the man holding Bates's face was Uncle Gabe.

DIVIDE ET IMPERE

"TJ, LUCY, I'D LIKE TO INTRODUCE YOU to the Commander of the Union Defense League," Artie said. "Jake, I believe you've already met."

Jake dove into Gabe's arms, which enveloped him in a giant bear hug. The room was silent.

"It's all right, Jakester," Gabe whispered. "It's all right."

"I didn't know if—"

"I know. I'm sorry. I know."

"How did . . . ? Wait, your voice." Jake noticed that Gabe's voice didn't sound like him. It was definitely Gabe, but the voice was Bates.

"Sorry." Gabe scratched his ear and pulled out a flesh-colored button smaller than a pea and dropped it in a tray on the table. "Better?" He was now speaking in his regular voice. "Voice modulator. Works with the Nano mask." He released Jake from his hug and turned toward TJ and Lucy. "I know you've got a million questions. And you deserve answers. But first I think proper introductions are in order." Gabe stepped toward Lucy.

"First, the young lady in the Budokai attack stance. You must be the world traveler, Miss García."

Lucy relaxed and offered her hand. "Lucy."

Gabe took her hand in both of his.

"Jambo."

Lucy smiled at Gabe's Swahili greeting. "Shikamo."

"Marahaba," Gabe continued. "Lugha moja haitoshi."

"Someone mind translating?" Jake asked.

"I said hello in Swahili, and she showed me respect as an elder," said Gabe. "The last part is just between the two of us." Gabe noticed the dried blood on Jake's lip and TJ's black eye. "You've had a rough night."

"There were some, uh, altercations," Jake stammered.

"It was dark," TJ said.

"And then we have young Mr. McDonald." Gabe turned to TJ, peeling the vase out of his still tightly clenched hands.

"TJ McDonald, sir."

"Well, Jakester." Gabe put his arm back around Jake. "What's that old line? 'If only we'd met under different circumstances.' I'm thrilled you're OK. I just wish you hadn't been sucked into this. This wasn't the time."

"What exactly is this?" Jake asked. "What's with the disguises? Who's Caleb Smith? Why didn't you—"

"All good questions. We'll get there. How about we eat and talk? Anybody hungry?"

TJ shot both his hands into the air.

"I think it was a rhetorical question," Lucy whispered to TJ.

"Not taking any chances," TJ whispered back.

Gabe spoke into his watch. "We've got some hungry troops up here. How long to get five dinners?"

"Ten minutes, sir," a voice called back.

"So, how about a little feast, League style?" Gabe asked. "If I remember right, tonight is spicy penne pasta, blueberry turnover, and if we're good, strawberry milkshakes."

TJ's face lit up. "He didn't say 'granola' once."

Gabe motioned for them to sit. TJ plopped down in one of the armchairs and then quickly jumped back up after something began to spark.

"Wow. Sorry about that," TJ said, picking up the almost invisible mesh mask.

"No problem," Gabe said, taking the mask from TJ. "These Nano masks can take a beating. Not like the old latex and makeup hack. These days, Department 5 gets a 3-D picture of your face, pushes a button, and there you have it."

"Genius," TJ said. "Who pays for all this?"

"Originally it was Lincoln's gold stash from the war. Now we have other sources. A few invisible foundations that care about freedom. Some hidden line items in a few countries' intelligence budgets. There's never enough and we never know who we can trust. I'm sorry I couldn't reveal myself earlier. We have tight levels of clearance, and the two agents that brought you in don't know about my Bates alias."

"So that was you at the museum and the Greystone and the Capital?"

"Not quite. Chicago was the real Bates. We intercepted him on the way to Springfield. It was me at the Capital, though. I was looking for you. But let's back up. Jakester, how exactly did you manage to track me down?"

"Club Thirty called to confirm your reservation," Jake said. "Also, the search history on my laptop."

"Ah, yes. Our secure tablets were frozen. Someone was trying to hack into them remotely," Gabe said. "I had to bug out fast and didn't think you'd be back until Sunday. Good work on your part, sloppy on mine. So, I think Artie's given you the basics?"

"Just a little," Jake said. "He told us about the Order of the Dark Lantern and the League. What does this Lantern group want?"

"It's pretty simple: power and wealth. They want to control the world's wealth and manipulate its governments for their own interests. Their roots go back to the Revolutionary War. When it became clear that the U.S. had won its independence, the leaders of the five most powerful families in Europe were outraged. U.S. independence had cost them significant wealth. They were concerned that others would follow America's example and rise up. The day after the Treaty of Versailles was signed, the five families met in Paris and came up with a simple strategy: They would work together to stir up conflict around the world so that people wouldn't unite. And that's what they've been doing ever since. They try to get people to hate, or at least fear, each other. They don't always even take sides; they just stir up trouble and profit from the wars and chaos. They call themselves the Order of the Dark Lantern because they control things from the shadows."

Gabe pulled a black disc from his pocket and put it on the

table. It looked like a rubber pocket watch with duct tape for a hinge. The cover had a small emblem of a shield with a single six-pointed star inside. He flipped it open and a glowing blue orb about the size of a tennis ball bounced into the air. TJ reached out to touch it but his hand passed through.

"Next-gen hologram," Artie said, adjusting the disc so they all could see the floating picture.

"The Lincoln assassination, the 1929 stock market crash, and World War II are just a few of their greatest hits. Pretty much anywhere you find chaos or ugliness on a large scale, you'll find Lantern fingerprints."

"I guess that explains *Star Wars Episode I*," TJ said.

"What?" said Jake. "If you're talking about Jar Jar—"

"Can we focus?" Lucy cut them off.

"Führerbunker," Gabe said. The floating orb flickered and turned into a grainy black image.

"Our biggest breakthrough came at the end of World War II. This was a tattoo found on the ankles of two bodies in Hitler's bunker. An upside-down pyramid with a black lantern circled by the words 'Divide et Impere.'"

"Divide and conquer," Lucy said.

"Exactly. 'Divide et Impere.'"

"Homeschool Latin." Lucy turned to Jake and TJ with a smile.

At that moment, an agent entered carrying five aluminum boxes, each the size of an iPad. He set the boxes on the table.

"Ahhh, dinner is served." Gabe stood up and motioned to a bathroom door near the elevator. "You can wash up in there." TJ was the last to emerge from the washroom. He had a pleased look on his face.

"I guess that's what the promise of food does to him," Lucy said.

"That, and the huge pump bottle of hand sanitizer in the bathroom," said Jake as TJ strode to the table rubbing his hands together.

Gabe said a quick prayer and then he and Artie pulled the lid off their boxes with a flourish. The kids followed. Inside each box were several brown plastic packages, each about the size of a postcard. The top one was labeled "Meal Ready to Eat: Spicy Penne Pasta." Another read, "Blueberry Cobbler Carbohydrate Enhanced." The smallest one was "Strawberry Dairy Shake Powder."

CLAVIS MAGNA

GABE TORE THE TOP OFF of a small package labeled "MRE Heater," poured it into his pasta bag, and shook it back and forth. He then poured the pasta into his mouth as if he were emptying the last caramel corn from a Cracker Jack box.

Jake and Lucy fumbled with their packets. TJ just stared into his box with his hands at his sides.

"Feel free to use the utensils," Gabe said. "I guess I'm just used to eating on the run."

Artie leaned over to help Lucy tear open her pasta. "MREs. Meals Ready to Eat," he said. "It's a military thing; food on the fly. It's not filet mignon, but it beats dung beetle dip, that's for sure."

"Dung what?" TJ asked with a disgusted look.

"You grab a handful of dung beetles," Artie said as he made a tight fist, "right out of their brooding chamber and you squish—"

"Perhaps," interrupted Gabe, "a recipe for another time.

Now, where were we? Ah, yes, the Lantern. Hitler's bunker turned out to be a gold mine of intelligence. We were able to wipe out the entire European operation. Next came South America and a few Nazi remnants."

Jake finished mixing his pasta and took a bite. It tasted like a mix of ramen noodles and day-old chewing gum. TJ was sniffing his and trying not to gag. Jake and TJ turned to see Lucy following Gabe's lead and gulping the pasta straight from the packet.

Lucy caught their stares. "It's a unit of food. What's not to like?" Jake reached into his pocket and pulled out a packet of Frank's RedHot sauce. He tore it open and squirted it into the pasta.

Gabe continued. "The five families are long gone. All that's left is a small but well-resourced splinter cell. But even while they've been shrinking, they've become more sophisticated—cyber-attacks, bio-weapons. We've even found evidence of cloning research."

"So how does last night fit in?" Lucy asked. TJ was frantically trying to squeeze a drop of hot sauce out of Jake's discarded packet.

"We don't exactly know, but we have a theory. It's linked to something they refer to as the Clavis Magna."

"The great key?" Lucy asked.

"Homeschool Latin has served you well." Gabe smiled. "The leader of this remaining Lantern cell is a particularly dangerous figure named Anarchus Kane. He seems to be obsessed with finding this Clavis Magna."

TJ gave up on the pasta and moved on to the blueberry

cobbler. He took a bite and gagged. "It tastes like Kool-Aid mixed with Play-Doh," he whispered.

"How would you—" Jake began to whisper back, but Lucy kicked him under the table.

"So they think the key is in one of these museums?" Lucy asked.

"In a way, yes. We don't think it's an actual key. There have always been stories that President Lincoln had more Confederate gold hidden away that only he knew about. Some believe that he carried a clue to its location on him at all times. We believe Clavis Magna is that clue. That gold would be worth hundreds of millions today."

"So the hat, the gloves—they're trying to steal everything the president had on him the night he was killed?" asked Lucy.

"Exactly," Gabe said. "Lincoln was known to keep notes, scraps of paper, even newspaper articles stuffed in his hat and elsewhere."

"Oh, yeah, that reminds me." Jake pulled the stained glove out of his pocket and set it on the table.

Artie jumped up. "You've got the gloves?"

"Kind of," Jake said. "I lost one when we were being chased." He turned the glove over and tried to look inside.

"Don't bother," Artie said. "We've been over the gloves in the past with an X-ray. Nothing on them other than his initials and the security chip the museum put inside. If there are any clues, they're not on the gloves."

"Last night makes a little more sense now," Lucy said. "But why are you in Springfield?"

"We intercepted a Lantern communication that they're coming here next."

"Here? This museum?"

"Not quite," Gabe said, turning and speaking again to the disc. "Fob."

An image of a small golden pyramid floated in the air. It looked like a large earring.

"It's called a watch fob. It's what gentlemen used to use to wind their pocket watches. This one was in the president's pockets the night he was killed. Do you know what else they found in his pockets?"

"A pocket watch," Jake said.

"You would think so," said Gabe. "They found reading glasses, a pocketknife, some cash, newspaper clippings and this fob, but no watch."

"Why would he be carrying the fob but no watch?" Lucy asked.

"That's what a lot of folks would like to know," said Gabe turning back to the disc. "Oak Ridge," he said.

A model of a stone tower slowly rotated in the air. It looked like a small castle with an obelisk like the Washington Monument rising up into the sky.

"Oak Ridge Cemetery?" Jake asked.

"It seems the Lantern believes Mr. Lincoln took the watch and the clue to his grave."

"Wait," TJ said, shaking his head. "You think they're getting ready to—"

"That's right. We believe Anarchus Kane is going to break into President Lincoln's tomb."

NAMES

GABE SNAPPED THE DISC SHUT. "It won't be the first time they've tried. Back in 1876, they almost got away with the body. Of course, security is a lot different now, but we've learned not to underestimate Kane."

Lucy noticed TJ's uneaten packet. "Not hungry?"

"Well, actually . . ." TJ eyed his packet.

"Don't mind if I do." Lucy grabbed TJ's pasta packet and gulped it down.

"MREs not doing it for you?" Artie said to TJ. "I'd get you a different flavor but I think the pasta is the best of the bunch. You should be glad it's not jambalaya night. Looks bad, tastes worse. If you've ever had a sick dog, I mean a really big one who can't hold his—"

"OK, OK, I think they get the point," Gabe said, cutting Artie off before he could go into detail.

"Anyway," Artie said, rummaging through a canvas backpack and pulling out a bag of pepperoni-flavored Combos and a pack of Slim Jims, "give this a try." He handed TJ a Slim Jim and dropped two Combos into his hand. "The trick is to chew them together with your eyes closed."

TJ popped the Combos in his mouth and took a bite of the Slim Jim.

"Close your eyes and chew," Artie said. "What do you taste?"

TJ chewed several times and began to smile.

"Pepperoni pizza!" TJ said. "Not bad."

"Ranger Pizza," Artie said. "For the busy warrior on the run."

"Artie's own invention," said Gabe, standing up. "And speaking of being on the run, we're setting up surveillance at the tomb. We don't know when they'll make their move, but we want to be ready. I'm headed over to the install. You kids will stay tucked in here tonight."

"What?" Jake jumped up. "We can help."

"Sorry. Not even close." Gabe was firm. "It's too dangerous for you and might compromise the team. You'll stay here. It's a secure facility and you'll be in good hands with Artie."

"But we're part of this quest now," Jake protested. "We can help."

"No debate," Gabe said. "You've already helped in huge ways. We're contacting TJ's and Lucy's parents. We'll meet up with them tomorrow. Your job now is to get some sleep. I'll see you in the morning." Gabe tousled Jake's hair and moved toward the elevator.

Jake reached out and grabbed Gabe's arm. "Uncle Gabe,

when you were . . . when I thought you were . . . I mean, I don't know what I'd do—"

Gabe locked Jake in a hug. "Me too, Jakester. Me too."

Gabe stepped onto the elevator and the doors closed behind him.

Artie dragged three military sleeping bags out of a closet and arranged them on the floor next to the fireplace. He pointed to a door across the room. "You know where the bathroom is. I'll wrap up with the guys downstairs and be back."

After Lucy and TJ finished, it was Jake's turn in the bathroom. Jake never thought getting ready for bed could ever feel this good. He wasn't just washing away two days of dirt, sweat, and blood; he was washing away a huge weight. They were safe. He was with Gabe. They would be home tomorrow.

When he stepped back into the room, Lucy and TJ were already in their sleeping bags.

"Last one in gets the light," TJ said.

"No problem, Thelonious," Jake said, flipping off the light and slipping into his bag.

"Ahhh, man," TJ said as Lucy laughed.

"It's pretty crazy what they can get in those reports," said Jake. "How many languages was that? English, Spanish, Swahili, and Nepali and what else?"

"Hindi and a pinch of Arabic," Lucy answered. "When you're little, you end up picking up a little bit of everything. It's not easy, though. I spent the first month at my school in Nepal saying 'I love you' to everyone when I thought I was saying 'Hello.'"

"Awesome," TJ said from the dark. "I bet you were popular with the boys."

"They thought it was hilarious. I was horrified. When we left, my nickname was still 'Love you.'"

So 'MOH-bile' and 'rubbish.' Which one of those languages did that come from?"

"Actually, none. I had a British tutor when we lived in Kenya. Soooo?" Lucy asked from the dark.

"Soooo what?" TJ asked.

"There's got to be a story. Thelonious Uriah Jordan Mc-Donald?"

"When my mom and dad first met at law school, my dad was wearing a porkpie hat and sunglasses. Mom said he looked like the jazz musician Thelonious Monk. It turned out that Monk was my dad's favorite, so it became a thing for them. Their first dance at their wedding was to one of his songs."

"So they named you after him?" Jake asked.

"It was my mom's idea. She used to love it at Monk's concerts when his band would be playing and he would jump up from the piano and start dancing around. She said that's what she wants for me. To do my best and enjoy every moment."

"Sweet Level 3 naming story," Jake said. "What about Uriah?"

"That part was from my dad. 1968 Olympics. Uriah Jones was the first black fencer to make the U.S. team."

"There's a fencing theme in your family," Lucy said.

"It started with my granddad. He was the first in our family to go to college, on a fencing scholarship. Then my dad did the same. I kind of didn't have a choice. There's a lot of early morning practices, but it doesn't hurt the old college app."

"And Jordan?" Lucy asked.

TJ laughed. "Mom didn't know about that one until after she got the birth certificate. My dad kind of snuck it in. He grew up in Chicago during the nineties. Enough said."

Lucy had no response.

"It's dark, but I can still feel your blank stare," TJ said.

"Michael Jordan," Jake explained. "Professional basketball player for the Chicago Bulls, six-time NBA champ, five-time MVP."

"Sure," Lucy said. "The shoes back at the museum."

"Yeah, the shoes," TJ said, "and then some. But wait a minute. What about you, Lucille? Don't tell me you're named after B.B. King's guitar?"

"Lucy Pevensie. My mom's favorite character from *Chronicles of Narnia*," said Lucy. "She says Lucy is full of courage because she's the one who most believes in Aslan."

"Top-notch. And the lion charm," Jake asked. "Aslan?"

"Aslan. My dad gave it to me for my fifth birthday."

"What about you?" asked Lucy.

"Ahem, well, curious thing. No story. I mean, I'd like to have a noble story, but Jake's just the name from the paperwork when Gabe adopted me. No epic legend, no love story. Not even a middle name. I guess they ran out of time. But how long does it take to give a kid a middle name? I guess I could add one now, but it wouldn't be the same, you know? So it's just Jake. Sorry, I guess that's a bit dull. No meaning."

"Well, 'Just-Jake' Herndon, I'd hardly call you dull. And if it's your name, it's real and it means something, wherever it came from," Lucy said.

"Yeah, maybe, I guess," Jake said, turning over. By the time he found a comfortable position, TJ was asleep and Lucy was already working into a snore. It didn't matter, not tonight. He was asleep within minutes. At first, he dreamt it was the first day of school. There was a pop quiz but the only thing he had to write with was a corn dog. He then dreamt he had a letter at home from the adoption agency telling him his real name. He drifted further to sleep.

NOT POSSIBLE

JAKE WOKE TO THE MOST OBNOXIOUS ALARM CLOCK he had ever heard. It shrieked, a vicious assault piercing his eardrums and making his chest thump. He then realized that he had even bigger problems. He was sliding along the floor. Someone had grabbed the hood of his sleeping bag and was furiously dragging him through the dark like a bag of garbage. He could hear boots running. He caught quick flashes of shadows moving around him. The alarm continued to pound. He thought maybe it was another dream. That thought ended abruptly when his body crashed into a wall in a very un-dreamlike way.

"Owww!"

A door slid shut, instantly cutting off the noise of the alarm, the sound of the boots, and the flashes of shadows. All was quiet. Whoever had grabbed him had stayed on the other side of the door. He squirmed out of the sleeping bag and stumbled to his feet, bumping into a wall. It felt soft, maybe rubber or plastic. A faint blue light slowly lit up the wall. It was just a soft glow, but since Jake's eyeball was only two inches from the wall, it almost blinded him.

"Whatthewhat?"

Jake jumped at the sound of the voice. He turned to see the faint outline of TJ sliding out of his own sleeping bag.

"You OK?" Jake asked.

"Yeah, I think I just bruised my arm on the landing. So who, what, and why?"

"I don't know," Jake said, trying to push on the door panel that had closed behind them.

"Where's Lucy?"

Zhaawww . . .

A grating, gravelly noise split the silence.

Jake and TJ spun toward the sound.

Zhaawww-hhhhhhhh-Zhaawww . . .

There was another sleeping bag, thrown a little further into the small room. Lucy was inside it, still sound asleep and snoring. Jake knelt down and tapped her shoulder.

"Lucy," he whispered. "Lucy, wake up."

Zhaawww . . .

"Please, allow me," TJ said. He found her ear and flicked it.

"Oww!" Lucy shot up from the sleeping bag, holding her ear. "What are you doing?"

"Sorry, necessary procedure," TJ said.

"What's going on?" Lucy asked, rubbing the sleep from her eyes.

"I don't know. I woke up to someone dragging me across the room. It was all dark, and some kind of alarm was going off. Next thing I know, I'm thrown in here and the door closes behind me." Jake walked to the wall and pushed. "It won't budge."

Suddenly the panel slid open and the deafening alarm returned.

A dark figure slipped into the room before the panel slammed shut again. The blue light framed the figure against the wall screen—high-tech armor, black helmet with a visor covering its face.

The figure pushed past TJ to the wall monitor and started tapping. The screen lit up with images of the lobby and hallways below. The figure turned back to the kids and flipped his visor up.

"Sorry for the rough handling," Artie said. "The thermal alarms downstairs are going crazy. Had to move you to the safe room."

The other wall panels came to life, filling with images from rooms around the museum. There must have been fifty different screens filling the walls.

"We're trying to isolate the source."

"Do you think this is the Lantern?" Jake asked.

"Not sure. None of the artifacts currently on site have been linked to the gold theories," said Artie, tapping one of the screens. A red frame flashed around an image. Artie spread the picture larger with his fingers. There on the screen was the unmistakable image of three Lantern soldiers moving through the entrance hallway.

"Well, it's not the first time they haven't made sense," Artie said. "The problem is that we don't have the muscle here to engage them. Most of the team is at the tomb."

Artie returned his attention to the screen where the three Lantern troopers were still standing in the center of the rotunda. "This isn't like them. They're normally in and out in a few minutes." The men began walking toward the Treasures Gallery. "OK, here we go." They walked right past the Treasures Gallery and continued down the hall.

"That doesn't make sense." Artie tapped the screen again. A view of the hallway came up. The commandos were moving toward the theater. They entered, pushed through the wall panel, and jumped onto the stage. They crossed directly through the hologram to the computer cabinet.

"Not possible," Artie said. One of them slammed a piece of putty onto the circuit board.

"What's not possible?" Jake asked.

"I don't think they're here for artifacts."

The other commando jammed what looked like a large battery into the putty.

"I think they're here for us."

THE DOOMSDAY DONUT

THERE WAS A BRIGHT FLASH OF LIGHT and then all the power in the building went out. A few seconds later the screen flickered back to life. The cabinet panel was swaying open and the Lantern men were entering the elevator. The screen crackled and went fuzzy.

"Field base is compromised!" Artie yelled into his watch. He removed a small flash drive and shoved it into a slot in the side of the monitor. "Running Trojan."

"Somehow they know we're here," Artie said, yanking the flash drive back out and moving toward the sliding panel. "It'll take them at least three minutes to hack the elevator. I've got one more wipe and we're getting out. Stay here!" He pressed the panel and slid through the opening.

The alarm was still shrieking as red warning beacons splashed off the walls of the dark Archives room. Jake, Lucy, and TJ watched through the doorway as Artie raced to a computer and shoved the flash drive in.

That's when Jake saw it. Halfway across the room, still sitting on the table, was—

"The glove!" Jake yelled to Artie. "The glove!"

But Jake's voice was drowned out by the blaring alarm. Even standing next to him, Lucy and TJ had a hard time hearing him. By the time they knew what he was saying, it was too late. Jake had sprinted into the room and grabbed the glove.

Artie had just finished the computer wipe and was heading back when he saw Jake. "What are you—"

An earsplitting explosion knocked Jake and Artie to the floor.

Pieces of glass and metal crashed down on their heads as five figures plummeted through the skylight.

Artie scrambled to his feet and pulled Jake up as they broke into a run. Three of the invaders rappelled to the floor. Jake and Artie dove for the safe room entrance, sliding in as bullets crashed into the door just as it slammed shut behind them.

Artie stood up and brushed off his pants. "Blastproof. But it won't hold forever."

He spoke into his watch as he crossed to the back of the safe room. "Trojan executed. Bugging out."

He opened a closet door, revealing a small spiral staircase. "All the way down." He grabbed each of the kids by the arm and shoved them into the passage before scrambling after them.

When they reached the bottom of the stairwell, they emerged into what looked like an abandoned garage. Old greasy tools were stacked along a wooden bench running the length of the room. Tires and car parts littered the floor and a blue beacon on the wall was flashing.

Artie walked over to a stained tarp and yanked it off, revealing a rusty, beat-up delivery van. It had three missing hubcaps and a faded Dangerous Delbert's Donuts logo peeling from its side. The windows were blacked out and it looked as if it had been junked about twenty years ago.

"Get in," Artie said, swinging open the van's back door.

The three kids hopped into the back and Artie joined them, slamming the door shut.

"Exodus," Artie called into his watch.

The interior van lights flicked on.

Jake had to blink and look again. The inside was entirely brushed aluminum and plasma screens. There were six black leather captain's chairs, each accompanied by the kind of headsets Jake had seen on helicopter pilots in the movies. Other than the occasional mess of frayed wires and duct tape, it was as high-tech as anything he had ever seen.

"These are the voyages of the starship *Enterprise*," whispered TJ under his breath.

"The official name is the Mobile Command Center, but I like 'The Doomsday Donut' better. Buckle up." A panel separating the back from the front opened and Artie jumped into the driver's seat.

The engine roared to life, the garage door opened, and the van screamed into the alley.

"Trojan complete. Baggage secure," Artie called out.

Panels on the interior walls slid back, revealing windows on the side of the van. Jake could see tall downtown hotels and office buildings whiz by before giving way to smaller shops and restaurants.

"So what's the Trojan thing?" TJ asked.

"A poison pill for the hard drives."

"So it wipes everything clean?"

"Mostly. It replaces the rest with fake data. They think our wipe failed, so they believe they've got real intel. Hopefully they bite and it leads them into a trap."

"Genius. Does it work?"

"We've only done it once before," said Artie.

"And?" Jake asked.

"Ever hear of Operation Overlord?"

Jake raised his eyebrows. "D-Day? The invasion of Normandy?"

"You're welcome," Artie said, smiling. "Right now, though, the billion-dollar question is how they found us. The entire field office is compromised."

They slowed to a stop at a red light. When a police car pulled up next to them, Jake, Lucy, and TJ dove to the floor. Artie glanced back and smiled at them with a small chuckle. "He can't see us." He waved and tapped on the window but the officer gave no response. "They're not really windows, just high-def monitors. We can have window view, or . . ." Artie tapped a button and the view outside Jake's window was replaced by a map of the city. "Bulletproof and immune to radiation, but outside they just see a tinted window."

As they turned onto a side street, Jake could see small bungalows and colonial houses lining each side of the road while a small park ran down the middle.

Artie spoke out again, "Donut ETA in five."

A voice responded, "SPEX confirm."

"Specs?" Jake asked.

"S-P-E-X. Our intervention squad. S is Surveillance. They monitor the location. P is Pursuit. They go after the bad guys."

"And E and X?"

"Extract. If you see them, you know something's gone wrong. But they get us out. They don't mess around. They always bring everyone home."

"OK, well, that's good. No one's died," TJ said with relief.

"I didn't say that. I said they always bring everyone home."

"Oh."

The van turned onto a gravel path alongside a tall wrought-iron fence. They slowed and passed through an old steel gate, a canopy of oak and maple trees hovering overhead. Moonlight broke through the dark clouds and bounced off a valley of white stones in the distance.

"Oak Ridge Cemetery," Jake said, realizing they were gazing at a sea of tombstones going all the way back to the Civil War. "The president's tomb."

"Yes, although I'm afraid you're not going to get the grand tour tonight. We're going in through the old gate."

The van slowed to a crawl as they banked onto a dirt path that became a dry creek bed. The woods on the side grew thicker as they turned through a small opening between two hedges and slowed to a halt.

Artie turned off the engine and opened the back door. "Everyone out."

They stepped out into the darkness of a dry creek bed. The

ground on both sides of the path rose quickly; a slope of over-grown bushes and trees led up to a small hill. Storm clouds were gathering overhead. Jake felt the air growing thicker.

Jake's eyes moved past the creek bed to the hill beyond. An imposing shadow loomed just over the crest, like the tip of an ancient castle watching guard over the fallen soldiers. A large terrace, each corner anchored by bronze Civil War stat-ues, gave way to a towering obelisk splitting the sky. It wasn't the first time Jake had seen President Lincoln's tomb, but to-night felt very different. It was as if the war had never ended.

They stood silently. There was nothing but the sound of crickets and a lone owl somewhere in the distance. Slowly, the bushes on both sides of the creek began to rustle. Six figues stepped out of the shadows, guns trained on Jake and the others.

"Salmon," Artie said.

"Portland," responded one of the figures.

"Chase," Artie said, completing the code word.

"Special Agent Jason Richards," said one of the men, low-ering his gun and reaching for Artie's hand. Gabe stepped out from the bushes.

"In the Donut," said Gabe. They piled back in the van and one of the Rangers closed the doors behind them.

"The Lantern broke into the museum. No interest in the Treasures Gallery; they headed straight for us."

"Well, Mr. Kane and friends seem to be full of surprises tonight."

Gabe motioned to Agent Richards who pulled up a screen on a tablet. "At 0100 hours someone hit the National Museum of Health and Medicine in D.C. All power and security was cut for three minutes. When it came back on, everything was back to normal, with one exception. They took the skull fragments."

"The what?" Jake asked.

"The museum's collection includes the bullet that killed President Lincoln and a few fragments from his skull."

TJ's eyes grew wide. "OK, I don't know what's creepier—that someone kept that stuff or that someone wanted to steal it."

"It's the Army's medical museum. They archive research on military medical procedures. The Lincoln autopsy was one of their projects."

Jake could see Gabe's face harden.

"That's not all, sir," Richards continued.

"Go on."

"At 0200 someone also broke into the Ford's Theater Museum in D.C. In and out in three minutes. The only thing they took was—"

"Don't tell me," Artie said. "The coat."

"That's right, sir."

Artie looked at Gabe. "They took the gloves from Chicago, the pillowcase from Philadelphia, and now the skull fragments and coat."

"Clavis Magna," Gabe said, pausing as if he couldn't believe what he was about to say. "The key doesn't have anything to do with the gold."

"If it's not about gold, what is it?" TJ said.

Gabe let out a very slow, deliberate breath. "We've had a secondary theory. It seemed too much of a stretch, even for the Lantern, but it's all lining up."

Gabe leaned over and locked the doors. He paused as if choosing his words very carefully. "What do you know about cloning?"

Gabe's question hung in the air for a minute as if no one knew what to do with it.

TJ spoke first. "Well, some would say that Bizarro Superman is a clone, but I would argue not. Then there was the ridiculous Spider-Man clone saga where someone cloned Spider-Man's girlfriend. And then there's the *Star Wars Clone Wars*, which is probably the gold standard for—"

"So, what you mean to say is 'nothing,'" Lucy said.

"It's basically the ability to make an identical copy of something. You extract DNA molecules from an organism and use that to make a copy," Gabe said, taking a seat.

"Hasn't it been done with animals?" Jake asked.

"Yes, and there are huge ethical questions around it. Is it safe? Is it right? Is it messing with God's natural order?"

"And you said earlier something about Lantern rumors," TJ said.

"Actually, I'm afraid it's more than that. We know they've been experimenting for years with something called 'Special DNA.' They've been mixing and matching DNA, trying to clone a kind of super-warrior. We recovered a file in a raid in Switzerland that indicated they want a particular profile. They want just the right mix—the molecules of someone cunning, proven to be aggressive, bold, even ruthless. We also recovered some of the bone fragments they had been using to extract DNA for their super-soldier."

"So you broke up their work. That's great," TJ said.

"Good, but not great." Gabe exhaled. "You've heard the phrase, 'The horse was already out of the barn'?" A couple of Lantern agents escaped during our raid. We thought they were guarding the project. It turns out they *were* the project. They were the first cloned embryos, all grown up, so to speak. And if that's not enough, there's one more thing: The source bone fragments they were working with, the one with the perfect assassin profile? Our tests matched them to one of the most notorious Lantern agents ever—John Wilkes Booth."

"Wait," said Jake, shaking his head. "Are you saying—"

"One of the two agents that escaped that night was Anarchus Kane. We believe he's the genetic clone of John Wilkes Booth."

The silence was thick.

"Not possible," TJ said. "I mean I like crazy sci-fi stuff, but cloning isn't that advanced. And even if it were, how could Kane be grown up already?"

"You can think whatever you want about what's possible," Artie said. "But up until thirty-six hours ago you would have said that about, well, everything that has happened in the last thirty-six hours. As far as Kane's age, we think they're using some kind of accelerated growth process."

"So tonight must be chapter two," Gabe said. "The gloves, the pillowcase, the skull fragments—there's only one reason Kane's going after these items and only these items. They all contain pieces of Lincoln's DNA, either in his blood stains or bone fragments. If the key that Kane wants is Lincoln's DNA, the whole Lincoln skeleton would be the jackpot. Pure source DNA."

"Wait," Jake said. "Are you saying—"

"I'm saying Anarchus Kane isn't going after Abraham Lincoln's watch tonight. Anarchus Kane is going after Abraham Lincoln."

CODE RED

"WHY WOULD HE WANT TO STEAL LINCOLN'S BONES?" Jake asked.

"Well, we know the Lantern has always thought Lincoln was a brilliant leader," Gabe continued. "Kane must think the Lincoln sample will help him complete his perfect model. Who knows? Maybe he even wants to upgrade himself."

"Upgrade?"

"Inject himself with Lincoln's DNA. Kane 2.0. Maybe he thinks he would be the perfect prototype, a cross between Booth and Lincoln."

"And the crazy train heads for freaky town," TJ said, shaking his head.

"There's also some evidence Kane suffers from memory echo. Basically, as a clone, he confuses himself with the original Booth. This might be some twisted idea of revenge in the name of Booth."

Artie tapped his watch. "OK, best guess is between 0300 and 0400. We need to lock down the baggage."

"What baggage? The hard drives?" TJ whispered to Jake and Lucy.

Gabe glanced at the screen on his watch, which had just lit up. "Survey, Pursuit, and Extract all confirmed. I think we're good to go."

"Sir, the baggage," Artie said.

"What's our safe house?" Gabe asked.

Artie tapped his watch again. "The vault."

"Wait. Are we the baggage?" TJ asked. "We're the baggage, aren't we?"

"OK. Tuck 'em in there, but I want you to stay with them."

"Wait a minute. Tuck us in?" Jake asked.

"It's what I said earlier. For your safety and the team's safety." Gabe turned back to Artie. "Take Agent Richards with you. Total RS from here on. Only break for a Code Red."

Jake, Lucy, and TJ followed Artie out of the van along with Agent Richards.

"OK, quick and quiet." Artie pushed a branch aside and stepped into the woods. They raced silently through the shadows, moving from tree to tree. The moonlight broke through cracks in the clouds, filtering through the rustling leaves of the giant oak and sycamore trees stirring in the building wind. They passed stone statues and tomb monuments weathered with age, their inscribed words and symbols barely visible. As they ran, Jake caught a glimpse through the thicket of Civil War tombstones scattered along the hillside.

They finally broke out of the woods and into a small

clearing. They stood at the base of the hill, facing a limestone structure carved into the side. It was about the size of a small garage but was as ornate as an old chapel. Greek pillars anchored both sides. "Oak Ridge" was carved into an arch across the top, and a double-wide iron gate guarded the entrance with a massive padlock.

Artie inserted a rusty key into the steel padlock. The padlock flipped open to reveal a small electronic pad. It beeped as he pressed his thumb against it. "Everyone into the vault."

They were met with a wall of cool, stale air as they stepped into the dark stone room. Agent Richards locked the gate behind them. "Vault of what?" TJ asked, coughing at the stench as he gazed at the empty burial vaults. "Dracula's summer home?"

Richards turned a brass knob on the marble wall and the entire wall pushed like a door. They squeezed through the narrow passageway into an even smaller room.

"We always have a secure location, a safe house, near every operation as a contingency," Artie said, flipping on a small flashlight. "This is the old receiving vault. It's where they kept Lincoln's body while they were building his tomb. The League used it as a safe house after the war but it hasn't been touched for over a hundred years."

As Jake's eyes adjusted to the darkness, ornate stone images of eagles, shields, and American flags carved into the walls around them came into view. Unlike the markers and statues outside, these hadn't been eroded by weather. On the back wall, the engravings of flags and stars gave way to a carving of a temple with an opened book in the middle.

Jake rubbed one of the carved shields on the wall. "Sweet carvings. This looks like the shield on Gabe's disc."

"Good eye. It's an earlier version of our League crest. When they added this chamber after the war, they marked it."

Artie stepped to the back corner and removed five bottles of water from a small backpack.

"So now what?" Jake asked.

"We wait for the all-clear or for next steps."

"What did Gabe mean by Total RS and Code Red?" asked TJ.

"Radio silence. No communication unless it's an absolute emergency. If the bottom falls out or someone's in grave danger, you call a Code Red. Otherwise, we can't risk anyone intercepting us," Artie said.

"So it's hurry up and wait." Lucy grabbed a water and sat down against the wall.

"It's the dirty little secret of covert operations," Agent Richards said, joining her on the floor. "Waiting."

"True," Artie said. "Long periods of boredom punctuated by moments of sheer terror."

The kids' faces went blank.

"Sorry, that's just an old war saying. We hardly ever get the terror part. There are exceptions, of course, like that open fracture I mentioned. You know, they say when you're in intense pain, the body kind of . . ." He looked up at the kids' empty faces. "But like I said, that's the exception. Really, we hardly ever get the terror part."

Awkward silence.

Jake stood up and slowly paced around the edge of the

room. Beneath the temple carving were three shields, each surrounded by twelve stars. "I get the League shield, but what's this Greek temple and the book?"

"Not sure," Artie said. "Probably early images of the Lincoln Memorial."

Jake took a seat next to Artie. "I've been thinking . . . about the cloning stuff. Do you really believe that?"

"I don't know. I just know I gave up being surprised about three missions ago."

"But even if they stole those things, the pillowcase and the gloves, how could they even be sure they're getting Lincoln's DNA from it? I mean, it's been over a hundred fifty years."

"DNA sequencer. We know they stole one, that's when all of this started. You can run any DNA—a human hair, a blood sample even, and compare it with any DNA on file for a match."

"Kind of like a fingerprint."

"Yes, but way more sophisticated. Kane's plan is pretty crazy, but I'm afraid he's living proof it can be done. And they've done it at least once more. I think you've had the pleasure of meeting #2."

"Slate!" TJ said. "I told you that was a superhero jump. That guy was not human."

"He's a working prototype of sorts, but definitely human. It appears they were experimenting with increased physical ability."

"And the laser eyes—he has laser eyes," TJ said.

Artie laughed. "Well, that doesn't have anything to do with cloning. They've got their own Department 5, of sorts.

Special contact lenses with Nano tech. They get data and communication delivered straight to their eyes."

"Whoa." TJ shook his head. "Google Glass on steroids."

"Basically. Also night vision. That's what you saw. We've been trying to reverse-engineer a pair for ourselves."

"So, the cloning," Lucy said. "They could be whipping up a whole batch of Slates or Kanes?"

"Not quite. They'll need to rebuild the lab we raided. And like we said, we pretty much dismantled their infrastructure. With just the one splinter cell left, it won't be easy. But the more DNA samples they have to work with, the faster their results."

"That's why they're going for the body," TJ said.

"Exactly. Stealing a bone fragment here, a bloodstain there is one thing, but getting a whole skeleton—that amount of source DNA would definitely turbo-charge things."

"So can this sequencer tell how old a stain is?" TJ asked.

"Only in broad ranges. It can tell if a stain is just hours or days old or if it's decades old, but not much in between."

TJ smiled. "Really. Well, good luck with the glove if they have it."

"What do you mean?" Artie asked.

TJ patted Jake on the back. "Young Mr. Herndon had a bit of a scuffle with a vicious brute at the museum that involved a little blood."

Lucy shifted and looked away.

"Hostile situation. The fog of battle," Jake said. "But maybe you're forgetting how you ended up on the floor of the plane bathroom."

"Debatable. I'm not fully convinced of that story. But you—there is evidence and it just happens to be on a priceless hundred-and-fifty-year-old relic."

"OK, someone fill me in," Artie said.

"Jake here got his—"

"It was totally dark," Jake interrupted. "And Lucy and I ran into each other."

"And she clocked him Nepali Kung Fu Catwoman style!"

"I had a bloody nose and some of it might have—well, it definitely got on the glove."

"The Lincoln glove?" asked Artie.

"Uh, yep," said Jake, pulling the other glove from his pocket. There's a little on this one but most is on the one we lost when they were chasing us."

"So," TJ smiled, "the Lantern guys are going to be quite confused if they have that glove and test it."

Artie stood up and walked to the far corner of the room.

"Scout to Base." Artie held one hand up for the kids to be quiet and spoke into his watch.

"Scout to Base. Code Red. Code Red."

RADIO SILENCE

"THEY'VE GONE GHOST," Artie said, turning to Agent Richards. "They don't have their sets on."

Jake had never seen Artie look so intense.

"You're sure, Jake? Your blood is on the glove, the one they got?"

"Yeah," Jake said. "But maybe it'll screw up their tests. They won't be able to read the stains."

"That's not it." He turned back to his watch. "Scout to Base. Scout to Base. Code Red." No response. "I'm going back to the Donut," Artie said, his tone becoming very serious. "Stay here with Agent Richards. No one is to leave this room. Not even to the outer chamber."

Jake squinted. "I don't get it. If Gabe's in trouble, maybe we can help."

Artie grabbed him by the shoulders and looked in his eyes. "Jake, listen to me. This is different. The Lantern might not be after what we thought."

"Yeah, not the watch—Lincoln's body. You said—"

"No, not the watch, not the glove, maybe not even the body."

"I don't get it. What could they—"

Artie stood up.

"I don't have time to explain right now." He turned to Richards. "I assume Gabe will want to get Extract over here. We'll stay RS, but I'll break it if I have to."

Artie stepped toward the passageway but Jake grabbed his arm.

"If Gabe's in trouble, you should tell us. We're not—"

"Listen to me. This is very important. You need to stay here."

"But if they're after Gabe I want to—"

"Jake, it's not Gabe."

"What? We're part of this now. We deserve to know."

"Jake! Listen to me. They might be . . . they might be after you." Artie disappeared through the passage and they heard the outer gate close behind him.

"OK. What does that mean?" TJ asked.

"I have no idea," Richards said, adjusting the duct tape on his communication watch. "But I trust him with my life. We'll just hold tight for next steps."

Jake walked to the corner of the chamber. He stared at the wall, looking dazed and pale. Lucy approached him. "Hey."

"I'm OK, I'm—" He caught Lucy's look and exhaled. "I'm . . . not exactly OK." Jake turned back to the wall. The silence was heavy in the vault's stale air. Finally, Jake spoke. "This is flat-out toxic. I wasn't exactly looking forward to this weekend, but it *could* have been my Big Do-Over. A chance to step up. Maybe some cheesy games, maybe even Level 2 new-kid junk. But getting shot at, almost blown up, or chased by some freak who might—we're not sure, but just *might* be after me, was definitely not on the list. I don't know what to think or do, but if this is seventh grade, I'm out."

"OK," Lucy said. "I mean, not OK, but really, that's OK."

Jake returned to blindly staring at the wall.

"What now? More hurry up and wait?" TJ asked. "I can live with the long periods of boredom. It's the sheer terror I'll take a pass on. If this nut-job Kane thinks he's Booth, he probably thinks I should be wearing chains and calling him 'master.' I thought we were way past that kind of crazy."

"Look," Richards said. "Everything's going to be fine. It's standard procedure if there's a logistics issue to pull back and regroup. We'll be fine."

TJ took a seat on the floor and pulled a bag of Combos out of his pocket.

Lucy raised her eyebrows.

"What?" TJ asked. "Gabe had an extra bag for an emergency. I think this counts." He turned to Richards. "So. Standard procedure? How many of these missions have you been on?"

"Well, they weren't all like this, but this is my nineteenth."

"And how many times have they called a Code Red?"

"Uhh, well, none."

Silence.

"Soooooooo," TJ said. "Combo, anyone?"

There was more silence, punctured only by the sound of TJ digging into the snack.

Jake stared at the wall carving. "I didn't notice it before, but it says something on this book." He used his hand to sweep away a layer of dust from the wall. As he brushed away the dirt, the faint outline of a few words emerged. "Evangelium vero something," Jake said, squinting and reading aloud.

"OK, I think I've had enough history lessons for tonight," TJ said. "And since most of it is from the Big Book of Crazy, I don't think it's going to be a lot of help on my SATs."

Lucy stood and grabbed a water bottle from the pack. "Not sure if it's hunger or boredom, but let me try one of those Combos."

TJ handed her the bag. It was empty.

"Really? What was that? Thirty seconds?"

"Sorry," TJ said, swallowing the last bite. "Growing boy, Chocolate Thunder, you know the drill."

Lucy walked over to Jake, who was still gazing at the book carving and mumbling to himself. He spit on his hand and wiped away more of the dust.

"That's gross," Lucy said. "Try this." She splashed a little water from her bottle on the wall. After a bit more rubbing, the inscribed words "Evangelium vero secundum Marcum" were clearly visible across the top of a fancy book. "Gospel of Mark." She smiled. "I never knew how handy Latin could be."

The rinsing also revealed that the shields inside the circle of stars were made of bronze, not stone.

"This has to mean something. I mean these old dudes, they did stuff for a reason, right?" Jake said.

"If you're thinking hidden Civil War gold, I'd say you've inhaled too much tomb dust," TJ said.

"No, but why would they make it like this?" He turned to Richards. "What did Artie say the League used this for?"

"Just a safe house for a few years while the tomb was built. Then they closed it up. Haven't used it for over a hundred years."

"I've been thinking. It's curious . . . Why is the temple split in two?" Jake stared at the wall, his lips moving silently.

"Ooookaaaay," TJ said, pulling up the backpack. "You two can do the ancient crossword puzzle. I'm going to see if they stashed any more Ranger Pizza in here."

Richards's watch crackled to life. "Scout to Baggage Handler. Scout to Baggage Handler."

"I really find that offensive," TJ said.

"Copy," Richards said into his watch.

"Urgent. The souvenir is infested."

"Repeat please," Richards said.

"The souvenir is infested. Destroy it. The souvenir is—*crrrrrrrrrrrr.*" The other end went dead.

"Scout." Richards tapped his watch. "Scout." Nothing.

38

A HOUSE DIVIDED

RICHARDS JUMPED UP. "Where's the glove?"

"What was he talking about?" Lucy asked.

"The Lincoln glove!"

"I've got it." Jake pulled the glove out.

"Infested? What, with lice or bugs?" TJ said.

"You might say that." Richards turned the glove inside out. For the first time, Jake saw a small computer strip on the inside of one of the fingers. It had a tiny dot that was glowing a faint orange at its tip.

"They must have reverse-hacked the security tag," Richards said, throwing the glove to the floor. "They've been tracking it."

He stomped on the glove. The dot flickered, but kept glowing. He stomped several more times. The orange glow finally died out. He picked up the shredded glove. "That should do it, but we can't take any chances. Be right back. Don't move."

He slipped through the passage and they heard him re-lock both locks.

"You know, the duct tape on his watch kind of affects my confidence in this whole thing," TJ said.

"So I guess we know how they tracked us to the Lincoln Library," said Lucy, "and the Greystone."

"My blunder," Jake said, shaking his head. "I shouldn't—"

The clang of the steel gate echoed through the chamber.

"Richards is back," TJ said.

The gate rattled again, much harder and much louder.

Jake put a finger to his lips. He dropped to the ground and crawled toward the passageway, peering around the corner. No one was there. The gate was still locked. He looked through the gate for Richards. No one. Just before he turned, something shiny caught his eye. He glanced back at the ground where Richards's shattered watch lay. The gate rocked as four arms reached through the bars and lunged for Jake. He fell backward, just escaping their reach. The arms flailed for him through the bars, but he tumbled further backward and scrambled around the corner into the back room.

"It's them, there's at least two!"

The gate rattled again.

The three kids stared through the dark at each other. TJ crawled on his stomach and peeked around the corner. A haze of bright red light shot through the gate and bounced off the walls.

TJ ducked back into cover, shielding his eyes from the light's blast. "They've got some kind of laser torch." The sound of a torch slicing through steel cut the air. TJ moved further back into the room. "They keep calling these safe houses. That must not mean what I thought it meant."

"House." Jake muttered the word to himself.

"Let's see: Scissors cut paper, paper covers rock, and I'm pretty sure laser torch blasts gate," said TJ, but no one was listening. Lucy was rustling through the backpack and Jake had turned toward the back wall. He was staring at the wall carving and mumbling.

"House," he repeated to himself. "It's not a temple; it's a house."

TJ grabbed Jake's arm. "Snap out of it." TJ picked up a flashlight.

"It's a house." Jake was running his finger along the carving. "That's got to mean something, right?"

The sound of one of the steel bars clanging to the floor bounced off the walls. TJ turned to Lucy. "We've lost him. How's your kung fu against bullets?"

"A house divided," Jake said.

They heard the torch fire up again.

"Hold on," Lucy said. "I think he's found something."

"House divided." Jake began turning the League shields. They rotated like the hands of a clock inside the twelve stars. "June 16 . . . Six . . . One . . . Six." He turned the shields so they pointed to the numbers six, one, and six.

Another bar hit the floor with a clang.

"1858. No. Too many digits." Jake mopped the sweat off his forehead with his forearm.

"Gospel of Mark. That must mean something," Lucy said.

"Mark. The house divided speech. That's it. Mark is the

book in the Bible that Lincoln used in the speech. 'A house divided against itself cannot stand.'" Jake was squinting as if trying to pull something from deep in his memory. He mumbled. "Two thirty-five. Mark 2:35." He turned the shields to two and three and five. Nothing. "What's plausible? What's plausible?"

The sound of the outer gate crashing to the floor rumbled through the chamber. A cloud of dust exploded into the inner passage.

USELESS

"WAIT!" Jake turned the shields to three and two and five. "Three twenty-five."

As soon as Jake clicked the third shield into place, a muffled grinding began behind the carving. The two sides of the house carving slid together and the wall pivoted in. The sound of boots filled the air as Lantern troopers stormed into the outer chamber. Lucy and TJ dove through the opening and Jake followed just as red lasers bounced off the stone wall as it closed behind him.

Jake rose from the cloud of dust, coughing. "The wall closed back. How did . . ."

A light flipped and Jake looked up to see TJ smiling and pointing his flashlight at an identical house symbol on the inner wall, this one split back apart. "So, just a hunch. I thought if you reversed it, it might close it back. You know you're not the only boy genius on this field trip."

Jake sat up, still coughing as he tried to speak. "I've . . .

never liked . . . the word 'genius.'" He coughed some more. "Ingenious, maybe, but genius—it gets thrown around so much."

"True," TJ said from above the dust. "But rather than throw out a perfectly good word, shouldn't we—"

"Guys!" Lucy interrupted. "Sorry to break up your vocabulary lesson, but what if that laser can cut through stone too?"

"Good point." TJ put his hand on Lucy's shoulder. "We might consider you for Genius Club after all."

Lucy turned to look around.

They were in a narrow tunnel, dark except for the glow from TJ's flashlight. TJ shone his light down the tunnel, but the beam disappeared well before it reached the end.

"I don't know where this goes," Jake said. "But anywhere that's away from them is good with me."

They walked single file through the cool, damp passageway, the strange silence broken only by their faint footsteps and light breathing.

After a few minutes, the tunnel ended at a narrow set of stone stairs. As they climbed up, the air began to grow clearer, less stuffy. After another minute, Jake could feel a slight breeze and hear the faint sound of thunder. Finally, the stairs took a turn and they entered a small stone room. It was just slightly bigger than a closet, with no furniture or windows. The only sign that they were now above ground was the smell of fresh rain and the sound of thunder coming through horizontal slats on a wall panel.

"Keep after 'em." A voice came from the other side of the wall.

TJ shut his light off. Jake stepped slowly over to the panel.

It looked like a louvered bronze door that had been closed with a lever, locking it shut from the inside. He squinted through the slats and saw the back of a pair of black boots impatiently tapping the ground.

"Well, get it open."

They were hearing only one side of a conversation.

"Either way I want the bodies."

The boots moved away. Jake could see that he was looking out over the monument entrance. The stairs must have led them to the old terrace entrance from back when visitors were allowed to climb the tower. He could just make out the legs of two soldiers standing on the dark balcony. A large duffle bag had been stuffed with something and lay next to the railing.

Did they already have it? The bag was big enough for a body, definitely big enough for a skeleton.

"They found them," one of the soldiers said. "Barricaded in the old vault. Probably buried alive. But we'll make sure."

"One less job for us," replied the other, taking a seat on the duffle bag.

"He's coming." The sitting soldier jumped to his feet and both men stood straight.

The crunch of boots on gravel cut through the air. Jake thought there was suddenly less air to breathe. *That smell again. A burnt match? Spoiled eggs?*

A set of boots passed by the screen.

"Well, gents. So far, so good."

Jake had heard this voice before. The figure tapped the bag with a stick. No, it was a cane.

"I see we've got our little treasure packed up."

Kane. He's here and he's already got the skeleton. We've got to tell Gabe.

Kane propped one foot on the bag, a hunter posing with his trophy. Thunder slowly rumbled overhead. There was a flicker of lightning in the distance.

"Storm's rolling in. How poetic." He took his foot off the bag and tapped his cane on the patio floor. "Load him up, boys."

Each man grabbed an end of the bag and heaved it up. One of them, however, lost his grip and the bag tumbled back to the stone floor. And then . . . it moved. The bag moved. Just a little, but it moved.

"Well, well. He lives." Kane stepped back toward the fallen bag. "Let's have a look, shall we?" He gave the bag a kick. It stirred and then rolled. Jake thought he heard a moan.

The Lantern troopers unzipped the duffle and pulled something from it, tossing it onto the patio floor.

"Stand him up, gents."

They lifted the body.

A clap of thunder erupted. Lightning flashed, illuminating Gabe's limp body. Jake lunged for the panel latch, but Lucy and TJ grabbed his arm before he could give them away.

The soldiers let go of Gabe's arms and he fell back into a pile on the terrace floor.

"I said, Stand him up."

They lifted Gabe back up, this time holding him steady. He slowly lifted his head to face Kane and then dropped it again.

"What's your name, old man?"

Gabe just stared back, his eyes only half open.

"Of course." Tap-tap. "The hard way." Tap-tap. He followed each word with a tap of his cane on the floor.

"I must say this is a bit of a letdown. I always thought a League agent would put up more of a fight."

He poked Gabe in the chest with his cane.

"But then, I guess you came prepared to be the hunter tonight, not the hunted." He laughed. "Dog chases car. Dog catches car. Car bites back."

Kane walked to the stone railing at the edge of the terrace, looking out to the Civil War tombstones.

"Quite fitting, don't you think? Here at this temple to your pitiful tyrant, we begin to make things right." Kane took several slow, deliberate steps back across the landing. He was just a few feet from the panel. Jake, Lucy, and TJ slowly eased away, pressing their backs against the wall.

He hopped onto one of the bronze statues at the corner of the terrace. It was a Union officer with his sword raised, leading his cavalry into battle. Kane ran his hand along the figure's outstretched sword. "A little trivia for you," he called down. "They made these statues out of melted-down Union cannons. Some kind of grand statement of peace. Pathetic. They didn't want peace, never did. Booth saw that. He knew."

A light sprinkle had begun, covering the terrace in a fine mist.

Gabe stirred and raised his head. He cracked open one eye and whispered, "Just like him."

Kane spun to look down at Gabe. "He speaks!"

"You're just like him."

Kane glared at Gabe, his eyes large and glazed over. "I consider that high praise. Booth was a patriot." His stare and intensity increased with each word.

"Useless," Gabe whispered.

Kane's face froze. His arms became taut, the veins in them bulging. His grip on the statue's sword tightened.

"You do not speak those sacred words. You do not speak them."

"Useless," Gabe repeated.

"You mock his words!" The steel sword snapped off into Kane's hands.

Jake pressed close to the panel. Someone needed to do something. Where were the League agents?

"Useless!" Gabe spit the word out again between gasps for breath.

Kane poked the air with the broken sword. With one hand he held his cane and with the other he swished the sword through the air. "You will not speak his words. You will not. You will not!" He wheeled toward a large bronze statue of Lincoln and sparks flew as he brought the sword down again and again on the president's likeness. Showers of sweat exploded from his hair as he flailed around. Each stroke left another deep gouge in the president's likeness. On the next strike, the sword snapped out of Kane's right hand and clanged to the terrace floor.

He looked down at his hand where a trickle of blood appeared. He gazed up at Gabe and smiled. Then he grabbed one end of his cane with his bleeding hand and tugged on the handle. It slid back with a click, revealing a sword as he slid it out of the cane. He dropped down and paced toward Gabe, slicing the air with each step.

No help was coming. This was it.

Kane cut through the air again and again. Jake's grip on the latch tightened. So did his face. He flinched with each swipe of Kane's sword-cane as the blade drew closer to Gabe's face. On the next swing, Jake broke through the panel and tumbled out onto the terrace floor.

ASCENT

JAKE'S ENTRANCE DIDN'T GO EXACTLY AS PLANNED. Not that he had much of a plan.

The soldiers dropped Gabe into a pile and turned their attention to Jake. The first soldier lunged for him, but he rolled out of the way at the last second and sent the man tumbling over the terrace wall. As Jake jumped up and moved toward Gabe's motionless body, he found himself staring into Slate's gray face. A small smile creased the clone's lips and his eyes glowed with a white light. Slate moved toward Jake but then suddenly went limp and crumbled to his knees. Jake scrambled to his feet just in time to see Lucy land a second roundhouse kick.

Lucy turned to look for Jake, but instead found herself staring into the rifle of the first soldier. Jake took the man out from behind, crashing into the man's knees and knocking his gun to the floor. Lucy dove for the gun but a gray hand snatched it out of her reach.

Slate had recovered. He smiled and raised the gun, first toward Jake and then toward Lucy, setting his aim on her. He pointed it right at her and—

Classshhhhh!

A bright spark flashed with the sound of clashing steel. The gun exploded out of Slate's hand and he crumbled to the ground, grabbing his wrist in agony. Wielding the other half of the broken cavalry sword, TJ stepped over Slate as he fell. He looked like a pirate. An angry nerd pirate. "Feats of strength *and* clever banter," he crowed. He swished the sword through the air. "The complete package." He kicked the gun over the edge.

Jake did a quick scan of the terrace. His eyes darted to where Gabe had been lying. Nothing. No Gabe. No Kane.

Something flashed in the corner of his eye. He spun around to see the swirl of a black coat disappear through the entrance panel.

Another flash came from the opposite direction. Artie was racing up the steps. Just as Slate regained his feet, Artie, Lucy, and TJ descended on him.

Jake looked back at the panel and then scrambled toward it. He dove through the entry and slammed the panel shut, locking the bar in place just as one of the soldiers lunged after him.

The chamber itself was empty and silent. In the background Jake heard the rumble of the battle outside and the growing thunder overhead. Then he heard a sound above him in the darkness of the tower. Something sliding, someone tugging. Like someone was dragging something . . . or dragging *someone.*

He bounded up the iron stairs. The ancient spiral staircase was steep and narrow, winding around itself as it rose higher up the obelisk. The sound continued as if on a beat. Every three seconds there was another sliding across the stairs.

Dust swirled with each of Jake's steps. It had been a long time since anyone had been on these stairs. The rumble of thunder grew stronger, echoing down the obelisk shaft. Jake pressed his hands against the cold railing as he climbed. Each step seemed to grow steeper as he fought to fill his lungs with the damp air.

The sound came to an abrupt stop. Kane was either resting or had reached the top. *What was he doing? Was he just trying to escape or did he have another plan?*

Jake slowed down, partly to catch his breath and partly because he wanted to make a quiet approach.

As he climbed higher, the air became more moist as mist, blown by the wind, began to strike his face. Flashes of lightning filtered down from somewhere above, leading each thunderclap with a burst of light.

Jake had always wondered what was behind the lookout openings at the top of the tower, but this wasn't how he'd wanted to find out.

The mist became thicker as he rose higher, as if he were entering the interior of a cloud. Thunder shook the walls and explosions of light bounced off each step.

He stopped. One last turn before whatever was waiting for him at the top. In the gaps between the peals of thunder he could hear the sounds of a battle still raging below. *What now?* He tried to slow his breathing. *Not possible.* At this point he wasn't thinking *noble quest*. He wasn't thinking *epic endeavor*. He was just thinking about Gabe. But what was his plan? *Save Gabe.* That was it. That would have to be enough.

Jake wiped his hands on his pants. He straightened his back, took a deep breath . . . and stepped around the corner. The pitch blackness of the room was broken by flashes of lightning exploding through the lookouts. The stark room was empty. It felt more like a prison cell than anything. And it wasn't much bigger. The limestone walls rose to a point just above his head. He was at the top of the monument.

Empty.

Then why did it feel like he was being watched?

A clap of thunder shook the tower as lightning lit up the room. The wind shifted and rain exploded through the lookouts, ricocheting off the walls like stray bullets. More lightning, more thunder, and with the next great flash, Jake saw him.

MALICE

KANE WAS SITTING IN THE CORNER against the wall, only about ten feet away. Gabe's unconscious body was lying in front of him. Kane didn't stir. He just sat there, totally still. His head was dropped, but his steely eyes were locked on Jake. He said nothing.

Rain sprayed through the room. A flash of lightning illuminated Kane's face. He was soaked in sweat and mist, his coal-black curls dripping onto his shoulders. He wiped his forehead and licked his bleeding hand, never taking his eyes off Jake.

"This is it?" he whispered. "An old man and a boy? You would think stealing their beloved tyrant would warrant a little more . . . effort." He nudged Gabe's body with his foot. Gabe didn't stir.

Jake took a step toward Kane.

"Ahhh, ahhh. I wouldn't." Kane reached from behind his back and rested the tip of his cane blade on Gabe's throat. He raised one eyebrow. "Take one more step and this sword will finish the job." He leaned over and wiped his nose on his sleeve.

Another flash of lightning exploded. Jake's eyes darted across the room, searching for a weapon. Nothing.

Kane rose to his knees, shoving Gabe back. Gabe was now slouched against the wall like someone who had fallen asleep in an airplane seat. Jake couldn't tell if Gabe was still alive or not. If he was, he didn't have much time. Jake could yell for help, but if someone below could have helped, they'd have reached him by now.

Kane slapped Gabe. Still no response. "I have questions for you, old man. But if you're not going to play along, I'm afraid *you're* the useless one."

Jake needed to get him to move away from Gabe. He needed to distract him.

"Well, then. Enough visitation. We'll just have to share this lovely sword. I'll take the handle. You can have the—"

"Useless!" Jake yelled.

Kane paused and shifted his gaze to Jake.

"Useless!" Jake repeated, a bit louder.

Kane's face became tight. His eyes narrowed and his lips pursed.

"Booth was right. And not just about his hands. *He* was useless!" Jake yelled again.

"NO! I STRUCK BOLDLY!" Kane took a step around Gabe and lunged toward Jake, his sword cutting through the air. "I STRUCK . . . HE STRUCK . . . BOLDLY!"

Jake dropped to his knees and rolled under Kane's swing. Kane's momentum rocketed him past Jake and caused him to tumble to the ground, dropping his blade. Jake wheeled around to grab it, but Kane quickly snatched it back.

He eased toward Jake, hunched over, dragging the sword low at his side as if he were pulling a heavy weight. "I STRUCK BOLDLY, I STRUCK, I . . ." He squinted his eyes as if straining to remember something. "HE . . . HE STRUCK BOLDLY, HE STRUCK, NOT AS THE PAPERS SAY." Sweat dripped from the curls of his hair onto his nose and face. The stench of sulfur grew stronger. He mumbled with each slow step. "HE WALKED, I WALKED WITH A FIRM STEP THROUGH A THOUSAND OF THE TYRANT'S FRIENDS, AND I . . . I STRUCK BOLDLY."

Jake stepped back slowly until his back was pressed against the stone wall.

Kane paused before he reached Jake. He straightened up. "I struck boldly. My action . . ." he grimaced. "My action was pure. I struck for my country." He turned and glanced back at Gabe as if considering unfinished business.

"BOOTH WAS A COWARD AND A TRAITOR!" Jake screamed.

"HE WAS A PATRIOT!" Kane retorted. "That bearded baboon was the coward! Hiding behind all those brave young men. We were groaning, groaning beneath his tyranny."

With each word, Kane swayed, slowly rocking back and forth. "I shouted, 'Sic semper tyrannis!' before I fired. I struck for my country. I DIED BRAVELY!"

It had been several minutes since Gabe moved and far too long since he had even made a sound. Jake knew he had to act fast.

"Booth deserved to die," Jake shot back. "SIC SEMPER IGNORAMUS! SIC . . . SEMPER . . . IGNORAMUS!"

Kane screamed and lunged, slicing the sword toward Jake's head. Jake dropped to one knee; he ducked and upended Kane, sending him into the wall. It was a move Jake had done hundreds of times in wrestling, just never when the other guy had a sword.

Jake spun around but Kane was already back on his feet, slicing through the air. Jake ducked and felt the rush of the sword pass just overhead. The madman swung again and again, forcing Jake to backpedal across the room.

Jake dropped and rolled, avoiding Kane's latest swing but ending up with his back pressed against the wall. Kane smirked and wiped a bead of sweat off the tip of his nose.

He swung again. Sparks flew as the sword glanced off the wall to Jake's left. He brought the sword down again, and more sparks showered from the wall to Jake's right. Kane lunged forward with the sword, just missing Jake's head and breaking the sword against the wall. Blinded with rage, the Booth clone lunged with his bare hands at Jake, who ducked only to have Kane latch onto the back of his neck. Jake dropped to his knees and spun around, sending Kane onto his back. Classic Beast Boy, perfectly executed.

Jake popped back up, ready to spring onto his attacker and finish the move. But Kane wasn't there. Jake spun around. Other than Gabe's body in the corner, the room was empty. Nothing. He took a step toward Gabe, but was intercepted by the full weight of Kane's body crashing into his back like a sledgehammer and slamming Jake to the stone floor.

He was only out for a second, but when Jake came to, he felt as if a boa constrictor were wrapped around his neck. He whipped his head from side to side, but with each turn of his neck, the grip only seemed to tighten. A rush of pain surged through his head as his lungs screamed for oxygen. He thrashed. Kane squeezed harder, lifting Jake off the floor and easing him backwards over the window ledge. A sharp pain shot through Jake's shoulder as the madman jammed him back onto the stone ridge.

The rain beat against Jake's face as he dangled backward over the ledge. The trees thrashed in the wind like monsters guarding the soldiers' graves below.

Jake flailed, searching for anything to grab, but each time his arms found nothing but air. Kane's eyes calmly stared down at him. Rain and sweat ran down Kane's face, revealing streaks of cold gray skin where his flesh-colored makeup was dripping off. Jake's lungs burned. A sharp pain shot through his head and his vision blurred. Everything was growing dark and fuzzy. No more air. The burning stopped. He couldn't keep his eyes open. Heaviness. Now silence.

Another flash of lightning erupted over the tower. A furious crash of thunder rocked the walls. Kane jerked up, responding to the explosion. Jake's eyes popped open. It was just enough. He lunged one last time, stabbing his arms upward and catching Kane's collar with one hand. Kane smiled and tightened his grip, his fingertips now meeting around Jake's neck.

Jake's other hand grabbed Kane's collar. He began to pull up, loosening Kane's grip ever so slightly as he swallowed a gasp of air. Jake bit the air, his lungs sucking in every bit of precious oxygen as he latched onto Kane. The clone tried to pry him off but as he did, he took one hand off Jake's throat. Instantly Jake used his last gasp to twist Kane's arm and spin him onto his side. A reverse Beast Boy. Illegal in seventh grade, but then again so were laser rifles and sword canes.

Jake gasped as the cool air filled his lungs and he rolled on top of Kane. His hands were now clenched on his attacker's neck. Jake stared directly into Anarchus Kane's eyes. There was no emotion there. Jake's own eyes were burning from Kane's sulfurous breath. His arms were on fire, but there was no way he was letting go.

Malice, said a voice in Jake's head. *Yes, that's what it is.* He was looking straight into the face of hate. It was all there in Kane's eyes—a family torn apart, one brother in blue, the other in gray, fighting each other. Another family—slave children ripped from their mother's arms. And his Uncle Gabe bruised and dying on the cold floor. Jake could hear Kane's desperate gasps. The madman was now the one biting for air.

Malice, the voice in Jake's head spoke again. *Finish the work.*

Jake eased the man out over the ledge.

There would be something right about this.

Finish the work. Malice.

Jake inched him further out. He wouldn't even need to push him. He could just loosen his grip. Just let go and let gravity bring justice.

He began to do that.

More lightning. More thunder. The rain pounded harder.

Finish the work. He began to let the man slide away. The voice broke through again, but this time clearer and more complete. *Finish the work, to bind up the wounds.*

Jake shook his head.

Finish the work to bind up the wounds. With malice toward none, and charity for all.

No, thought Jake. *Not charity. Justice. For Gabe, for the families, for everyone. Just let go. Let him fall. Justice.*

Malice toward none. Charity for all. Charity for all.

He looked into Kane's eyes one last time. It was all still there. The rage, the hate, the malice. But this time he saw something else. The lightning was like a flashbulb, creating a picture of Jake's own face in Kane's glassy eyes. It was all there—the rage, the hate, the malice. All coming from Jake's own face.

"No," he whispered. He loosened his grip. He let go . . . and grabbed for Kane's arms, pulling him up and heaving back into the room. They spilled onto the stone floor.

The rumble of boots echoed from the stairwell as Artie and four League Rangers raced into the room. They descended on Kane near the ledge as he squirmed and gasped for breath.

Jake stumbled across the floor to the pile that was Gabe. He grabbed onto the old man and rolled him onto his back. No movement. He clutched his hands. They were cold as ice.

The silence was like nothing Jake had ever heard. There was plenty of noise—Kane gasping for air, Artie calling for more help, the crack of lightning, and the rain washing in, but Jake could hear none of it. It was like a dream without sound.

He reached back for Gabe. A Ranger stepped in, pulling Jake off the body while a medic dropped to the floor. They said something, but he couldn't hear. A blur of arms pointing and faces yelling, but no sound. Jake struggled to get back to Gabe but the Ranger held him tight. The Ranger was saying something to Jake, but his words were disappearing into the fog like everything else.

And then, the eyelid. He twitched. First one, then the other. Then Gabe's chest rose and fell with a single breath. "Jakester," he gasped.

DANGEROUS DELBERT

JAKE BROKE FREE FROM THE RANGER and collapsed into Gabe, who coughed as he choked for air. The medic cradled the commander's head while he slipped an oxygen mask on him. For the next ten minutes Jake sat silently next to Gabe, watching him slowly suck in fresh air and regain his strength. By the time Gabe was ready to stand, the thunder and lightning were retreating into the distance. Jake and the medic carefully lifted Gabe to his feet and began the slow descent to the base of the tower, arm in arm.

By the time they reached the landing, the storm had faded and two Union agents were placing several Lantern troopers into an SUV. TJ and Lucy were huddled on a silver tarp draped across a wall at the monument's edge. They were drenched, but other than a few cuts and bruises, they were OK. When Jake, Gabe and the medic emerged from the tower, they eased Gabe down onto the stone wall. TJ and Lucy ran to Jake, knocking him to the ground in a wet awkward heap.

"Sorry," TJ said as they struggled back to their feet. "Not a lot of group hugs in fencing. Need some practice."

Four League Rangers emerged from the stairwell, escorting a handcuffed Kane. He was silent but stared at Jake with an icy gaze as they led him away.

"What's next for him?"

"We're not taking any chances. Secure League facility. We'll work with the government. There's a lot to figure out," Artie said.

The sun was just beginning to rise over the monument as they took a seat on the stone wall next to Gabe. A medic finished wrapping a large bandage on Gabe's head.

In the circular drive, just beyond a large, bronze Lincoln bust, a van had pulled up and Union agents were beginning to unload silver suitcases. An agent walked past with a wet-dry vac while another one carried what looked like two blacked-out ski goggles with headphones duct-taped to the sides.

"So you guys did all right down here?" Jake asked.

"Yes," Artie said. "It seems Mr. McDonald knows his way around a sword."

"I'd like to think ten years of Saturday mornings is worth a few MMS."

Everyone gave TJ a confused look.

"Mad Medieval Skills," TJ said.

"And then, of course, there's Miss García."

"MJS," TJ said.

"OK, I give up," said Artie.

"Mad Jungle Skills," TJ said, making awkward karate moves with his hands and feet.

"I'll take that," Lucy said with a smile.

"Quite a night. One of the Lantern agents got away, but Agent Richards is OK and we grabbed the other two," said Artie. "And Mr. Lincoln's remains are safe and secure. That, plus Kane and Slate, makes a banner day."

"And speaking of Anarchus Kane," Gabe said as he put his arm around Jake, "Mr. Jake Herndon didn't do so bad either. I was drifting in and out up there. How did you pull him off me?"

"Classic mistake. He did it to himself. I saw how crazy he got when you used Booth's dying word against him, so I tried it again."

"Did I hear you yell 'Sic semper tyrannis'?" Gabe asked.

"Almost. I told him Booth deserved to die. I yelled, 'Sic semper ignoramus.'"

"'Thus always to idiots'?"

"It seemed to rankle him," Jake said.

Gabe broke up laughing.

"Well, it worked. That, plus seven years of wrestling above your weight," said Artie.

"MRS," TJ said.

"You know that wrestling is spelled with a W, right?" said Lucy.

"Mad Rail Splitter Skills."

"SPLITTAHHHSSSS!" Jake and TJ raised their fists in the air.

Gabe turned to Lucy. "Do you have any idea what that's about?"

"Unfortunately, yes. I just refuse to acknowledge it."

"OK then," Artie said as the agents behind them moved

into the stairwell with their cases. "They should be done adjusting things here in the next ten minutes. There'll be a news story about some vandalism of the statues, but that's about it. Time for us to hit the road."

By the time they reached the end of the walkway, the rising sun was glistening off the large Lincoln bust. "You know, there's an old myth," Gabe said, pointing to the shiny worn nose on the face. "Some think if you rub his nose it's good luck. It's a nightmare for maintenance who have to patch the hole rubbed into his nose every few years, though, so I guess it's not good for everyone."

A black SUV pulled to the curb as TJ reached up and rubbed Abe's nose.

"Breakfast anyone?" Gabe asked. "I know this little donut place." As they piled into the SUV, TJ had a sly smirk on his face.

"What are you looking so pleased about?" Lucy asked TJ.

"That was my wish."

"Wish?"

"Rubbing Abe's nose. I wished for donuts," TJ said.

"I don't know what concerns me more," Lucy said. "That you believe in that kind of thing, or that you would use your wish for a donut."

"Hey, you can go back and rub it for world peace if you want, but I'm going for an Honest Abe."

They pulled into a parking lot under a giant donut wearing a black hat and sunglasses. They were back at Dangerous Delbert's, and once again the smell of fresh donuts swept over them. They took their places in line behind a mix of hospital

265

workers and cab drivers. TJ browsed the racks behind the counter while Beverly filled the orders.

"And there we have it!" TJ exclaimed, nodding to the top rack. It was a large chocolate iced donut, filled with whipped cream and topped by a glob of more whipped cream the size of a tennis ball.

"Cream inside, chocolate outside, and BAMMM! An explosion of bonus cream on top. It's like eating a cloud of happiness."

When the last person in front of them was served, Lucy stepped to the counter. "Do you have anything that's, I mean, a little less sugar?"

"Well, we killed the Lumberjack. Couldn't sell a single one. We're trying a bran muffin today," the woman said.

"Are you kidding me?" TJ said, turning to Lucy. "It's a donut shop. We beat the crazy storm troopers. Embrace the joy."

The line had begun to grow behind Lucy as she interrogated the lady about the ingredients. TJ began anxiously bouncing on the balls of his feet.

Lucy ignored him. "Is it healthy?"

"Sure, if you want it to be, honey. It's the closest you're gonna get here."

"OK, I'll take one. And an orange juice."

"Great. Finally. Yes." TJ stepped to the front.

"Good morning, Beverly. I'll have two Honest Abes and a chocolate milk. How about you join me in the goodness, Jake?"

"Hmmm. I think I'll have—" Before Jake could give his order, a large man wearing a Dangerous Delbert's apron and a paper hat bounced out the kitchen door. He walked toward Gabe with a serious look.

"No more donuts! All out of donuts. Especially for you."

"Well then, I guess we'll take our business elsewhere," Gabe said.

The man broke into a grin and pulled Gabe in for a hug. "It's been a while."

"It has indeed, Delbert. I brought some young first-timers."

"Jake, Lucy, and TJ, meet Dangerous Delbert himself." Gabe turned back to the man. "Are you still frying 'em up yourself back there? I would think you'd have some help by now."

"Quality control, my friend, quality control." He slapped his hands together, sending a cloud of powdered sugar into the air. "Perhaps your young guests would like to see a batch being made?"

"We'd love to," Gabe said. "Come on, kids. A quick tour of where the magic happens."

"But my donuts," TJ murmured.

"They'll still be here. Don't be rude," Lucy said, grabbing TJ's arm and pulling him toward the kitchen door.

As soon as they pushed through the double doors into the kitchen, Delbert and Gabe picked up their pace, almost speed-walking. They snaked around a set of industrial kitchen equipment, the cook calling out the names like a tour guide running short on time. "Five-quart jelly pump, stainless steel bench, dough roller, large-capacity frying bin." He rattled them off in machine-gun style, not even glancing as he cruised past.

Jake, Lucy, and TJ had trouble keeping up as they entered a small storage room. "Ten-pound bags of highly active yeast, thirty-pound bags of pastry flour, bittersweet chocolate."

He raced past the boxes to the exit, pushed it open, and hurried through. They stepped into a small parking lot where five Dangerous Delbert's delivery vans were backed in, waiting for their next shipment.

He continued his speed tour. "And then these little boxes of deliciousness are loaded and delivered to your neighborhood store," he said, while opening the back door of the van and shuffling Gabe, Jake, Lucy, and TJ into the back. "Happy deliveries!" he said, slamming the door shut as the engine roared to life.

The inside looked exactly like the van from the previous night, the only exception being a stack of donut boxes in the corner. As they pulled onto the street and sped away, the window monitors came to life, projecting a view of the outside.

"Wait a minute—" Jake said.

"Strategic redundancy." Artie answered his question before he could ask it. "There's more than one Doomsday Donut."

TJ lifted the lid off the top donut box. His smile dropped into disappointment. The box contained another set of the blacked-out ski goggles with headphones duct-taped to the sides.

"Sorry," Gabe said. "As you've seen, sometimes a donut van isn't really a donut van."

"So, Dangerous Delbert?" Lucy asked.

"Longtime Union agent. Handles vehicle dispatch. Also makes a mean donut."

"Yeah, well, I wouldn't know about that part," TJ said, shooting Lucy a look. "Apparently it would have been rude to actually eat one."

"Sorry. I didn't know we were bugging out. But you're welcome. I probably added a day to your life," Lucy said.

"An extra day for eating a bran muffin? No, thanks. I'd rather die with a donut in my hand."

"We decided to make a quick transfer. Security protocol," Gabe said. "And now we're off to home." Gabe wrapped his arm around Jake and turned to TJ and Lucy. "We've contacted your parents. They'll meet us at the Greystone. They know you're OK and we've given them a topline. We'll brief everyone together—what you can and can't say—and then we'll give you your cover stories."

"OK, but I'm counting on the courageous tomb fight for my college essay," TJ said.

"I'm afraid you're going to be disappointed. You were at the museum when it blew up, but not much more than that."

The houses and suburbs outside gave way to farms and open fields. Jake felt his eyes getting heavy, and within five minutes they were all fast asleep.

PRESERVE AND PROTECT

IT WAS FOUR HOURS LATER when Jake awoke to the van slowing to a stop in the alley behind the Greystone loading dock.

"End of the line," Gabe said as Artie stepped out. They entered through the back door and made their way down the hallway.

Amy, the hotel concierge, opened a door labeled "Employees Only" as they approached. "Welcome back, Commander."

"Thank you, Agent Miller," Gabe said.

It was a simple room, just a small kitchen at one end and a folding table surrounded by metal chairs at the other. There were four adults sitting at the table. A distinguished-looking black man with a neatly trimmed gray beard and a tweed sport coat sat close to an equally distinguished-looking woman. Next to them was a young, beautiful Hispanic woman, unmistakably an older version of Lucy, sitting by an athletic-looking man with slightly graying hair in jeans and a T-shirt.

All four leapt from their chairs and rushed to the kids.

TJ's mom smothered him in a tight hug. "Thelony, we were worried sick." She actually lifted him off his feet.

"Mmmphh. Mmmmphh." TJ struggled to breathe until his dad intervened and loosened his mom's grip.

After a few minutes of hugs and tears, Gabe asked everyone to take a seat at the table. He motioned to two agents at the back of the room. Jake recognized them as Greystone parking attendants. The agents nodded and left the room, locking the door behind them.

"I know you have a lot of questions," Gabe said as he took a seat at the table. "But before I get to the answers, I want to let you know that you have some very special kids. They were not only rescued this weekend, but they did some rescuing of their own. You should be very proud."

TJ's mom put her arm back around him and squeezed.

"I'm going to answer some of your questions, but not all of them. I hope by the end you'll understand."

Over the next hour Gabe briefed them on the museum heist, and explained that he worked for the university. He didn't mention the League or its history. He also didn't mention the Dark Lantern or anything about cloning. He assured them that the thieves had no way of finding out their children's identity.

After reassurances that they would get more information in the morning, it was time for the families to go home.

"Oh, and one more thing—TJ." Gabe reached into a bag that had been sitting on the table and removed a Dangerous Delbert's box. "For you."

"I'd like to think that it's donuts," TJ said. "But what's really in it?"

"I think you've seen too many spy movies," Gabe said. "Sometimes a donut box is just a donut box."

TJ cracked the box open to find a six-pack of Honest Abe donuts and a small tube of hand sanitizer. "Breakfast of Champions!"

Everyone stood up. The kids looked at each other. Jake didn't know what to say. He felt like he was saying goodbye to two old friends. From the looks on their faces, Lucy and TJ felt the same.

"This isn't a farewell," Gabe said. "We're regrouping tomorrow for a full debrief. And then there's the little matter of seventh grade."

Amy led TJ, Lucy, and their folks into the lobby while Gabe slid the service elevator cage open and stepped on with Artie and Jake.

When the elevator came to a stop on the twenty-first floor, rather than sliding the cage door open, Gabe tapped the keypad. After he clicked through a series of buttons, the elevator went dark. A blue neon light flicked on. Jake felt something move behind him and he turned to find a back door he'd never known existed sliding open.

They stepped into a large attic space about the size of a basketball court. Wood beams framed paneled walls that angled to a peak about twenty feet above them. A bank of plasma screens was suspended from the cathedral ceiling, displaying a mix of video from New York, London, and somewhere in India.

Dozens of people wearing League IDs around their necks were gazing into computer monitors and tapping on touch screens.

"Welcome back, Commander!" a young woman said as she carried a stack of file folders past them.

"Thank you," Gabe said, leading Jake and Artie past a mismatched collection of tables running down the middle of the room. Some of them were old library tables like the ones in Jake's apartment, while others looked like someone had scrounged steel worktables from an old factory, but all of them were well-worn and battered. An odd mix of electronic guts from handheld computers, yellowed Civil War battle maps, and rolls of duct tape was scattered across the tables. A small printer was spitting out a fake passport.

They paused as they reached a large wooden door that might as well have been salvaged from a castle. At the top was a stained glass panel of the League shield and the words *Preserve and Protect*. Gabe opened the door and they entered a round office. A mix of old books, Civil War artifacts, and high-tech gadgets filled every inch of the floor-to-ceiling bookshelves. A rather beaten-up love seat patched by duct tape was positioned in front of a small stone fireplace across from two old leather chairs. They took seats in front of the fireplace.

"Well, Jakester. I know you've had a lot thrown at you. It's hard to absorb. I also figure there's still another piece you're probably wondering about."

"At the vault," Jake said. "Artie said they might be after me."

"Yes, well," Gabe said, "that part's a bit tricky. In fact, most of our team don't have clearance on this. When you told us that the glove had your blood on it, that changed the game. Artie told you about the Lantern's DNA sequencer?"

"Right. What's that have to do with me?"

"Well," Gabe paused and cleared his throat. "If the Clavis Magna is Lincoln DNA, there's something that would accelerate Kane's plan a lot faster than a hundred-and-fifty-year-old skeleton. If he could ever get his hands on living DNA—not old bone fragments but a living, breathing DNA sample—it would be a breakthrough beyond his wildest dreams."

"Living DNA?" Jake was more confused than ever.

Gabe leaned forward. "Jake, my great-grandfather was Allan Pinkerton."

"The president's secret agent?"

"Yes, founder of the League. When the president was killed, my great-grandfather made a vow, a vow that became our mission."

"To preserve and protect," Jake said.

"That's right, to preserve the Union," Gabe nodded.

"And protect the people," Jake said.

"Not quite. To preserve the Union and to protect . . . the family."

"The family?"

"When Mr. Lincoln died, my great-grandfather promised the president's widow, Mary, he would do whatever was necessary to ensure the safety of her family. Mary ended up with only one grandson, Abraham Lincoln II. When Abe II was sixteen, he was studying in Paris and the League foiled a Lantern attempt to kidnap him. His dad, Robert, asked the League for help protecting his son, the sole carrier of the Lincoln name. Later that year, they faked his son's death in London and Abe II went into the secret protective custody of the League. He grew up as a League agent, and so did his children, and his children's children.

"The League preserves the Union and we protect the Lincoln bloodline. We are still keeping both vows today. Jacob, I adopted you because I love you, and also because of my pledge. You've always asked about a middle name. You do have one. It's always been here waiting for you.

"Jacob Lincoln Herndon, you are the great-great-great-grandson of Abraham Lincoln, the sole surviving descendant of the sixteenth president of the United States."

Jake sat still. "What? How can . . ."

Gabe moved next to Jake, putting his hand on his shoulder. "This is a bit sooner than I planned to tell you, but it's obviously time."

"But then, my parents—"

"Your parents were two of our best agents," Gabe said. "They died during a mission not long after you were born."

Jake stared at the floor. No one said a word. Gabe put his arm around Jake. The only sound was the air coming through vents. Finally, Jake looked up. He wasn't crying but his eyes weren't dry either. "Was it the Lantern?"

"We have our suspicions, but we don't know exactly."

More silence. Then Jake nodded his head. "So if Kane had identified the blood on the glove," said Jake, "the live sample would be me?"

"Yes. To them, you would be *the* Clavis Magna," Artie said. "Good for them. Not so much for you, I'm afraid. You see, to extract such a large amount of DNA from you, they would need to—"

"Yes," Gabe interrupted. "I think he gets the idea."

Gabe stood up. "Over the years, each descendant has become a League agent and raised their children under League protection. You're the last of the line, though. The good news is that it's over. Kane and Slate aren't going anywhere. We're mopping up a few stray agents, but I think we can consider the Lantern snuffed out."

"But Kane saw you," Jake said. "He knows what you look like, and TJ and Lucy . . . and me. He can tell someone."

"Department 5 has a little patch for that," Artie said. "The goggles with the headphones you saw will take care of that."

"They wipe their memory?" Jake asked.

"Not exactly. Re-Visors work more like Photoshop or the 'find and replace' on a computer document. They selectively overwrite faces and images in someone's memory with something else. We just have to catch it while the memory is still fresh."

"What about Governor Haven, the presidential candidate?"

"Clean, at least as far as we can tell. And the police too. Bates and a few other Lantern operatives infiltrated the department last year, but the police are cleaning that up."

Gabe stood up and stepped toward the door. "So, Mr. Jacob Lincoln Herndon, we have a lot to catch up on. But right now, I think you should meet the rest of the team. Many of them you already know, just in different capacities."

It was after midnight when Gabe and Jake finished. As they stepped back toward the elevator, Jake noticed a tattered banner just above the door:

With malice toward none, with charity for all, with firmness in the right as God gives us to see the right, let us strive on to finish the work we are in, to bind up the nation's wounds, to care for him who shall have borne the battle and for his widow, and his orphan, to do all which may achieve and cherish a just and lasting peace among ourselves and with all nations.

A. Lincoln, March 4, 1865

They walked back through the elevator and exited the other side into their apartment. Jake's mind was still reeling when his head hit the pillow. It was so much to think about. Artie, Gabe, Kane, the League, the Lantern, his parents. What more was there that he didn't know? The questions swirled, but that didn't stop him from drifting into a deep, deep sleep.

LAST DAY OF SUMMER

"IS HE DEAD?"

Jake was lying motionless in the grass, but he could still hear the voice. Even among the sounds of the buses and taxis rushing behind the park, he could hear the voice.

"Not dead. Maybe mostly dead, but not all dead." TJ leaned over and flicked Jake's ear.

"Hey!" Jake jolted upright on the picnic blanket.

"Sorry. Necessary procedure," TJ said. "See what I mean?" TJ turned to Lucy. "Definitely not all dead."

"What happened to the crucial day of chilling?" Jake said. "We agreed to a day of chilling."

"I don't recall a vote on that proposal but if it involves Yoo-hoos, I could be persuaded," TJ said.

"All I know is school starts tomorrow. I don't want to waste the last day of summer," Lucy said, as she began to pack the blanket and Frisbee into a backpack.

"As you wish, your highness," TJ said, standing up and bowing deeply.

"That's two *Princess Bride* references in less than a minute. I'm calling a foul."

"Foul?" TJ said.

"Yes, a violation of our agreement, a penalty, an infraction of some sort," said Jake.

"OK, I'll pull it back. I guess I'm just feeling a bit Westley after all the courageous swordplay." TJ threw the backpack over his shoulder as they walked across the grass.

"Westley? How many times do we need to review this? You're way more Inigo Montoya than Westley," Jake said, pausing and looking at his reflection in the giant mirrored bean sculpture. "If anyone would be Westley, it would be me."

"Wait a minute! Why would you be Westley? I'm Westley to my bones. Is this a race thing?"

"I can't believe you don't see this. You're totally Inigo. The attitude. The underlying hostility."

"Oh, that's ripe. Let's get an objective opinion." They caught up to Lucy, who had continued walking. "OK, Princess Buttercup, what do you think? Who's more Westley?"

"I have no idea what you're talking about, but if you ever call me that again, I'll reintroduce you to my foot."

Jake and TJ stopped in their tracks and stared at her.

"OK. It's time we deal with this," TJ said.

"I agree. Essential. Critical. Could be Level 3," Jake said.

"What's so critical?" Lucy asked.

"Well," TJ said, "you may have killer kung fu moves and can haggle for a granola bar in six languages, but you are lacking some very crucial knowledge for a rising seventh grader." He turned to Jake. "How much time do we have?"

"It's one o'clock. I'm back on school time tonight, so I figure we have until nine," said Jake.

"OK, Netflix marathon. We don't have much time but we can't go straight to *Princess Bride*. Just a few essentials: *Toy Story*, *The Avengers*, and *Spider-Man*," TJ said.

"I'm not sure about that," Jake said. "I mean, you're a little heavy on Marvel, and I don't think she can fully appreciate it without a foundation of the early Lucas and Spielberg stuff."

"Wait . . . ? Are you saying that Pixar and Marvel stole from *Star Wars*?"

"I'm not saying *stole*, but you have to admit there's some references that are important."

"I'm suddenly looking forward to precalc," Lucy mumbled as they descended the steps into the train station.

EPILOGUE

AN ELDERLY BUTLER CARRIED A SILVER TRAY down a long castle corridor somewhere in the Swiss Alps. He passed gold-framed oil paintings and ceremonial swords decorating ancient stone walls. He paused at a large wooden door and then entered the room cautiously.

A huge antique table dominated the center of the room. On one side of the table were five large chairs, almost as big as thrones, each with a different crest engraved on the back.

Five old men sat silently in the chairs, their silhouettes framed against a row of soaring windows that looked out onto a cavernous valley and snow-capped mountain peaks in the distance. Each of the men was wearing an expensive suit and an impatient face. On the wall in front of them was a massive plasma screen displaying a map of the world. Red lantern symbols blinked brightly on over a hundred locations spread around the globe.

The butler placed the silver tray on the table before quietly leaving. One of the men rose and pulled five folders off the tray.

"We'll get to the reports from Paris, Beijing, and New York, but first I'd like to go over these glove tests and the Chicago train station photo. I think you'll find them very interesting."

The five men leaned forward as the map on the plasma screen was replaced by a medical chart and a grainy security camera image of the back of Jake's head.

* * *

We've had some creative fun with history in this book, but you might be surprised by what's true.

You can explore some of the stranger truths and check out other bonus content at LeagueAndLantern.com/bonus.

ACKNOWLEDGMENTS

I'm so thankful we're not designed to do life alone. If I've left a name off of this list, please forgive me and know it has nothing to do with you being less than incredible and was simply a terrible mistake brought on by the fog and fury of doing this for the first time.

* * *

Many years ago on a journey to a faraway land that had been ravaged by fighting, I made my way into the countryside to an ancient castle that had somehow survived. It was there on the walls of an inner chamber that I first encountered the words "Nihil Sine Deo." To my Creator, the Maker of noses, Inventor of story, and Giver of impossible adventures: Nihil Sine Deo.

Dad and Mom, the original Delbert and Beverly. Your love and support never fade.

Nancy. You are an incredible gift in every way.

John and Grace. This is as much your story as it is mine. You are each a little Jake, a little Lucy and a little TJ, in all the best ways.

To our extended families, with love and gratitude: Randy, Ann, Ashley, Alexis and Adeline. Colleen, Larry and Laura, John and Amy, Randy and Liz, Ashley, Charley, Lauren and Ethan, Kyle, and Evan and Chelsea. And in loving memory of Jim.

Jim Bechtold. You are a brilliant strategist, a great encourager, and a rock.

Brian and Libby Tome, Jim and Vivienne Bechtold, Tom and Nancy Shepherd, Jerry and Betty Rushing, Paul and Usha Sklena, Darin and Pamela Yates, and the amazing Crossroads community.

The early encouragers: artists, authors, readers, and waymakers. Jeff Davenport, Steven Manuel, Laurel Brunk, Dave Little, Rachel Henry, and Todd Henry among them.

My editor, Steven Bauer. You are a storyteller and a teacher in the absolute best sense of those words. Thank you for guiding, shaping, challenging, and encouraging.

My designer, Clare Finney. Thanks for your eye, your wisdom, and your guidance.

My cover illustrator, Joe Slucher. A great artist and a wonderful, patient creative partner.

Marketer extraordinaire Mike Halloran.

Storyteller of light and sound, full of talent and heart: Tate Webb.

Tate Lucas, Abby Sutton, Chris Sutton, and the Dot Dash team.

My secret weapon and wordsmith, John Wells.

My copy editor, Stefanie Laufersweiler. If there are any errors in the book, I can assure you it's because I cheated and made just "one more change" after she had finished.

The awesome and insightful student readers who made this book better: Ava, Brenden, Chanse, Dove, Eden, Elise, Emma, Ethan, Filia, Julia, Katherine, Madeline, Memory, Molly, Owen, Paige, Seven, and Sydney

Leaders and Artists generous with their time, energy, and talent: Julie Arnold, Steve Babbitt, Nancy Beach, Chris Beard, Rich Bennett, Chris Bergman, Charlie Bollman, Noel Bouché, Juliette Brindak, Phil Cooke, Bryan Daniel, Dan Egeler, Lou Grieci, Jackelyn Viera Iloff, Paul Lauer, Mac McQuiston, Tim Mettey, Randall Murphree, Rick Schatz, Brian Steege, Vance VanDrake, Bob Waliszewski, Jonathan Robert Willis, and Tim Winter.

The wonderful partners at Collide, Maple Press and Ribbow.

Encouragers and Supporters many times over:

Gerry and Jenny Albers

The Basil Family

John and Kim Brannon

Tim and Laurel Brunk

Rob and Susan Busch

Michael and Loann Burke

Ray and Joan Conn

Phil and Kathleen Cooke

Ben and Kami Crawford

Michael and Susannah Croci

Don and Connie Donovan

David Falk

Paul and Susan Fisher

Dan and Leigh Gorman

Mark and Connie Greene

John Handlesman

Dr. Bradley Jackson and Lynn Watts

Jill

Brad Johansen

Peter Junoy and Holly Ledyard

Tim and Grace Kerr

Artie and Lisa Kuhn

JD and Sue Landgrebe

Dave and Holly Little

Steven and Dora Manuel

Russ and Gretchen McNamara

Daniel McNeil

Tim Mettey

The Meyer Family

David and Angie Miller

Rick and Wendy Mitchell

Randall Murphree

Gail Nolte and Phyllis Hafer

Evans and Cathy Nwankwo

Bill and Alli Patterson

Kurt and Beth Platte

Larry and Patsy Plum

Steve and Shannon Plymire

Carroll and Kathy Roberts

Jim and Barb Ruh

Karma Christine Salvato

Edgar and Leiza Sandoval

Paul and Shalie Schacht

Greg and Karen Simpson

Tonya Steely Tierney

Steve and Kim Wanamaker

David and Kelsey Warren

Philip and Megan Winchester

Mr. Nate Workman and Dr. Julie Workman

To Gary and the team at IJM, to Don Gerred, and to everyone defending the weak and the fatherless and upholding the cause of the poor and the oppressed: Thank you.